David Ambrose read la
internationally in theatre
website on www

ALSO BY DAVID AMBROSE

A MEMORY OF DEMONS

DAVID AMBROSE

POCKET
BOOKS

LONDON • SYDNEY • NEW YORK • TORONTO

First published in Great Britain by Simon & Schuster UK Ltd, 2003
This paperback edition published by Pocket Books, 2004
An imprint of Simon & Schuster UK Ltd
A Viacom company

1 3 5 7 9 10 8 6 4 2

Simon & Schuster UK Ltd
Africa House
64–78 Kingsway
London WC2B 6AH

www.simonsays.co.uk

Simon & Schuster Australia
Sydney

A CIP catalogue record for this book is available from the British Library

ISBN 0-7434-4075-7

Typeset by Palimpsest Book Production Limited,
Polmont, Stirlingshire

Printed and bound in Great Britain by
Cox & Wyman Ltd, Reading, Berkshire

A MEMORY OF DEMONS

PART ONE

'SUSPICION'

PART ONE

1

Tom Freeman contemplated the white-coated figure perched on the end of his bed. 'I'm afraid it's a death sentence,' was all he remembered of what the doctor had just said.

Then he heard, 'That's a certainty – unless you make some big changes in your life.'

So, there was an 'unless'. But did he want an 'unless'? Wouldn't he rather just die, and as soon and insensibly as possible? He tried to say as much, but could only make a rasping noise in the back of his throat. He reminded himself that he was in a neck brace and his jaw was wired. In addition, he was encased in plaster for three broken ribs, a fractured shoulder, a cracked hip and a broken leg. It was a miracle, he had been told, that he was alive.

The doctor, who was in his mid-thirties, only a year or two older than Tom, went on: 'At some point your liver or pancreas will go, or your kidneys, maybe the whole lot. Not to mention the brain damage that becomes inevitable with that level of sustained drinking. And all of this is without even mentioning your coke habit.'

He paused, his gaze focused solemnly on Tom's eyes, hoping to see that his message was hitting home and having some effect. Tom stared back in defiant silence. It was his firm belief that everyone had the right to go to hell in their own way. In fact, it was just about the only thing he believed in – his one article of faith. He just wished he could get his mouth to formulate the words so that he wouldn't have to listen to any more of this pious monologue which was really starting to piss him off.

'Of course,' the doctor was saying, 'the good news is that you're unlikely to die from any of those drug- or alcohol-related conditions, because you'll probably get yourself killed in some dumb accident before that. Like last night. You must have been hit by a passing vehicle – most likely a truck, from your injuries. You probably don't remember anything.'

Tom tried to shake his head, but the doctor held up a hand in alarm.

'Don't try to move your head! You were pulled out of a ditch over on River and Pike. Somebody had called in to report a corpse. When the paramedics arrived, their first response was that you had no vital signs, then they found a pulse. They revived you in the ambulance, though nobody thought you would live – yet here you are.'

Tom started to ask where the hell River and Pike was, but once again had to abandon the attempt.

Besides, what did it matter? It would mean nothing to him. He would have no memory of how he got there.

He knew he was in Albany, but the last place he remembered before that was Manhattan – some club in Tribeca where he'd known one of the musicians, and somebody had started talking about driving up the Hudson Valley. There was a rock festival, they'd said, just outside Albany. The next thing he remembered was the limo. Some lunatic had hired a limo. Whose idea had that been, he wondered? He suddenly had a horrible feeling it had been his. He remembered that a bunch of them had piled in, and there'd been a bar which, now he thought about it, they'd stopped at least a couple of times to replenish on the way. Plus of course they'd had all the usual drugs.

That much came back, but that was all. They must have reached their destination, though he had no memory of arriving. What, he wondered, had happened to the others? It was unlikely he would ever know, because he had no idea who they were. He could not remember even a single face. The whole thing was a blur of booze and coke and more booze, followed by a few more reviving lines of coke, plus pills and joints . . . until he found himself in this place, trussed up and suspended from hooks and pulleys like a carcass in the slaughterhouse. Who the hell did he have to fuck to get a drink around here? Not that he was going to be able to fuck anybody in his present state. Which boded badly for a drink.

The doctor looked on, arms folded patiently, waiting

for whatever dialogue Tom was having with himself to come to an end. When he saw Tom's gaze flicker up to meet his own once more, he delivered his final warning. 'You're going to recover physically. I told you it's a miracle that you're alive. It's also a miracle that you've done yourself no permanent damage – at least not yet. You still have a chance. It's up to you.'

Once again Tom tried to speak, but managed only an angry grunt. What he had wanted to ask this fresh-faced prig in front of him was whether he'd been born sounding like a summer camp religious counsellor, or whether he'd taken a course in that crap along with anatomy and pathology?

'Try to get some rest,' the doctor said. 'It'll be a while before you can talk, but we'll fix you up with a pad and a pencil soon as we can. Is there anything you have to tell me right now? Anything you need? Give me one blink for yes, two for no.'

Tom thought for a moment. Of course there was something he needed; a large vodka with ice and a line of coke would do nicely. But he knew he wasn't going to get that, so he blinked twice in the simple hope of being left alone.

As though reading Tom's thoughts, the doctor nodded his acknowledgement, said, 'I'll see you later,' and left.

Tom lay paralysed, beginning to feel his body itch and ache, and wondered how long this could go on before he went mad.

2

The drugs helped, of course – painkillers mostly, power-ful enough to take the edge off going cold turkey. Perhaps they slipped him something else to get him through it; he didn't ask, just waited impatiently for the dispensary nurse to make her twice-daily rounds with the little paper cup of pills and capsules that made his life in that place tolerable.

But as his physical injuries healed, they started decreasing the dosage. The young doctor, whose name Tom knew by then was Richard Pierce, was perfectly aware of the effect this was having.

'No, absolutely not, I'm sorry,' he answered in response to Tom's urgent pleas for increased medication. 'I'm here to get you well and back on your feet, and that's all I'm promising. The rest of your problems you're going to have to take care of yourself. There's an open meeting of AA held in this hospital three times a week. Go and check it out – right now, in your wheelchair.'

Tom muttered some angrily dismissive response. He

gave short shrift to the well-meaning hospital chaplain who stopped by to talk with him, and was needlessly offensive to the psychiatric counsellor who asked if there was anything she could help him with. In a perverse way, he was convinced that the more unloved he made himself amongst the people caring for him, the sooner they would make an effort to discharge him and let him get on with his life.

His life. What was it worth, his life? There was not one person in the world who would be grieving now if he had died in that ditch. Nor was there one person whose presence in the world made him positively want to go on living. He could not envision a future worth striving for, nor did he deceive himself that he could ever return to those heady days of a decade or so back when life's possibilities had seemed endless. With a brilliant degree in journalism and political science, and membership of Phi Beta Kappa, all doors had been open to him. Banking, the media, politics – all beckoned. Perversely, and perhaps fatally, he had chosen to ignore those heady opportunities and to take a shot at his undergraduate dream of making films. It was now or never, he told himself. If he failed, he could always fall back on something in the 'straight' world.

To begin with, the compromises he made were so small he almost didn't notice them. Besides, what was wrong with advertising and PR work? You learned your craft that way. A lot of great directors had started like that.

Some, however, stayed there. Tom, after five years, was proving to be one of them.

To a casual observer he was a big success. He was working hard and earning large amounts of money – far in excess of most of his college contemporaries. But in his heart he knew he was going nowhere. Perhaps that was why the drinking got such a hold on him, and then the drugs. But drink and drugs came with the job; they were part of that world, everybody did them. He could handle it, Tom told himself and anyone who asked. But soon it was handling him. He started doing bad work, and then the offers started drying up.

As his money dwindled, he got occasional freelance work to keep himself afloat, but he achieved little and was paid less. Even before this last episode he was close to broke and living way beyond his means. Now he didn't even have the courage to call his bank to find out how bad the damage was. Luckily his health insurance hadn't lapsed and would see him through his hospital-ization. But after that he would be on his own in every way, a burnt-out case with a great future behind him.

The depression he entered in that painfully uncom-fortable orthopaedic bed gradually darkened into an all-pervading anger with the world and himself for being part of it. There was a black hole at the centre of his life, something into which all the promise he had once shown, all the talent he had squandered, had vanished for ever. Now, he decided, he would vanish into it him-self. It was the only thing to do. The ultimate implosion.

He had noticed the 'Staff Only' elevator from his wheelchair on the way to physiotherapy every afternoon. It was wide enough to take a stretcher or even a whole bed, and he could see from the indicator above the doors that it ran from the basement to the summit of the building. Oddly, he only ever saw it in use once. He asked the nurse pushing his chair about it, and learned that there was a more convenient central bank of elevators in the new wing of the building. It was all Tom needed to know. This was the chance he had been looking for – heaven-sent, he thought with bleak amusement.

A week later, he was able to make the journey to physiotherapy alone on a walking frame, and was encouraged to do so. He decided he would wait a while longer to explore the elevator, until he had the strength to deal with whatever obstacles he might encounter on the upper level. There could be steps, locked doors or windows, parapets. When the time came, he would be ready, prepared in mind and body. It was surprising how the fact of having a goal in life, even if that goal was self-destruction, made all the frustrations and discomforts he was subject to more bearable. The knowledge that he had made his decision brought him an extraordinary peace of mind.

Ten days later he had swapped his walking frame for two light alloy crutches. His muscular strength was returning and he was starting to move around almost nimbly. He decided it was time. Late one afternoon, which he had noticed was one of the quieter times in the hospital's routine, he checked the corridor in both directions, and pressed the call button. He waited, trying to blend innocently into his surroundings, as hidden machinery whirred and eventually the wide doors parted. He got in quickly and pressed the top button, willing it to respond before anyone came around the corner and spotted him. As the doors came together with a soft shuddering motion, he heaved a sigh of relief and realized he had been holding his breath.

The elevator rose smoothly, without stopping, and opened onto a narrow corridor. It was deserted, but he had the impression that this was the usual state of affairs up here. There were no distant sounds of ringing phones or voices, no echoing footsteps, no impression of life going busily on around corners or beyond the few closed doors he could see, and which he guessed were probably storage rooms.

He walked a few yards until he reached an intersection where identical corridors split off in opposite directions. He carried straight on until he reached the next corner, where he saw what he was looking for. To his left, three steps led up to a reinforced-glass partition beyond which he could see an expanse of blue-grey cloudy sky. There was a door in the partition, and he mounted the steps praying that it would be open. He shook the handle; it didn't budge. He was cursing softly and looking around for another way, when he saw a key protruding from the lock in front of him. He turned it, and the door opened effortlessly.

His first instinct on the far side was to fill his lungs with fresh air for the first time in weeks. He had forgotten how different it smelt and tasted from the atmosphere inside. But it was only a momentary response; he reminded himself that he was not up there to feel good about life, but to end it.

He looked around. The flat surface of the roof was dotted with ventilation ducts and larger structures housing elevator and air-conditioning machinery. Beyond all that he could see a parapet of brick, topped with flat concrete flagstones, no more than two feet high. He hobbled over to it, dropped to his knees, and peered down.

Below him lay the parking lot. Two cars had just pulled out, leaving him with an oil-stained hard surface that would annihilate him on impact. It was perfect. Luck was on his side this afternoon.

It took him a moment to realize he was hesitating. And several more to realize why. First of all, he had the odd impression that something had changed, stealthily and silently, without his noticing, while his attention was elsewhere. Something had changed, but what?

Something in him? Or something around him?

Was it possible that, having got right down to the wire, as it were, he had discovered that he didn't really want to die? That his despair was an illusion?

He thought for some moments before he identified where this strange new feeling was coming from – the same place at the back of his mind as his decision to end it all. But this wasn't a decision. It was a need. He wanted something badly, something more than death.

He realized what it was. He wanted a drink.

The fact was, he wanted a drink more than he wanted to die.

3

'My name is Tom. I'm an alcoholic.'

'Welcome, Tom. Good to have you with us.'

It was the open AA meeting that Dr Pierce had told him about. He had found the initial confession, 'I am an alcoholic,' amazingly easy to get out, almost as though he had been wanting to say those words, without knowing it, for a long time. They were four words that changed him, and changed the world he lived in.

What most surprised him was the warmth of the group, and the welcome they offered him. They were men and women of various ages and from obviously different walks of life, from executives to artists to blue-collar workers. They didn't ask questions or want anything from him, not even his second name. All they wanted was to hear his story, and have him listen to theirs.

Some of those stories, he soon realized, had been told many times and were now polished performance pieces. Others were stumbling, inarticulate attempts to express painfully won self-knowledge. Everyone was listened to with the same thoughtful respect, and everyone was thanked with the same warmth for his or her contribution.

Throughout the remaining period of his physical recovery, Tom went to these meetings several times a week. He gained in strength and confidence and clarity of mind. But the real change had taken place on that first day. He changed, he realized, because he had wanted to. There was no other way.

Then, one day, something happened that would alter all the days that came after it. He was on his way back from a physiotherapy session, walking down a hospital corridor with the help of a cane. The sun was streaming in through tall windows and reflecting off the white walls and polished floor. It gave a shimmering quality to the figure walking towards him, like a form taking shape as it stepped out of a mirage. At first he supposed it was a nurse, then he saw that she was wearing not a uniform but a cotton dress and simple flat-heeled pumps. She had a dancer's walk, light and fluid, yet every step was firmly connected with the ground. As she came closer he could see that her dark blonde hair was drawn back in a ponytail, which emphasized the almost perfect symmetry of her features. She had a strong jaw, a generous mouth, and green eyes that seemed to pull you into an orbit of their own once they fixed on yours. He must have been staring at her, from the way she turned her frank gaze back on him. It was a moment before her mouth opened with the surprise of recognition.

'Tom Freeman! What are you doing here?'

'I was about to ask you the same thing.'

They had stopped, facing each other, people hurrying past them in both directions.

'I was just visiting my cousin,' she said. 'She's been having her wisdom teeth out.'

'You live here? In Albany?'

'About twenty miles away. A little place by the river. Saracen Springs. And you?'

'Oh, I was just passing through.'

She looked at his cane, and took in the painful stiffness of his body. 'What happened to you? Did you have an accident?'

'Yes,' he said, his mouth twisting into a wry smile, 'rather a long one.'

'Tell me.'

'D'you have time for a cup of coffee?' he said.

'Yes, of course.'

They sat on lightweight aluminium chairs at a Formica-topped table in the hospital canteen. It was ten years since they had seen each other – a lot of time to cover.

'I heard everywhere that you were doing fantastically well in advertising,' she said. 'Then suddenly nobody knew where you were or what you were doing.'

'Well, now you know,' he said, mentally noting that she had kept track of him, which was something he would never have expected. He and Clare Powell had been friends in college, though they had never dated. He had always been slightly intimidated by her – attracted by her beauty and her openness, but sensing a refinement and a reserve in her that made him nervous. Besides, she had been going out with someone else, a boy from an old Boston family. Old money, Tom always thought, would suit her better than any other kind.

'You married Jack, didn't you?' he asked, noticing that she wore no wedding ring.

She glanced down, as though following his thoughts, to her unadorned finger. 'Yes,' she said, a note of self-consciousness creeping into her voice. 'We divorced three years ago. It was all quite civilized, we just went our separate ways.'

'I'm sorry,' he said, telling himself at once he was a hypocrite. 'Any kids?'

She shook her head. 'I think we both suspected on some level that it might not work. We were too young. Anyway,' she shrugged, 'no children. You?'

'Kids? No – I haven't even been married.'

She gave that little flashing smile of hers that had always made his heart beat faster. That smile, he used to tell himself, was something she bestowed on everybody. It was just part of the way she was with people, so he had no reason to feel special when she turned it on him. But now here he was, alone with her in these drab, colourless surroundings, and that smile was making him feel very special indeed.

'Ah, yes,' she said, 'you always were the dashing bachelor.'

He blinked a couple of times, meeting her gaze but feeling awkward and a little stupid, the way she always used to make him feel. 'Dashing'? Was she making fun of him? Or flattering him? Flirting with him, even? He cleared his throat, shifting his position to reduce the pins and needles in his left leg.

'More like crashing,' he said, with a self-deprecating laugh, 'as in crash and burn.' He wanted to get this out of the way. He wanted to make sure that this lovely and desirable young woman knew the kind of mess he had made of his life. 'They tell me I'm lucky to be alive,' he said. Then, still looking at her, he added, 'I'm beginning to agree with them.'

The look between them extended, and became a kind of understanding.

'I always thought you'd have to burn out a little before you really hit your stride,' she said.

'You did?'

She nodded.

'Well,' he said, and again let the silence lengthen until they were both quite sure what was going on between them, 'who'd have thought it?'

4

After the break-up of her marriage, Clare had left New York and travelled in Europe for six months. Then she returned to rent a small house in Saracen Springs, because it was a place where she had been happy for an important part of her childhood: when she was seven, her father, who taught political science, had taken up a post at Albany University. Ten years later he had been appointed to a full professorship in California, and they had moved again. But she had kept some good friends from those early years, and was currently working for one of them in a business consultancy he had set up. Clare specialized in small-firm start-ups, many of them the second and third generation of dot.coms keen to benefit from the painful lessons learned by the first generation of dot.bombs.

The more he thought about it, the more amazing Tom felt was the coincidence that had brought them both to this place at this time.

Sometimes, though, he found himself giving way to

a superstitious fear that it was all too good to be true, that he had been far luckier than he deserved and he would be made to pay somehow. But he quickly banished such negativity as simply an echo of the bad days. He could never go back to being who he was. He was a different man now.

Tom and Clare were married as soon as he was able to remain upright for the brief ceremony without the use of a cane. Her parents flew in for the event, plus her sister, a portrait painter who lived on Cape Cod, and her brother who was a doctor in Miami and came with his wife and three young children. Tom enjoyed the feel of having a family around him, since he had none of his own. He was an only child, and his parents were divorced by the time he went to college. His mother had since died; and his father, a marketing executive for a soft drinks conglomerate, was remarried with a new family and living in Asia.

The newly married couple moved into Clare's rented house, which was fine for the two of them though not big enough to start the family they both wanted. But the most important thing for the time being was to get Tom's career jump-started. He put out feelers to old friends in the advertising business, and got a sympathetic hearing but not much else. The fact was, he knew perfectly well, they saw him as yesterday's man.

Undeterred, he tried other avenues. With Clare's help he put together a prospectus for a company of his own and they started looking for investors. Then he had a brainwave. He saw that an old friend of his, a promoter in the music business, was putting out tours of old rock bands that appealed both to the nostalgia market and to a surprising number of kids. He made a call and was given permission to go along with a couple of them, just himself with a video camera.

Travelling for weeks at a time with a bunch of hardened rockers was an experience designed, as he and Clare had foreseen, to put anybody's dedication to sobriety beyond a casual test. Tom came through not only without a slip but without a moment's temptation. The first week on the road he checked out a couple of local AA meetings, but more out of habit than need. After that, he didn't bother.

The footage he got was sensational, and the result was a documentary that got invited to Sundance, started picking up prizes, and was sold to television throughout the world. He also started getting calls from companies that wanted to be in business with him.

Although he wasn't making the kind of money he had once made in advertising, he was enjoying his work and life a lot more. He and Clare took out a mortgage on a beautiful colonial-style white clapboard house on a leafy avenue. Besides, money went a lot further in Saracen Springs than it did in Manhattan, to which he commuted several times a month for meetings.

They had barely got the carpets down and the curtains in place when Clare announced, to their mutual delight, that she was pregnant.

5

Julia Katharine Freeman weighed in at six pounds twelve ounces. Because she was the first child of a woman over thirty, her parents had taken their doctor's advice and had all the tests available. Aside from being reassured that their baby was healthy, it meant they had not needed to waste time thinking about boys' names when they knew for sure they were having a girl.

The first time Tom and Clare brought their daughter home, she seemed to positively gurgle her approval of the light, brightly painted room they had prepared for her overlooking the leafy garden.

'I think we got it right,' Tom said, watching her happily batting a small hand at the delicate mobile suspended over her cot.

'I think we did,' said Clare, catching his eye with a smile.

Throughout the following weeks and months, Julia did her share of screaming through the night, catching small infections, and giving her first-time parents one or two stomach-churning scares. The worst was when she crawled into a linen cupboard and fell asleep, leaving them frantically searching the house for what seemed a lifetime but in fact was a little under twelve minutes.

Making friends between baby and household pets was one of the subjects they had read up on. The best advice, endorsed by friends who had tried it, was to place the child on a rug with the pet or pets in question, and let them get on with introducing themselves to each other – while, of course, keeping a careful watch to make sure things didn't get out of hand. But both Sam, their black Labrador, and Turk, their Siamese cat, seemed delighted by this new addition to the family. Turk initially tried to feign lofty indifference, but soon began to purr with satisfaction as the small pink hands learnt how to pat and stroke him without poking him in the eye or pulling his whiskers too hard.

Clare had continued working through almost the full term of her pregnancy. She had planned on taking at least a year off to look after Julia full time; then, perhaps with the help of a nanny, she thought she might ease herself back into work, much of which she could anyway do from home. But that was a decision she would make later.

She had still not gone back even to part-time work by the time Julia had her second birthday, which was around the time she started to talk. Her first word out of nowhere one morning was 'melon'. Why she should have made that choice baffled and amused them both.

David Ambrose

They weren't even sure that she'd ever seen a melon, let alone tasted one.

'I don't believe she said the word at all,' Clare maintained. 'It was just a baby noise, like poo-poo or coo-coo.'

'No, she was really making an effort,' Tom insisted. 'It was something she was trying to say.'

'OK, so let's see if she says it again. Come on, sweetie, talk to Mommy and Daddy. This is Mommy . . . this is Daddy . . .' The three of them were sitting cross-legged on the floor of Julia's room one Sunday before breakfast, with old Sam sitting off to one side, his tongue lolling out of his mouth, observing the ritual with genial curiosity.

'Mommy . . . Julia . . . Daddy . . . Mommy . . . Julia . . .'

Both Tom and Clare repeated this mantra several times, tapping each other or Julia herself on the chest to demonstrate which name applied to whom. The child watched with bright-eyed interest as first her father's finger, then her mother's, moved around their little triangle. She quickly caught on to the idea that they wanted her to repeat what they were saying. And so she tried.

'Mom-ma . . . Dad-da . . . Mom-ma . . . Da-da . . . Mom-ma . . .'

Clare let out a squeal of delight and swept the child into her arms. 'She did it! She's talking! Oh, aren't you a clever little girl! You're talking!'

They continued with the exercise, wanting to be sure

that this wasn't just some fluke but that Julia really had grasped the idea of what communicating in words was all about. Certainly, it was clear that she had got the hang of Mommy and Daddy; what she had more difficulty with was her own name.

Clare repeated, 'Mommy . . . Daddy . . . Julia . . .'

'Mom-ma . . . Da-da . . .'

'Julia,' Tom finished for her when she stopped yet again, unable to go further. He tapped her softly on the chest several times to emphasize that this little person right there was Julia.

She seemed to understand. She fixed him with an intense wide-eyed gaze, then copied his gesture, tapping herself on the chest.

'Mel-on-ee,' she said.

Tom and Clare looked at each other, more amused than anything else. 'Does she know any Melanie?' he asked.

Clare shook her head. 'I don't think so.'

'*Julia*,' Tom repeated, turning his attention back to his baby daughter. 'Mommy . . . Daddy . . . *Julia*.'

The child frowned. This was starting to confuse her.

'Mom-ma, Dad-da,' she said, more firmly than before, waving an arm at each of them in turn to make absolutely clear that she had got the point they were trying to make. Then she hit herself on the chest with an open hand, and repeated, 'Mel-on-ee.'

This time their smiles, Clare's and Tom's when they looked at each other, were replaced by mild concern.

Was there something wrong with the child's hearing?

Clare said, 'She got "Mommy" and "Daddy" all right. Maybe she just can't say "Julia" yet.'

'Then how come she can say "Melonee", or "Melanie", or whatever it is?'

Clare thought a moment. 'Maybe it's Susan,' she said. Susan was the girl who babysat for them once or twice a week. She was the fifteen-year-old daughter of a neighbour, smart and totally reliable.

'You mean Susan calls her Melanie?'

Clare shrugged. 'Maybe Susan's got a friend called Melanie. Maybe she's heard them talking on the phone and made the wrong association. I don't know. I'll ask Susan. It must be something like that.'

They looked at their daughter, and she looked back at them, her face reflecting the puzzlement she saw.

'Julia,' Clare repeated softly, but with an undertone of quiet urgency, resting her hands lightly on the child's tiny shoulders.

'Julia,' Tom echoed as she turned to look up at him, searching his face for confirmation of what her mother was trying to tell her. 'Julia.'

She looked back at her mother, then back at Tom. Abruptly, her face lit up with one of those dazzling infant smiles of recognition where all doubt is swept aside and everything is suddenly right with the world.

'Joo-ya,' she said, swinging her arms and clapping her chubby hands in front of her. 'Joo-ya.'

6

He could not remember where or when he'd had that first drink. *As every alcoholic knows, the first drink is the only one that counts. The others just follow on, drink after drink, with no end in sight. It's part of the disease: a pattern. If for some reason you forget where it leads, that first drink, you start again . . . and pretty soon you find out.*

Of course, Tom knew perfectly well that you don't really forget. What you do is push the memory down into your subconscious and slam the lid. And suddenly the lid becomes a bar stool.

Which was why, however many drinks later, he found himself stumbling through a tangle of undergrowth and wild grass, falling on the muddy earth, picking himself up and struggling on. Up ahead of him the ground rose towards a few straggling bushes that seemed to mark the limit of what might once have been a garden. All he could see beyond that was a cold slate-grey sky.

He made an effort to clear his befuddled brain and recall where he was and how he got there. But his mind remained resolutely

27

blank. He could remember nothing of the last few hours. Or was it more than hours? Days, even?

He looked back in the direction he had come from – and for the first time saw the house. It sat, like an exposed tooth in a well-worn gum, on the far edge of the hollow he was struggling to climb out of. It looked abandoned, not quite a ruin, but with its windows broken or boarded up and tiles missing from the roof. There was a strange tower at one corner, like an imitation-Gothic castle.

What was that place? Why did he have to get away from it as though his life depended on it? He knew that something had happened in there. Was it something he had done? Or something done to him? His mind was blank, all memory wiped out by shame or shock, or fear of discovery . . .

The sound of a car passing by was so close that it startled him. Instinctively he flung himself to the ground. He heard the hum of tyres on a slightly damp road, but could see nothing. It was followed by the sound of a heavier vehicle, a truck maybe. He figured that the road must be just beyond the crest of weed-choked trees and bushes up ahead.

He knew he had to get away from there unseen, which meant he must be careful of that road. But why was he so afraid? What was he running from? Why couldn't he remember?

He looked up at the sky again. The clouds were low and a pale light was slanting from the horizon. It could not be long after dawn, which meant he must have spent the night, or part of it, inside that house, on the far side of the half-rotten door that he could see swinging in the light breeze on its hinges.

What had happened in there? What had he done?

The thought of going back to find out filled him with a ter-

ror so overwhelming that it made him almost physically sick. He staggered on, not caring as foliage and branches scratched his face and hands and tore his clothes. He fought his way through until he reached the road, which was deserted now. He started down it, only half-consciously taking in the bleak post-urban sprawl of empty warehouses and crumbling factories with their smokeless chimneys stabbing skywards. This was not a place where people lived or worked any more, just passed through on their way to somewhere else.

Still he felt afraid of being seen, so he continued to run, possessed only by the insane thought that if he ran fast and far enough, he would become invisible . . .

He must have blacked out at some point, because the next thing he remembered was opening his eyes and finding himself in a darkened room. He sat up sharply, disoriented, his heart beating fast. Then he saw the familiar red figures of the digital clock beside his bed. They read 3:30 a.m. But how did he get there? How long had he been there? It was not possible that the horror he had just lived through had been a dream.

Instinctively he turned in search of Clare's sleeping form, but her side of the bed was empty. Where was she? What had happened to her? Had she been part of what he had been running from? Had he left her behind in that terrifying house?

There was a sound, a soft footfall. He turned, and saw her standing in the door, a robe loosely tied at her waist.

David Ambrose

'Sorry,' she said, 'I tried not to wake you.'

He absorbed the sight of her with a mixture of relief and fear. 'What happened . . . ?'

'Julia was crying. She's sleeping now.'

'I mean . . . How did I get here?'

She looked puzzled. 'What d'you mean? You were asleep.'

'No, I . . . I wasn't . . . I was . . .'

He swung his feet to the floor and stood up, feeling none of the sharp knife-thrust of pain that he might have expected after soaking his brain in alcohol the way he must have done. His thoughts were clear, his hands and vision steady.

'Tom, what are you doing?'

He was picking up his shirt and jeans from the armchair in the corner where he sometimes left them. There was no caked or drying mud on them. Nor on any of his jackets when he opened the closet where they hung. His shoes sat in neat rows on the angled ledge below. What had he done with those torn and filthy things he had been wearing?

'Tom?'

She came up behind him, and he turned. 'I don't understand. I was running through this overgrown garden, through mud and dirt . . .'

'Darling, you were dreaming.'

'No, it was real . . . I was running from this house . . .'

'*This* house?'

'No – a house I'd never seen before. Something had

30

happened there, but I don't know what it was. I just knew I had to get away.'

'It was just a nightmare. Come back to bed.'

'Not *just* a nightmare. I . . . I'd been drinking.'

'Oh . . . one of those.' Her robe fell open as she slipped her arms around him and pressed the soft warmth of her body against his. 'You told me you still dream about it sometimes, but the nice thing is you wake up sober, no hangover. Look at you – you're fine.'

'It was just so . . . frighteningly real.'

'Come back to bed.'

She led him by the hand, pausing only to let her robe fall to the floor. 'You and Julia both,' she said as they slipped beneath the covers. 'Bad dreams, that's all.'

He held her close, saying nothing.

7

Next time Susan came over to babysit, Clare asked her about Melanie. But the teenager knew nobody of that name; nor, so far as she remembered, had she ever used the name around Julia. But as Julia never mentioned it again, and was quite happy to respond to her own name instead of insisting she was someone else, Tom and Clare forgot about the whole thing.

For almost a year.

Tom was in New York for a meeting at WNET, the public broadcasting station. They liked a proposal he had put to them for a series of interviews with artists – writers, painters, composers – about where they'd grown up. The department heads he had come to see agreed that it could 'have legs' and gave him an order for six programmes. As he was leaving the sleek black building on West 33rd Street that houses WNET, his cellphone rang. It was Clare.

'Darling, you're not still in your meeting, are you?'

'No, I'm heading for the station. What's up?'

'It's not serious, but Julia's in the hospital.'

He stopped walking. Someone bumped into him and cursed angrily, but he paid no attention.

'What happened?'

'They're not sure if it's an allergy or something she ate. She was nauseous and running a fever. Linda rang me and I came right home.' Linda was the nanny they had hired when Clare had resumed part-time work three months earlier.

'But she's in the hospital?'

'They want to keep her under observation overnight.'

Tom was walking again, the phone pressed to his ear. He could tell from Clare's voice that there was something she wasn't saying.

'Are they sure it's not serious?'

'Quite sure. She's upset, that's all.'

'How d'you mean, upset?'

He heard her hesitate. 'She was a little . . . confused.'

'Confused how? What d'you mean?'

'She didn't know who I was. She kept saying she wanted her mommy. She didn't know me.'

Without noticing it, Tom had started walking briskly along 33rd towards Eighth. Now he started to run. He turned left, heading north, and flagged down a cab. He told the driver to get him to Grand Central as fast as he could. He was supposed to have lunch with a publisher who wanted to put out the artist interviews in book form if he swung the TV deal, but he would call him and explain.

When he reached the station he found there was a train in twenty minutes. As he waited, he left a message with the publisher's assistant, then called Clare back.

'Can you talk?'

'Yes. I'm with her, but she's asleep. Wait a minute, I'm just going out of the room . . .'

'Is Bella there?' he asked. Bella Warne was Julia's regular paediatrician.

'She was. She's coming back later when they get a second lot of test results.'

'What did she say?'

'Only that she could rule out the worst things, like meningitis, or some virus that attacks the nervous system. There's no sign of motor or brain impairment.'

'But she didn't know you. You said Julia didn't know you.'

'At first. It was only for about a minute. I think it was the fever. It was alarming, that's all.'

He saw that the gate had opened and passengers were starting to file down to the platform. He followed them, telling Clare that he would go straight to the hospital from the station, but she should call him before then if there was any news.

His phone didn't ring for the next hour. Nor did it ring on the fifteen-minute drive from the parking lot where he'd left his car to the Charles A. Martin Memorial Hospital on Bingham Road. A nurse at reception gave him directions, and when the elevator doors didn't open immediately, he took the stairs two at a time to the children's floor.

Julia was awake now. She looked pale and subdued, but otherwise normal. She greeted him with an enthusiastic 'Daddy!' and gave him her usual kiss and hug.

He had made eye contact with Clare the moment he entered. A flash of mutual reassurance passed between them. Nothing new had happened, but he could tell from the way she took his hand how glad she was to have him there. She had been badly shaken.

'Now, young lady,' he said, sitting down, 'what are you doing in bed at this time of day?'

Julia seemed remarkably calm, almost passive. 'Have they given her anything?' he asked Clare.

'No tranquillizers. Something to get the fever down, that's all. Her temperature's normal now.'

'Daddy, look . . . !'

She pointed to a round Band Aid on her arm, obviously where a hypodermic had been inserted.

'Just to take a blood sample,' Clare said, and squeezed Julia's hand. 'You were very brave, weren't you, darling?'

'It hurt.'

After that, they mostly tried to make jokes, doing everything they could think of to make the child laugh. Clare had told her simply that she must have eaten something that had made her sick, and the doctors wanted to find out what it was so that she wouldn't do it again. She seemed quite unconcerned by the prospect of having to stay there overnight, though that was partly because her mummy would be staying with her.

They waited till a nurse came in to check her temperature again before stepping outside to talk. They had already agreed that Tom would stay there for the rest of the afternoon while Clare returned to the office to clear up a couple of things.

'It's my fault,' she said as soon as they were alone. 'I have to stop working.'

'Why? How is this your fault?'

'That thing about wanting her mommy, and me not being her mommy . . .'

'Oh, come on . . .'

'I'm serious. I think she felt I'd deserted her. I'm *not* her mommy any more, not the way she wants.'

'Are you saying she got sick and ran a fever because you went back to work?'

'Maybe it's psychosomatic.'

'And her not knowing you was just an act?'

'I don't know. How could a child of that age . . . ?'

She gave a sigh of deep weariness, almost despair. Tom took her in his arms.

'Look, she's fine now. You can see that, can't you?'

'Yes, but . . .'

'But nothing. Let's not do anything hasty – all right?'

After a moment she said, 'All right. It's just that . . .'

Her voice shook. She was close to tears.

'Tell me.'

'She was screaming. It was one of the nurses who

calmed her down. I didn't know what to do. I've never felt so terrified and helpless in my life. I just backed away till I felt myself pressing against the wall. Then suddenly she calmed down. The nurse pointed at me and said, "You know who this is, don't you?" She just looked at me for a long time, then said, "Mommy."'

'So?'

'It's just this feeling I had . . .'

'What feeling?'

Clare turned her eyes up to his, searching for a sign that he understood what she was telling him.

'That she didn't mean it. She was just saying it to please me.'

8

In the two hours he was alone with her, Tom tried everything he could think of to draw the story out of Julia from her point of view. He got nothing more than a bare statement of the facts.

'I felt sick. My tummy hurt.'

'Then what happened?'

'We went to the hospital.'

'Who did you go with?'

'With Linda.'

'Was Mommy there?'

'Mommy came after.'

He was convinced she had no memory of the events Clare had described. Certainly he got no sense that she was telling the story to please him. Even though Clare told him she had only felt it for a moment, it had left a deep mark on her, which wasn't surprising. It was a terrible thing to happen.

But the child had a fever. She was delirious. That was the obvious explanation. The only one.

A nurse came in to check Julia's temperature again. He waited anxiously, but it was normal. The fever had been brief and showed no sign of returning. And Julia's spirits were picking up. She said she was hungry. He left them fixing up what the nurse was going to get her to eat, and slipped into the bathroom.

As he washed his hands, Tom contemplated his face in the mirror. It was true what his friends had told him – those who'd had children years ago: it changed you like nothing you could imagine. Everything suddenly took second place to that tiny, fragile life that you had brought into the world, and which you would sacrifice yourself to protect without a second thought.

Was that just the power of genes? A blind force dictating the survival of the young and procreant over the old and spent? Or was something else going on? Were love, concern and the aching tenderness of parenthood more than just tools thrown up by evolution to keep things moving relentlessly and meaninglessly on?

Did it matter either way? All he knew for sure was how little he knew. He wasn't religious, at least not beyond the acceptance of 'a higher power' that was part of the twelve-step programme that had so crucially helped him towards sobriety almost five years earlier, but he certainly felt that life was more than just a chemical process. Since the birth of their daughter, they had both felt convinced, in a strange and indefinable way, that something more was going on.

The first thing he heard as he stepped back into the

room was the nurse's laughter. 'You're teasing me,' she said. 'Your name isn't Melanie. It's Julia.'

'Melanie!'

Julia was sitting up, a favourite soft toy clutched in her arms, a big smile on her face, enjoying herself.

'All right, I'll call you Melanie if you want me to. But I know you're really called Julia.'

'Melanie!' Julia countered gleefully, like a tennis player lobbing the ball back over the net, content to keep going until her opponent grew tired and gave up.

'Look, your daddy's here. Why don't we ask him what your name is?'

Julia hadn't heard Tom come in. She looked around sharply, almost guiltily. In that moment, he understood what Clare had been talking about. Suddenly there was something between them, his daughter and him-self, something alien. It was a strange and disturbing feeling.

'Who's Melanie?' he said, trying to keep his tone light, as though he wanted to join in the game. 'I can't see anyone here called Melanie.'

Julia's face relaxed into a coy smile. She began to rock the toy, a monkey, in her arms, saying nothing.

'Is this Melanie?' he said, sitting on the edge of the bed and pointing to the little monkey.

She shook her head, and pressed her face down into the toy as though wanting to hide from his questions.

'I'll be back with your tea in a few minutes,' the nurse said brightly. 'Can I bring you anything, Mr Freeman?'

'No,' he said absently. Then remembered his manners and added, 'Thank you. No, I'm fine.'

The nurse went out. Tom didn't say anything for a moment, then sat on the edge of Julia's bed.

'Why did you say you were called Melanie?' he said, still keeping his tone light, as though simply asking her to explain the rules so that he could join in the game.

She didn't answer, just shook her head again, all the while keeping her face buried in the little monkey, which she was now squeezing tightly.

'Do you know someone called Melanie?' he asked, running his hand lightly over her hair as he spoke.

She kept her face buried, as though afraid to look at her father. He knew he mustn't press too far. Yet he had to get some kind of answer. He couldn't just leave it there.

'Was it a game?' he said.

She nodded her head vigorously, almost too quickly, as though willing to agree to anything that would end this conversation. And he, of course, had offered her the perfect way out. All just a game.

'Look at me, darling,' Tom said.

She lifted her face towards him, her expression solemn now, and a little wary.

'It's all right, I'm not angry. I just want to know who Melanie is.'

'Melanie gone,' she said, in a voice so soft it was almost a whisper, and strangely more babyish than her normal one. 'Melanie gone now.'

9

You are so selfish, how can you do this to me. I was young and I had a right to a career.

Did you hear me? I told you you bought your guilt with me then with him and now it doesn't work any more. It's over. Stop now. I will not let you put him in hospital for a treatment I know wouldn't work. You've got him I have him then. There's nothing he could want with me. There might be something here in him all the same. There I told him all her knowledge I collected I bought at the drama he knew so much the grown-up needs.

Dr Bella Warne regarded the couple thoughtfully from behind her desk. 'It's not unusual for a child to have an imaginary friend,' she said. 'Especially an only child. In fact it's quite normal.'

'It's not exactly an imaginary friend, Bella,' Clare said, refusing to have her concern dismissed so lightly. 'Julia says she *is* Melanie. It's more like a multiple-personality thing.'

Dr Warne reflected on this for a moment. She was a large-boned woman with straight dark hair and an unsmiling face. Only her eyes, which could be penetrating or kindly as the occasion demanded, hinted at the sharp intelligence behind them.

'All right,' she said, 'I'm going to give you a rational explanation which has nothing to do with *Three Faces of Eve* or anything else you might have watched on late-night television.'

She raised a placatory hand when she saw Clare about to protest. 'I know – it's natural you fear the worst.

42

You wouldn't be parents if you didn't. But let's just think about what happened. You said "Melanie" was the first word she used, after "Mommy" and "Daddy".'

'Actually it was before,' Tom said. 'She was trying to say something that sound like "melon". Anyway, whatever it was, it sounded like a word, so we started trying to teach her "Momma", "Dadda", and "Julia". She got "Momma" and "Dadda" just fine, but Julia was a no-no. She kept hitting herself on the chest and saying, "Me Melanie".'

'So you started this name-the-family game after she said "melon".'

'Yes.'

'Had you been eating a melon, or talking about it? Was there a melon in the room?'

'Absolutely not. That's why I thought it odd she was trying to say the word.'

'Maybe she wasn't. Maybe it was just one of those sounds that come out of babies' mouths. But because you picked up on it and started teaching her *your* names, she thought that "melon", or something like it, must be her own.'

'As you say, it's rational, Bella,' Clare said, not yet ready to yield her point, 'but it doesn't explain where that whole Melanie thing came from yesterday.'

The doctor looked at her levelly, taking her concern seriously. 'I think it does, Clare. Children remember the oddest things. She might well recall that you'd given her the impression that her name was Melanie, then told her it was something else. So she thinks she has a choice of names.'

Clare regarded her sceptically. Recognizing the look, Bella's face relaxed into a smile that started at the eyes and spread a surprising warmth over the whole of her somewhat forbidding face.

'All right, it's only a theory, but it's a plausible one. All I'm saying is, I really don't think you have anything to worry about.'

The three of them walked from Bella's office to Julia's room. She was dressed and ready to go home. After hugging the nurses and Bella, she walked out of the building holding her mother's hand and still clutching her favourite stuffed monkey.

They talked it through, and Clare eventually relented on the idea of giving up her career. What finally tipped the balance was her fear of turning into an over-protective mother. Besides, Julia was due to start pre-school soon, so she would be spending less time at home.

Tom made another trip into New York to see the publisher he'd stood up the previous week. They sketched out a deal and as much of a schedule as they could at this early stage. It was after seven when he got home, but he knew the moment he saw Clare that something was wrong. She was tense and pale. She hadn't called him, she said, because it was still nothing to panic about. But it was troubling. It had happened again, the 'Melanie' business.

Clare had been going upstairs, passing Julia's door, when she had heard her talking. She had stopped to listen – not meaning to eavesdrop, but simply out of that tender curiosity any parent has about the mysterious imaginary world of their children. She supposed that Julia was playing with her toys and dolls, hosting a make-believe tea party, perhaps, the way Clare remembered doing in her own childhood.

She heard the word 'mommy', followed by a pause, then Julia said several words she couldn't quite make out. She edged closer to the half-open door, and saw the child talking on her bright yellow toy telephone. Clare knew perfectly well that children talk to imaginary people on toy phones all the time; that is why toy phones are made. But there was something about the concentration that Julia was putting into the conversation that made Clare listen more closely.

'When Mommy goes to work,' she heard, 'Linda looks after me.' There was a pause, followed by, 'Daddy goes to work, too, but sometimes he stays home.'

Julia fell silent again, nodding once or twice as she listened to the phone, then finally she said, 'I like Linda . . . Yes . . . No . . . I do . . . I love you too, Mommy . . .'

At that moment she noticed Clare in the door, broke off her conversation and hung up. Embarrassed at being caught spying on her own child, Clare came into the room and knelt by her, bringing their eyes level.

'Who were you talking to, darling?'

Julia dropped her gaze and didn't answer.

'Were you talking to Mommy?' she asked brightly, trying to communicate her willingness to play this game by whatever rules Julia chose.

Julia nodded solemnly in response, still not looking up.

'What did Mommy say?'

'She said, "I miss you, Melanie".'

Clare froze. 'Melanie?'

Julia looked up in sudden alarm, like someone who has betrayed a vital secret by a slip of the tongue.

'Mommy doesn't call you Melanie,' Clare said, 'do I?'

Still the child did not reply, just continued to gaze fearfully into her mother's eyes as though caught out in some awful lie and awaiting a sharp scolding.

'Darling, it's all right,' Clare said, reassuring her. 'Mommy isn't angry. Just tell me why you said I called you Melanie.

The child twisted her fingers for some moments, painfully embarrassed, as though searching for a way to explain herself. Eventually, she found one.

'Not you,' she said. 'My other mommy.'

10

He was standing in a cellar. A faint light filtered in: looking up, he saw a tiny skylight, too high and too grimy to see out of. The floor was uneven, hardened earth, with stones embedded in it here and there. The walls were old bare brick, crumbling in places.

He had no idea how he had got there. All he knew was that something terrible had happened in that place. Something he did not want to remember.

Something he had done.

But what was it? His mind was a blank. He was in shock – that was why he could remember nothing.

He knew the answer was close by, somewhere in the darkness. All he had to do was take a step into the darkest of the shadows, and he would know.

But he was paralysed by fear and could not move. He clung on to the thought that he must not give way to panic, but trying to avoid it was like holding his breath under water; his lungs were on fire with pain and about to burst. Suddenly he was retching for air, crouched over with his head between his legs and trying

47

to vomit; but it passed. As his breathing steadied he was seized with only one thought: to get out of that place.

He looked around once more, and saw an opening. It seemed as dark at first as everywhere else, but then he persuaded himself he could detect a hint of light in the distance. He started towards it, breaking into a run, bruising himself and scraping his hands on the rough walls as he went. He stumbled around one corner, then another, and found himself in a long passage with a door at the end, half rotten and hanging off its hinges so that daylight showed through the cracks in it. He stopped.

For some moments he did not move, his headlong dash for freedom suddenly restrained by the fear of what might lie in wait outside. He edged forward, making no sound, listening. All he could hear was the whistle of a light wind, but no movement and no voices. He pushed open the ruined door a cautious inch or two, so slowly that anyone watching would hardly have observed the movement. He peered out, and saw an overgrown tangle of weeds and grass. The ground rose away from where he stood, reaching a few straggling bushes that seemed to mark the limit of a garden. Beyond that, all he could see was a slate-grey early morning sky.

Suddenly he knew where he was. He stepped outside and began to climb, following what might once have been a path, but was now overgrown and slippery with mud. He lost his footing and landed on his hands and knees. As he picked himself up, he looked back, and saw the house he had just left: abandoned, boarded up, and with that strange imitation-Gothic tower at one corner he remembered from last time, it sat on the far edge of the untended, run-wild garden he was struggling to climb. Something about it *made him think, as he remembered from last time, of an exposed tooth in a well-worn gum.*

Last time? But how could there have been a last time? Unless last time was some kind of prophetic nightmare, a glimpse into his future, and now he was living the real thing.

But he didn't believe in ESP or anything like that. He never had. So this must be . . .

'Darling? What is it? Are you all right?'

He felt a hand on his arm, and pulled away with a shout – 'No!' – of rage and fear.

'Tom!'

It was Clare's voice. In the darkness. He was back in the darkness, in that awful house.

A light went on. He saw her hand on the bedside lamp.

'For heaven's sake, you were having a nightmare.'

'No, I . . .'

Again he felt her hand on his arm, but this time he didn't pull away. 'I'm sorry, I . . . I thought I was . . . I was in this house . . .'

'*Which* house?'

'Some place . . . I don't know what or where . . .'

He raised a hand to his forehead to steady the dizzying sensation he felt as he sat up.

'You were struggling like a madman.'

'I was . . . running from . . . something . . .'

He realized as he spoke that he was still out of breath, and his heart was beating fast.

'From what?'

'I don't know . . . it was just a dream . . . crazy . . .'

'Are you sure you're all right?'

'I'm fine. Sorry I woke you. Go back to sleep.'

They both settled down. Clare switched out the light. For a while they lay side by side in silence, until she said, 'Why don't you tell me about it?'

'There's nothing to tell,' he said, then added, 'Besides, I don't want to sleep alone.'

'What d'you mean?'

He sensed the movement as she turned towards him in the dark. 'You know the quickest way to empty a room, don't you?' he said. 'Tell people your dreams.'

She laughed and reached out for him. They rolled into each other's arms, and thought no more of talking.

11

'Brendan Hunt is the man to see,' Bella Warne said. 'He trained at the Mayhall in Boston before settling for a quieter life. He's first class – published a couple of very highly regarded papers in the last few years.'

Using her influence, she got them an appointment in two days. Dr Hunt was about Tom's age, with thick sandy hair, an open, fresh face, and graceful hands that remained clasped in his lap as he talked, even when he leant forward to ask a question of Julia. He wore a tweed jacket over an open denim shirt, and had an easy manner that immediately put both parents and child at ease.

'You know who this is, don't you?' he asked Julia, indicating Clare.

'Mommy,' she replied, with the kind of smile that said this was a silly game, but she was happy to play it.

'And this?' nodding Tom's way.

'Daddy.'

He paused a moment, letting her replies hang lightly in the air before moving on.

'Do you have another mommy and daddy?' he asked.

Julia looked down at the floor, as if suddenly unsure how to deal with this.

'It's all right. You can tell us.'

'Yes,' she said, without looking up.

'Are they here now?'

She shook her head.

'Where are they?'

'I don't know.'

'Can you tell us what they look like? Maybe you can draw them for us.'

Julia looked up now, but at him, not her parents. When she spoke, it was as though they were no longer in the room, and she had something important that she must make this stranger in front of her understand.

'My daddy's gone away.'

Hunt showed no flicker of response, just kept his relaxed, friendly gaze focused on her earnest face.

'Not this daddy. Your daddy's here.'

Without hesitating, Julia said, 'My other daddy.'

Again Hunt offered no response. Tom looked neither right nor left, though he sensed as much as saw Clare's anxious glance in his direction.

'And what does your other daddy call you?'

'Melanie,' the child said, with a slight inflection at the end, almost as though it was a question, though quite obviously it wasn't. She was simply unsure of whether she ought to be saying this.

'That's fine,' Hunt said, leaning slightly closer and

creating a sense of intimacy between them. 'Now why
don't you go and play next door with Nurse Rogers, then
Mommy and Daddy will take you home in a little while.
OK?'

Julia went happily into the game- and toy-stocked
room next door, under the kindly supervision of the mid-
dle-aged nurse. Brendan Hunt turned to face the worried couple across his desk. His office was wood-panelled
and comfortably furnished. Framed degrees and testi-
monials hung on the wall behind him, but the other walls
bore a collection of original paintings, mostly abstract.

'I'm quite sure we can rule out any physical basis for
this,' he said. 'We'll do further tests, including a brain
scan. In fact, we'll do whatever we have to or whatever
you feel you want us to. But the truth is I have a strong
sense that this is nothing more than a child's imagination running riot – or if not quite a riot,' he added with
a smile, 'at least threatening to disturb the peace.'

'But *why*?'

Clare's question was charged with the frustration of
someone who can see everything with perfect clarity,
except the sense behind it.

'I think if I see her a few times, we may be able to
find that out. Why don't we start with you both telling
me something about yourselves?'

Tom and Clare had prepared for this, working on
the assumption that if a child has psychological problems, it's more likely to be the parents' fault than the
child's. They had searched their memories and their

consciences long into the night to think of things they might have done to provoke this condition in their daughter – if, indeed, 'condition' was the right way to describe it. Clare continued to blame herself for returning to work too soon, but Tom would have none of it. He, on the other hand, could never forget that he was an alcoholic. It was a disease, admittedly, and not a sin: not something he had an obligation to feel guilty about. But like all alcoholics, like addicts of whatever kind, he was acutely aware of the effects his problem could have on other people's lives, especially those closest to him. He had not had a drink in five years, so neither Clare nor Julia had been exposed to the worst aspects of his disease.

But were there other aspects? Other ways of doing damage? He couldn't be sure. Maybe, he told himself, there was something about the mindset of the addict that makes them dangerous to other people even when sober. Maybe they, or at least some of them, are just lethal human beings.

Hunt listened to all of it – their fears and hopes, their guilt and their confessions – with a professional, non-judgemental equanimity, occasionally pausing to take notes but never interrupting, except for the occasional question that would help draw out what they were trying to say, or clarify something that they had not yet managed to wholly understand themselves. Only when they had finished did he raise his gaze to theirs and offer them a gently reassuring smile.

'What I normally suggest with a child this young is a form of play therapy. And it's most valuable if it's fairly intensive, maybe three times a week, or even daily to begin with. That's what I suggest with Julia, at least for the next couple of weeks, then see where we go from there.'

'Would we be part of that,' Tom asked, 'or would you see her alone?'

'You can be present if you wish, certainly if Julia prefers it, which is often the case for the first session or two. But even a child as young as Julia sometimes needs to say things that she might not know how to say in front of her parents. And part of the therapist's job is to keep those things in confidence, if appropriate. I always give parents an outline of what's going on in treatment, but not necessarily a detailed record.'

'How do you define appropriate?' Clare asked.

Hunt sat back. 'That depends. Obviously if the child asks you not to tell the parents, then you don't. At least not right away. Or unless there's something of overriding importance that leaves you no choice. There are no hard and fast rules.'

'Do you ever tape sessions?' Tom asked.

'It depends on the case. Sometimes it can be helpful, if I'm seeing the child alone, to play the parents a tape afterwards. That's something I may do with a very young patient, though it can be counterproductive with an older child – again, the confidentiality thing.'

Tom and Clare looked at each other. By some tacit

David Ambrose

communication between them, it fell to Tom to turn to Hunt and say, 'All right, whatever you think best – we'll go along with you.'

12

Julia had her first full session two days later. Her parents had decided it was a little heavy having both of them there, so Clare went the first time and Tom the second. 'Play therapy' turned out to be just what it sounded like. It took place in a room which was bare of everything except chairs, a table, a soft carpet and plenty of pillows. There were various drawers on one wall, each of which contained different sets of toys. Every child who came had his or her own drawer which was ritually unpacked at the start of every session, and packed up again at the end.

A large part of the first session, Clare told Tom afterwards, consisted of Julia making a selection of the toys that would go into her drawer. Hunt guided her unobtrusively towards a choice that would encourage her to act out her 'double life', if that was what it was. By the time Tom sat in on the second session, she already had 'mommy and daddy' dolls for Clare and himself, plus two more dolls for her imaginary parents. He noticed that while the dolls for her 'real' parents, Clare and Tom, were kept very much together and were obviously a couple, the imaginary parents were apart, with the father as a kind of token figure playing little or no role whatever.

Neither Tom nor Clare tried too intensely to decipher what all of it meant. Hunt told them that it was too early even for him to form any clear-cut ideas. What was obvious to the parents, however, was how much Julia liked and trusted the amiable psychiatrist with his easy manner. Clare sat in once more on the third session, but after that the child was quite content to be left alone. Whichever parent took her to the clinic for her session merely spent an hour or so in a comfortable waiting room reading a book or magazine. Afterwards, Hunt would give a brief summary of progress.

'I'm using a very light form of hypnosis,' he told Tom after one session about two weeks in. 'That sounds more dramatic than it is. Children are good subjects for hypnosis because of their imagination. I use it simply to help focus and concentration.'

'Do you mean she's in a trance?'

'No, no. You wouldn't even know she was hypnotized. She moves around quite normally, eyes open. Why don't you sit in next time and see for yourself?'

It was Clare, not Tom, who did as Hunt suggested. All that happened, she told Tom afterwards, was that he told Julia to imagine she was on a magic carpet that would carry her anywhere she wanted to go. Then there was a magic hat, a magic ring, and even a magic toy dog that told her secrets only she could hear.

There was no doubt that Julia was enjoying herself enormously in these sessions. Her parents also got the impression, not just from the reports Hunt gave them as the weeks went by, but also from the way Julia behaved at home, that things were going well. One thing Hunt had told them at the outset was that they should never, under any circumstances, ask Julia any questions about her imaginary family.

'Inviting her to talk about them only validates them for her. And if she does talk about them, the best way to respond is by changing the subject. I think you'll very soon find that they disappear entirely from her conversation. What I'm getting her to do is, quite literally, pack them up in her drawer and leave them there. When she starts a session by unpacking only those things that represent her life with you and nothing else, then we'll have achieved pretty much what we hope to.'

It took three months to reach that point. When therapy is successful, Hunt said, it ends not with a bang but a whimper. There's no dramatic overnight change; you just realize one day that a problem you used to have isn't around any more. Like the memory of physical pain, mental pain too is hard to recall. Her parents could not know for sure whether Julia had been in pain or suffered mental anguish of any kind, but Brendan Hunt thought not, and advised them against asking her about it because that risked reopening a can of worms that had now been successfully closed. Certainly, she had never appeared to be overly disturbed by her fantasies about a second or alternative family, except of course for that one time in the hospital when she had called out for her mommy and, however briefly, refused to accept Clare in the role. The pain then, and for the most part since, had been Clare's and Tom's.

But now it was in the past, and that was all they needed to know. They were grateful to Brendan Hunt; grateful to each other for having weathered the storm; grateful to have their adored daughter to themselves again.

Over the next five years, Julia Freeman grew into an extremely pretty, bright young girl. The blonde curls of childhood became long, soft tresses that she kept in place with an Alice band – the kind of ribbon seen in early illustrations of *Alice in Wonderland*. Her parents always felt she had something of an Alice in Wonderland quality about her: a natural sweetness of nature combined with a quick mind and endless curiosity.

She did well at school, where she was popular with pupils and staff alike. She didn't care much for sport, except for swimming, which she was good at. Also, she liked horses and was learning to ride. Not being short of friends, she was never lonely, though there were times when she chose to be alone. She would read, curled up in her room, for hours on end if something caught her imagination. Tom and Clare were both quietly pleased when they realized that watching television had become for her more of a social thing than a solitary occupation. Her friends would come over, or she would visit them, and they would watch their favourite programmes or play some computer game together. Alone, she preferred books.

Tom and Clare didn't so much decide against having another child; what they said was if it happened, it happened. The fact that it didn't happen upset neither of them greatly. If they had been younger it might have been different. But by the time Julia turned eight, Tom had turned forty and Clare was about to. Tom's career had continued to thrive, and Clare had resumed hers full time, also with success. They had remained in the same house because they loved it, but they had acquired a pied-à-terre in Manhattan which made business meetings easier and was useful for weekends when they felt like seeing a show.

Sometimes, in quiet moments, or on those thankfully rare occasions when he found himself sleepless at four in the morning, Tom would still wonder how long it could all go on. A nagging voice at the back of his head reminded him that no life goes unscarred, no happiness unblemished. We know all the worst things that can happen to us and those we love – disease, pain, premature death – yet we hope, irrationally, to escape them.

But how can we? The only answer is to live now, he would tell himself at the end of these pessimistic interludes, because now is the only time we ever live. Do not brood on what might have been or what might come. Celebrate what is. And in what is, he knew, he was a truly fortunate man.

13

He knew where he was, even though he had closed his eyes and dared not open them. So long as the shadows of the cellar were replaced by total darkness, he need not acknowledge the horror he had seen, and which he now struggled to forget. Even the worst freak show conjured by his blind imagination was no match for the awful reality that he knew would assault him if he opened his eyes again.

The first thing he had to do was get out of this place. That shouldn't be impossible, even with his eyes closed. He knew where he was well enough: he had been here before, though he wasn't sure exactly why or when.

He took a step, then another – and brushed against the rough brick surface of a wall. He turned, this time holding his hands out tentatively in front of him, and moved in what he felt sure now must be the right direction. He counted his steps silently . . . one . . . two . . . three . . . four . . .

Suddenly he faltered and gave a gasp of pain as he almost turned his ankle. Before he knew it, his eyes had opened on a reflex stronger than his will to keep them shut. He saw now the *familiar floor, just as he remembered it, made of hardened earth with stones embedded in it, some round and smooth, some with sharper jagged edges. It was one of these that he had stumbled on.*

But now, as he raised his eyes to peer through the frozen shadow-play of semi-darkness, he saw again the thing, that awful shape, that he had been trying so hard to pretend was not there.

Even now, as he watched her lying there, he tried to tell himself she was asleep. But he knew otherwise. He knew she was not sleeping. He knew that she was dead. He knew that there was no escape from this, no going back. A fatal line had been crossed.

How did it happen? The shock had emptied his brain. He was too stunned to think.

Had he been drunk? On drugs? If so, he was sober now – horribly sober.

He knew that it was no excuse, but he desperately wanted to believe he couldn't help it. Did he go mad? Was he temporarily insane?

Who was she, anyway? He forced himself to go closer, looking down at her, short skirt riding up above her waist. Without thinking, he dropped to his knees. He was about to pull the skirt down, impose some kind of modesty, when he stopped himself. What was the point? What difference did it make now?

He felt the panic rise up through his body, impossible to fight. He thought he was going to vomit, but the feeling passed, leaving him with a single thought of dreadful clarity: that everything he had ever been or done was, from this moment, worthless. This mad and senseless act was now the definition of his life, the only thing that mattered. It would never leave his thoughts, awake or sleeping – if he ever slept again.

His one desire was to get out of there. He told himself that if he ran far and fast enough, he might yet escape this unbearable reality. But where could he hide?

He became aware of a faint light filtering in from somewhere above and to one side. Still kneeling, he turned in its direction, rising once more to his feet as he did so. He did not take his eyes off that tiny skylight, too high and grimy to see out of, until he stood beneath it, in the place he recognized.

Only then did he look back into the deepest shadows. He could see nothing, but he knew now what was hidden there.

He started to run. As he stumbled down the passage towards the light beyond the broken door, a voice was screaming in his head: 'You're dreaming! It's only a dream! You're having a nightmare!'

It made no difference. Because this time he was living it. This time, there would be no escape.

The terrified wailing sound went on for some time before he realized it was the sound of his own voice. It felt like an age before he was able to convince himself that he was awake now, and it had only been a nightmare. He had not killed anyone. How could he have imagined such a thing, even in his wildest dreams?

Wildest dreams. This had been the wildest of them all. But he was awake now, back home with Clare at his side.

Except, he saw as he turned, she wasn't there . . .

Of course, he told himself, she had gone to check on the baby . . . But their daughter was no baby now. She would be nine next birthday. What was wrong with him . . . ?

Something else struck him as he looked around. This was not his own bed. It was not even his own house. He was in a strange place he did not recognize . . . The panic took a grip on him again, reaching up from somewhere in his gut to tighten around his throat. He took a deep breath, forcing calmness on himself.

He remembered now, finally. He was in New Orleans, the Hotel Richelieu on Chartres Street. He had come down two days ago to talk to some jazz musicians about a film.

Thank God.

That awful dream. Where did it come from? Hell – or himself? Or some hell in himself? He jumped as the phone rang at the side of his bed. He reached for it and hit a switch to glance at his watch. It was just after 6 a.m.

'Tom?' It was Clare's voice. 'I'm sorry to wake you. I know it's early.'

'Darling? What's happened? Is something wrong?' He didn't need to ask: he could hear the tension in her voice.

'It's Julia. Don't worry, she's not hurt or sick. It's nothing physical.'

'What's happened?'

'It's that Melanie thing again. I think you'd better get up here.'

14

It was coming up to Easter when the father of one of Julia's friends called up with a proposition. He and his wife were taking their daughter, Charlotte, to Niagara Falls for the long weekend, and wanted to know whether the Freemans might care to join them on the trip. Julia, it transpired, had already told them she was keen to go, though oddly enough she had said nothing about it to her parents. Anyway, Clare and Tom thought it sounded like a good idea, so they agreed.

Then a problem came up with Tom's schedule. He was planning a documentary about jazz piano, and one of the key people he had to talk with down in New Orleans could only see him over that Easter weekend. He felt bad about cancelling, but Clare encouraged him to go. He knew that she and Julia would be in good company and well looked after.

Tom had a sound man and cameraman with him, and they had pretty much shot everything they needed the night before he got Clare's call. He got a flight out at nine thirty. Clare met him off the plane and as she drove him back to the hotel they went over in more detail some of the things she'd told him on the phone.

'It's that quiet obsessiveness that's so scary – just insisting that her real name is Melanie, and that her "real family" live somewhere around here.'

'Around here?'

'That's what she said.'

'Did she say where?'

Clare shook her head.

'Did you ask her?'

'I was going to. Then I thought about what Brendan Hunt said about not encouraging her in the fantasy.'

'You're right.' He thought a moment. 'I guess the first thing we need to do is get hold of Brendan Hunt.'

'I should have done that already.' She looked over at him with an anguish in her face that he had not seen before. 'I'm sorry,' she said, her voice breaking. 'I've not been much use.'

'You've done fine. Don't worry – we'll get through this.'

Her eyes were back on the road. She wiped a hand across them to clear the mist that had come over them. Tom saw that she was biting her lip on the inside. He reached out, touching her face lightly with his fingers. 'I mean it. We'll be fine.'

They were silent a while, then he said, 'It started last night? Just out of the blue?'

She nodded. 'We were ordering dinner, the five of

us. Julia said she wanted meatloaf. You know Julia and meatloaf, or steak or ribs. I thought she'd made a mistake and said maybe she'd like chicken or pasta. But she insisted she wanted meatloaf. I said, "But you don't usually eat meatloaf. You hate it." She looked at me in a strange way, as if she was challenging me to accuse her of lying, and said, "I'm Melanie now."'

'And her friend Charlotte – you said she was in on the whole thing?'

'It turns out Julia had told her that was why she wanted to come here – because she had this secret family close by. Charlotte was sworn to secrecy – you know how kids are.'

Tom thought about this. He wasn't sure he knew anything about kids. Maybe he'd started too late in life. Maybe he and Clare were both out of their depth. It certainly felt that way right now.

'The incredible thing,' Clare was saying, 'is the way she just carries on playing with Charlotte, or doing whatever we're doing, as though nothing had happened. Except that if anybody calls her Julia, she just says her name is Melanie.'

'It sounds almost like a game.'

'It's more than a game.'

When they got to the hotel they found Julia, Charlotte and her parents in the heated indoor swimming pool. It was obvious that the parents realized something was quite badly wrong, but they didn't really understand the situation and were a little embarrassed by it.

The moment Julia saw Tom, she started running towards him with her arms flung open, calling out, 'Daddy, Daddy!'

He held her tight, not caring about the damp stains spreading over his coat. He didn't know why he said what he said next. It just came out, forced from him by the emotion that was threatening to choke him, and the sting behind his eyelids.

'Am I really your daddy?' he said.

She looked at him with a kind of playacting surprise, as though he was teasing her.

'Of course, you're my daddy!' she said, and gave him another hug around the neck and pressed her cheek against his. 'I love you, Daddy.'

'What about your other daddy?' he said.

She didn't say anything, so he prompted her.

'Do you love your other daddy?'

She shook her head. 'He's not like you.'

Tom caught Clare's anxious gaze, then asked: 'And what about your other mommy?'

Julia pulled away a little so she could look Tom in the eyes. There was a smile on her face.

'Oh, yes,' she said, 'I love my other mommy.'

15

The evening was strained but, oddly, not difficult. Clare had spoken with Charlotte's parents. They had understood as much as anyone could, and had agreed to go along with whatever Tom and Clare suggested.

Tom had managed to talk with Brendan Hunt on the phone. Over the years since Hunt had treated Julia they had run into him pretty regularly. Saracen Springs was a community in which their social circles tended to overlap. Hunt had always been anxious to hear how Julia was getting along and was pleased to know that she'd had no further problems. But he had never seemed worried about her, certainly never suggested that it might be useful for him to see her again. As far as he was concerned, the episode was over and she was fully recovered. Whenever he and Julia met, whether in the street or in a restaurant or at the house of some mutual friend, she had always greeted him like a favourite uncle, obviously happy to see him again.

Hunt listened in silence as Tom explained what had

been happening over the phone. 'I can't offer much of an opinion without talking to her,' he said when the story was finished. 'When will you be back?'

'I'm going to get the first flight we can. It's a little tricky, being the holiday period.'

'It's probably a good thing to get back here if you can. In the meantime, don't challenge her, don't accuse her of talking nonsense. At the same time, don't play along with her.'

'What about her friend Charlotte?'

'What about her?'

'She seems to be part of the whole thing. Should we separate them?'

Hunt was silent a moment. 'I don't think so, not at this stage. Just do your best to keep things on an even keel till you get back here.'

Tom got seats on a plane late the following morning. On Hunt's advice they didn't tell Julia they were going home early, which made them both feel a little awkward and dishonest. But that was better than getting her upset and having to deal with the problem all night, which Hunt said was a risk they ran. Far better, he had said, to cook up some story about an emergency in the morning just before they left for the airport.

Clare had kept the double room which she and Tom had originally booked, along with an adjoining room for Julia. They all three gathered on the big bed after supper and watched television. When Julia began to fall asleep, Clare suggested she turn in. The child slipped off the bed without objection, kissing both her parents before heading for her own room, rubbing her eyes. In the door she stopped.

'Daddy,' she said, turning back, 'will you take me to my mommy's house tomorrow?'

Tom felt Clare's eyes on him but avoided meeting them. 'We'll see,' he said evasively. 'Let's see what happens in the morning.'

'No – promise now,' she said, with an edge of reawakened determination in her voice.

'Let's talk about it in the morning,' Tom repeated feebly. 'We're all tired now. I think we should go to sleep.'

The child looked at him with an odd mixture of distrust and acceptance. It was as though she was debating whether to argue, or let the matter drop. She chose to let it drop.

When her door was closed, Clare rolled with weary gratitude into Tom's arms. They lay in silence for a while. Then Clare spoke in a little voice, as though afraid both of the words she was speaking and the thought behind them.

'Pam said something tonight, after dinner.'

Pam was Charlotte's mother, a sympathetic, kindly woman. Tom waited for Clare to go on, but when she did not, he prompted her.

'What? Tell me.'

Clare pulled away from him and sat up on the edge of the bed with her back to him, as though needing to put some distance between them before she could say what she had to.

'She said that she'd read something a long time ago, some article, about children who were born with memories of past lives.'

She paused again, but this time it was Tom who deliberately said nothing. She turned to look at him with a question in her eyes. She needed a reaction from him.

He dropped his gaze from hers, thinking how strange it was that he found it so hard to look at her in that moment.

'Memories of past lives – reincarnation? Is that what we're talking about?'

He was aware of making an effort to sound calm, almost casual, neither shocked nor offended by the idea. In fact he was asking himself whether, on some unconscious level, the thought had not already crossed his mind.

Clare shrugged. 'I don't even know if they're the same thing. Maybe you can be born with the memory of somebody's past life without being that person reborn.'

He made some noncommittal noise. At some point, without noticing, he too must have swung his feet off the bed, because he now found himself pacing the floor. 'Let's not get too far ahead of ourselves,' he said. 'If every child with a vivid imagination is going to be accused of being a reincarnated soul . . .'

'No one's accusing her. It's just a possibility that maybe we should consider.'

'You're right. Sorry, I didn't mean to . . . it's just that an idea like this takes some getting used to. The first thing we need to do is spend some time with Brendan Hunt and get his perspective on all this.'

They knew that sleep was not going to come easily to either of them. Clare started packing, while Tom went through his email. It didn't take long, and he was about to sign off when he had an idea. He brought up a search engine and typed one word into the find box: 'Reincarnation'.

He was not prepared for what came up. There were over two hundred thousand responses. Mostly they came from addresses like Beliefnet.com, Spiritweb.org, Mystica.com, and Tarotplanet.com. There was a lot of material from the Theosophical Society, much talk of karma, various ongoing debates about why Buddhists accepted the doctrine but Christians didn't; and, frankly, a number of contributions from the sort of people he would have hoped never to find himself alone in a room with.

All the same, when he thought about it, he realized that he had always considered Buddhism the sanest of all religions. Buddhists didn't worship icons and they didn't bludgeon people's heads because of quarrels over dogma.

But they believed in reincarnation. From the Dalai Lama on down.

Could he really understand that idea, he asked himself, as anything more than a metaphor? Because a metaphor would not do. It was only the shadow, a reflection of something else, a way of using one thing to illuminate another. This thing had to be the real thing or nothing at all.

When at last they went to bed, they lay awake in the dark, talking softly, in circles.

16

Julia said nothing at breakfast about the proposed visit to her 'mommy's home' that she had been so keen on the night before. Nor were there any references to 'Melanie' or her 'other life'. She didn't even object when Tom announced that they were going home a day earlier than planned. He and Clare had agreed that if she made a scene they would be quite open with her and tell her that they wanted her to see Dr Hunt.

But in the event she just nodded matter-of-factly, almost as though she had been expecting the announcement. Then she said she would like to go and play with Charlotte. Clare went with her. They had agreed, as a precaution, that they were not going to let her out of the sight of either one or the other of them until they were on the plane. They didn't really think that she would run off in search of this imaginary mother, but they weren't about to take the chance.

Tom stayed behind to take care of their bags and to check out, then he went out to the play area where he knew they would be. There was an indoor area, with a pool, and an outdoor one with no pool. They were outdoors. Charlotte's father was supervising the girls on slides and roundabouts – stuff for kids a little younger than themselves, but because there were two of them they were having a good time.

Their mothers sat at a table nearby, drinking coffee. Tom sat down with them and poured himself a cup. It was as ordinary a scene, at least outwardly, as you would find anywhere: families on vacation having visited the tourist sights and now keeping the children entertained.

Clare was telling Pam about Tom's trawl on the Web for stuff on reincarnation and how much of it he had found. Pam admitted she knew nothing about the subject: it had just stuck in her mind after she read that one article years ago. Like Tom and Clare, she didn't find it something she could believe in literally. She seemed anxious and strained, constantly glancing over to where the girls were playing. Tom wondered if she was afraid that Charlotte might catch the condition from Julia, then immediately reproached himself for the peevish tone of his thought. If he were in the position of Charlotte's parents, he would feel the same: what was happening here was too strange to be entirely casual about.

In fact both sets of parents were keeping their eyes on the girls pretty constantly, as though afraid they might vanish if left unobserved for a moment. Then Tom noticed that something was happening between Julia and Charlotte's father, Harry. Julia was talking to him in the earnest way children have, backing up some request with a wealth of circumstantial detail so that he would have no reasonable excuse, so she thought, to refuse what she was asking.

Harry listened solemnly, while his own daughter waited quietly on one side. This was nothing to do with her. Tom watched as Harry crouched down to respond to what Julia had said. As he spoke, he gestured in Tom's direction, as though referring her to her parents for whatever it was she wanted.

Tom and Clare were on their feet at the same time. 'It's all right,' Tom said, 'let me.'

Clare sat back down, but kept her eyes on her daughter as Tom started over, making an effort to look casual, as though he was just being sociable. As he walked, he saw Julia glance at him out of the corner of her eye. She dropped the subject that she had been so eager to persuade Charlotte's father about, and returned to playing with Charlotte. She led the way up the ladder of a helter-skelter which they had already skimmed down several times with shrieks of laughter.

'What was all that?' Tom asked.

Harry stood with his hands in his pockets, looking perplexed. 'It was weird. She suddenly started on about how I had to take her to visit her mommy. She said her daddy wouldn't take her, so please would I? We could just pretend we were going for a walk, and Charlotte could come too, but we should go get my car.'

'What did you tell her?'

'I said we shouldn't do that without your permission, so I suggested we go talk to you about it. But she wouldn't do that. She said you'd just say no.'

Their silence was broken by the girls' laughter as they reached the end of their ride, and started around the back to go again.

'OK, thanks, Harry,' Tom said. As he spoke, he glanced Julia's way. She was paying him no attention and seemed absorbed in her game with Charlotte. At the same time, he saw Clare get up from her table, leave Pam, and start towards them.

'It's all right,' Tom said when she got nearer. 'Crisis averted.'

'What happened?'

He explained – with Harry hovering in the background to verify and elaborate on everything he said. Tom would have liked him to shut up, but it was hard to tell him. Besides, he was so conscious of the pain in his wife's face every time Julia's 'other mommy' was referred to that he had no thought but for her.

Clare looked at her watch. 'I think we could get out of here,' she said. 'I'd rather wait a little longer at the airport.'

'You're right,' Tom said. 'Let's go.'

As he turned to call Julia over, he heard Pam's voice. 'Charlotte – where's Julia?'

The next thing he saw was Charlotte getting off the slide – alone. He felt his heart miss a beat as fear shot through him like an electric shock.

There was no sign of Julia.

His attention, the separate attentions of all four adults, could not have been distracted for more than a few seconds. Yet she was gone.

Clare was already running across the grass, calling her name. Pam ran over to Charlotte and put her hands firmly on her shoulders.

'Where is she? Did you see where she went?'

The child shook her head, alarmed by the feel of adult panic around her.

'Charlotte, we're not blaming you,' Tom said. 'Please, just tell us if you know anything.'

She looked up at him, blinking, as though convinced that she was going to be unfairly held responsible for something she had not done.

'She said she had to go home.'

'Where did she go? Which way?'

Charlotte pointed towards a hedge behind a climbing frame in the shape of a fort. Tom ran towards it. Close up, he saw that there was a gap big enough for a child to slip through, though too small for an adult. He ran along it, looking for a way around.

'Tom, over here!'

He looked back and saw Clare waving him towards her. She had found a gate and disappeared through it before he got there. Harry was right behind him, but paused to shout back to Pam, 'Stay with Charlotte. I'll help them find her.'

Clare was frantically searching the parking lot when

Tom caught up with her, but there was no sign of Julia.

'She can't have got far,' Harry was saying a little breathlessly. 'It was just seconds.'

Tom looked around desperately for some clue to where she might have gone, trying to think himself into his daughter's mind. Then, about five hundred yards away, below where they were standing, he saw a handful of long-bodied green buses manoeuvring around a handful of concrete islands and covered pick-up points. 'Harry – your car!' he shouted. 'Mine's out front!'

Charlotte's father pulled a key from his pocket. 'Here. It's insured. I'll check around the hotel.'

Tom snatched the keys from him and was already behind the wheel before Clare jumped in beside him. 'Where are you going?'

'Down there. Look! She wanted Harry to drive her but he wouldn't, so she's taking the bus. That *must* be where she's headed.'

The car, a big sedan, was already moving, tyres protesting as Tom spun the featherlight powered steering this way and that, not giving a damn for the angry shouts from pedestrians and a couple of raised fists it got him. He made an illegal U-turn, bounced over a divider, and headed downhill. 'Does she have money?' he asked Clare.

'Enough to take a bus. She had her pocket money with her.'

The road down to the bus terminal curved gently to the left. There was an intersection coming up, and he tried to get there before the lights changed, but had to slam on his brakes at the last second. Neither he nor Clare was wearing a seatbelt; Clare grabbed the dash with both hands to stop herself being thrown forward.

'Sorry,' he said. 'Are you all right?'

'Yes.'

She spoke without looking at him. Her eyes were scouring the distance for that small figure in a blue and yellow tracksuit with a white ribbon in her hair.

'Better buckle up,' Tom said.

They both did. When the lights changed to amber, the car was already moving. He was driving badly, but it crossed his mind that if a cop pulled him over, he could probably enlist him in the search. It might be the best thing that could happen.

The terminal, when they reached it, was more complex than it had looked from above. Regular traffic was routed around the edge, and he couldn't find a way in.

'Stop – let me get out and look.'

Clare shot out of the car and stepped up on a concrete island, craning her head to get an overview of the place. People and vehicles crisscrossed in all directions. It was impossible to get a clear view of anything.

Then he saw her, subliminally almost, just a flash of colour before she disappeared again, leaving him unsure whether he had imagined her or not.

'Over there!' he called to Clare, getting out of the car and pointing. She was already running. He sprinted after her. He heard the roaring engine before he saw

the bus about to run him down. He managed to pull
back, almost deafened by the horn's blast. He ran
around the rear of it, but by the time he emerged the
other side he could see no sign of either Clare or Julia.

He ran to the next island, and looked around in all
directions. He caught sight of Clare so far from where
she'd been that he didn't know how she'd got there so
quickly. She was trying to attract his attention, waving
and pointing. He started to follow, but another bus got
in his way.

At one of the windows he saw, unmistakably, his
daughter's face. She didn't look at him; she showed no
sign of seeing him; and she flashed by in a second.

But it was her.

17

Without taking his eyes off the bus, he swung the car over and pushed open the door for Clare to get in.

'You shouldn't have waited,' she said.

'Don't worry, we've got her.'

He pulled abruptly into traffic, accompanied by more angry honking, but he kept the bus in clear view. They followed it through two sets of lights, neither of which was red long enough for one of them to get out of the car and go pound on its door. At the third set, a truck jumped a light and got between them.

When they got around the truck, they found themselves following two buses in place of one, with nothing to tell them which was which. Tom thumped the steering wheel.

'Shit!'

'It was the one on the right.'

'How can you tell?'

'Just from where it was.'

'You're wrong.'

85

Suddenly they were fighting like married couples everywhere over who knows the way and whose fault it was they went wrong. Only this time it wasn't funny. They both became acutely aware of that at the same moment, and fell silent.

Clare reached over for his hand. 'I'm sorry,' she said. 'My fault.'

'No.'

They drove in silence, and in silence they observed each bus choose a separate pre-selection which would take them in opposite directions. They had to make a choice.

'Which one?' he said.

'I don't know. Which do you . . . ?'

'Right,' he said.

'Right.'

He swung the wheel to follow. The road led up into tree-shaded avenues which branched off into residential streets.

'Try to pass it,' she said.

'There isn't room if he doesn't pull over.'

An oncoming car forced the driver of the bus to pull over a yard or so, but before Tom could get past he had drifted out again. Tom hit the horn, to no effect. He hit it again. Perfectly framed in his rear-view mirror, the driver's left hand extended a defiantly uncivil finger.

Clare placed a restraining hand on Tom's arm. 'Wait till he stops. He'll have to soon.'

When he did, moments later, Tom swung the car past

and pulled across the bus's nose, blocking it. He saw the driver tense and reach for something under his dash as Tom ran towards him.

'I'm sorry,' he said to the driver, waving his open hands to show that he had no intention of attacking him. 'We're looking for our daughter. She's eight years old.'

Clare had run to the other side of the bus where three or four people were getting down. As soon as the way was clear, she ran up the steps and inside.

'Hey, lady!' the driver called out indignantly. But she was already halfway back, checking every seat.

Tom came around and started to climb the steps. The driver reached under his dash again. Tom could see a radio, and a knuckleduster next to it.

'Look,' he said, 'we just want our daughter, that's all.'

The driver relaxed a little. 'How old did you say she was?'

'Eight.'

'Well, she's not on this bus.'

Tom looked down the centre aisle. Clare was already returning with disappointment on her face, shaking her head.

'OK,' Tom said. 'I'm sorry.' Then added, 'Thanks,' as they got off. The driver hit a button and shut the doors, glad to be rid of them. Curious faces peered down from the windows as they ran to their car, made a quick turn, and headed back in the direction they had come from.

'It's *got* to be the other one,' Tom said. 'It *had* to be one of those two.'

He took a right that looked like a short cut back to the road they had left. He was acutely aware that the other bus could by now have taken some untraceable route, but left that fear unspoken. So did Clare, though he was quite sure she shared it.

They found the main road and drove for several minutes. Then Clare said, 'It must have turned off.' Her voice was taut with anxiety.

Tom didn't say anything, just kept driving.

'Turn back,' she said.

'In a minute.'

'It can't have come this far . . .'

She stopped, because quite suddenly, as they rounded a long curve in the road, a bus like the one they were looking for came into view.

'Oh, God,' she said, 'is it the same one?'

Tom didn't answer, just pulled out to overtake. As he did, it began to slow. It was making a stop. He pulled up in front, not blocking it this time, and they both ran to the door where a couple of people were getting off and one waiting to board. The driver was less aggressively paranoid than the last one, and listened with an open, understanding expression as Tom explained their problem and Clare checked out the passengers.

'Your wife won't find her back there,' he said. 'She got off at the last stop.'

'Where was that?'

'About a mile back. I thought it was kind of unusual, a little girl that age on her own. I asked her if she was all right, but she said her mommy was waiting for her.'

Clare had rejoined Tom just in time to hear the last part. She didn't react; she was used to it now, too distraught to feel pain any more.

'Thanks,' Tom said to the driver. They ran back to the car, scrambled in, and made a U-turn. After a mile, just as the driver had said, they saw a shelter that marked the last stop. There was nobody about, nobody to ask if they'd seen a little girl a few minutes ago. Tom stopped the car and they looked around.

'She could be anywhere,' Clare said.

'Not if she's still on foot.'

'Why wouldn't she be?' Clare shot back, straight out of that pit of nightmare thoughts that any parent must be tortured by when a child goes missing.

'Let's drive around,' Tom said, 'block by block. We'll work outwards from here.'

'I'll start over the other side,' she said, already half out of the car.

'If we lose each other, meet back here in fifteen minutes.'

She nodded briefly, taking his words in only subconsciously. Her eyes and thoughts were elsewhere. She did not even shut the car door before she started to run across the road.

18

It was a modest, respectable working-class neighbour-hood. The clapboard houses were mostly well kept, though some could have used a little repair and a coat of paint. Children's toys were strewn here and there, along with the occasional line of washing. Cars were parked in driveways, some of them up on bricks where their owners could work on them. There was a lot of greenery, clusters of trees softening the gridlike struc-ture of the place.

A couple of times Tom stopped to ask people if they'd seen a little girl in a blue and yellow tracksuit. They hadn't. After ten minutes of circling, he knew he wasn't going to find her, and headed back towards his meeting point with Clare. There was no sign of her, but he was a couple of minutes early. He knew he couldn't just sit there and wait, so he pulled over the road and began searching on the far side, hoping to see Clare somewhere.

Three blocks in, he saw her in the distance, running.

He accelerated towards her and honked. She glanced over her shoulder, but kept on running, signalling him to catch her up. As he drew level he leaned across and pushed open the passenger door. She was in before he'd even stopped, pulling the door shut, breathing hard.

'Somebody thinks they saw her five, maybe ten minutes ago, heading this way.'

She pointed to a smaller road that curved off and up a slight incline. Tom swung onto it. They both held their breath as they curved left for a hundred yards, then followed the road up and to the right. That was when they saw her ahead, a little figure marching along with that odd sense of purpose that children have when they know exactly where they're going and what they have to do. She was unaware of them until Tom braked hard alongside her. When she saw them, she flinched and backed away.

Tom was out of the car almost as fast as Clare, who was already squatting down, hands on Julia's shoulders, when he reached them. He could see that Clare wanted to shake the child in anger and hug her for joy at the same time. Tom touched his wife gently on the arm. He didn't know why. To reassure her, perhaps. To remind her he was there. Or maybe he was trying to draw the pain from her, to take it like a lightning conductor and disperse it in the earth beneath his feet. At any rate, it seemed to release something in her. She pulled Julia to her, holding on to her as though afraid to let go ever again.

'Where are you going, darling?' Tom said, trying to not frighten the child, trying to show her he wasn't angry.

She looked at him, still clasped as she was in her mother's arms. 'To see my mommy,' she said.

Tom saw Clare's shoulders bunch as she fought to control the pain this gave her. He crouched down next to them, bringing his gaze level with Julia's.

'Let's get in the car,' he said.

He saw her try to pull away from Clare, suddenly distrustful of them both. And he saw Clare slacken her embrace but still hold on to the child. He reached for Julia's hand.

'Let's go.'

'No!'

She pulled free of his grasp, looking hurt and angry, as though she suspected he was planning to betray her. In a way, he supposed, he was. All he wanted was to get her away from there. To get all of them away from there.

But Clare saw how impossible that was even before he did. She looked at him and he knew, without her saying anything, that she was right. What could they do? Carry her away, screaming? Kidnap their own daughter? They had come too far. It was too late.

'Where is your . . .' she began, turning back to Julia, but couldn't finish the sentence. 'Where is it you want to go?' she asked instead.

Julia stuck out her small arm, rigid and uncompromising, pointing up the street. 'There's a windmill,' she said, 'then my house.'

A windmill didn't seem to make much sense to either of them. But they were past arguing.

'Let's go in the car,' he said, offering his hand again. Julia remained suspicious. 'We can walk if you like,' he said, 'or ride in the car. It's up to you.'

She took a moment to make up her mind, to be sure she could trust him and that this wasn't some kind of trick. Then she reached for his hand and obediently climbed into the back of the car while he held the door for her.

Tom and Clare tried not to look at each other as they got in the front. There was a strange embarrassment between them. The invisible wall that had been growing around Julia these last two days was now threatening to separate the two of them in some way that they could not fully understand. They both knew that it was something they should fight – *must* fight – but they didn't know how. What they did feel, strongly and unspokenly, was that this was neither the time nor place to make a stand.

He drove slowly, like someone searching for a specific address or street number. He could see Julia in his rear-view mirror, alert and filled with anticipation. The houses they were passing now were on the lower end of the social scale, more rundown than those nearer the main road. Some of their windows were cracked and patched with board, the cars outside them older and rustier.

'Look,' she said suddenly, 'the windmill.'

Her parents looked in the direction she was pointing. Sure enough, on the top of a house they were passing, was a curious contraption, a kind of home-made weathervane in the shape of a windmill.

Julia now became excited and started jumping up and down, shouting, 'There's my house! There's my house! There's my house!'

It stood back a little way from the road. Several trees, tall, thin and undernourished, grew around it in an unplanned straggle. It looked as if somebody made an effort to keep the place clean and tidy, but it needed money spending on it. But there were no broken windows, and the lace curtains that hung in them on both floors had been washed not long since.

Julia was out of the car and running before Tom even thought of hitting the door lock. Not that keeping her trapped in there would have achieved anything. He realized with a sickening sense of immediacy just how out of control their lives had become in the last hour. They were doing everything they had said they were not going to do – *must* not do – but she had left them no choice.

Tom looked at Clare, and a moment later she looked at him, but their eyes did not meet. They were hoping, and at the same time admitting what a forlorn hope it was, that one of them would know what to do next. Certainly, he felt out of his depth in a way he never had in his life before.

Suddenly, without being conscious of having moved, he found himself running up the path after Julia, wondering what he would do when he caught her. Clare was with him. 'Julia,' he heard her call out, 'come back.'

Julia paid them no attention. Before they could reach her she had stepped up on the low porch and pulled open a screen door. When the door beyond turned out to be locked, she hammered on it with her open palm and shouted, 'Mommy! Mommy! Mommy!' It wasn't the cry of a child running away from something and looking for protection. So far as Julia was concerned, her parents might as well have not been there. Even when they caught up with her and both of them reached out to pull her back, she didn't react.

The door was already opening. Tom looked up at the face of the woman who stood there.

19

She probably wasn't more than thirty, but she had the washed-out look of somebody who had already learned to expect little from life but disappointment and frustration. She was actually quite attractive, but the sullen expression on her face defied anyone to think so, let alone to think of mentioning it. She wore old jeans with scuffed trainers and a shapeless sweater.

'What's going on?' she asked sharply, her aggrieved look moving from the strange couple in front of her to the child with them.

Julia, totally unafraid, looked right back at her and said, 'Where's Mommy? I want my mommy.'

The woman looked at Tom and Clare. 'What is she talking about? What does she mean, she wants her mommy?'

'It's hard to explain,' Tom began uncertainly. 'We don't understand it. We're her parents, and . . . I'm sorry, this is a mistake.'

He took hold of Julia's hand, this time resolved to

carry her to the car by force if necessary. She tried to shake him off, but he held on firmly.

'Where's Emery?' she demanded.

A puzzled look came over the woman's face. 'Emery?' she said. 'What about Emery?'

'His house has gone.'

Julia pointed her free hand accusingly at a pile of clapboard near the door, where Tom saw an area of paint marginally less worn by the elements than the rest. It would have been about the size of a dog house.

The woman, shaken, called over her shoulder into the house. 'Joe, you'd better get out here.'

'Who was Emery?' Clare asked.

The woman looked at her, as though focusing on her properly, on all of them, for the first time. 'Emery was my sister's dog,' she said.

Julia didn't move. She was staring straight up at the woman, a frown darkening her face as she made sense of what she was hearing.

'Jennifer?' she said after a moment. Her tone was tentative, like someone seeing an old friend or a member of the family for the first time in years, yet not quite sure if it was really them.

The woman caught her breath. 'How do you know my name?'

'It's me, Melanie.'

Tom feared the woman was about to faint and moved towards her. But the man she had called for appeared behind her and caught her. She was deathly pale, her eyes half shut, her hand going to her head to stop it spinning.

'What's going on?' the man demanded, then looked challengingly at Tom. 'Who are you?'

He wore working clothes and was around forty. He was well built, with close-cropped hair and the aggressive attitude of a man who would lash out instinctively at anyone who threatened his dignity or self-esteem. In other words, Tom estimated, someone to be careful of.

'You don't know us,' Tom said, 'and I don't believe we know you. I apologize for disturbing you. This is very difficult to explain, but our daughter thinks she knows this house.'

The man's hostile gaze fell on Julia. 'She what—?'

Again the child did not flinch. She glared right back at the man in front of her with a lack of fear bordering on contempt. There was something in her that Tom had never seen before, a kind of defiance, an anger that was older, more adult than her years.

'Does the name Melanie mean anything to you?' Tom said.

The woman, who had started to recover herself by now, answered softly. 'Melanie was my sister.'

The man, Joe, extended a thick forefinger from a meaty fist. 'You people better leave,' he said, 'and I mean now.'

'Fuck you, Joe!'

Tom barely had time to register the fact that Julia had spoken before he realized that Joe's fist was now an open palm, sweeping towards Julia's head with a force that could break her neck.

With a strength and speed he didn't know he had, Tom grabbed the man's wrist and blocked the blow – 'Don't even think about it.' he said. The words came from some atavistic depth in his body. The two men were locked eye to eye, and Tom had laid hands on him first. To a man like that, it was a licence to kill. But he saw that Tom meant business, and he hesitated. However, he wasn't a man to back off easily.

'Joe, please. . . !'

The woman was pulling him back, her efforts all but useless against his brute strength. After a moment he relaxed and lowered his fist, but didn't take his eyes off Tom.

'We didn't come here to cause trouble,' Tom said. 'In fact I don't even know what we're doing here. We're still trying to figure it out. We're just trying to understand.'

He turned to where Clare crouched with her arms wrapped protectively around Julia.

'You said Melanie *was* your sister's name?' Clare asked.

The woman nodded.

'What happened to her?'

'Nobody knows. She disappeared nearly ten years ago. Walked out of the house and never came back.'

The slam of the screen door made them all turn. Joe disappeared into the darkness of the hall, emerging almost at once with a leather jacket that he was pulling on.

'I've got to go to work,' he said, starting towards an old Chevy parked near where Tom had stopped. 'And I better not find you people here when I get back.'

They watched him go. For some reason nobody said anything until he had made a U-turn with a screech of tyres and disappeared from view. It was only then that they realized Julia too had disappeared.

Clare and Tom experienced another of those surreal moments of panic like the one they'd had at the hotel, when she had vanished as if by magic from under their noses. They both looked around, calling her name. It was Jennifer who noticed a movement in the house.

'She's inside,' she said.

They ran in after her. Julia was just disappearing up the dark staircase that led off the cramped hall. Their feet clattered on the uncarpeted wooden steps. There was no sign of her on the landing. Tom and Clare had no idea which way to turn, but Jennifer started pushing open various doors one after the other, revealing sparsely furnished rooms, a couple with unmade beds, one serving simply as a storage space for household junk. There were two or three still to go, but she stopped in front of one as though suddenly sure that this was where the child would be. Yet she hesitated before pushing open the door.

'Julia?' Tom called out. 'Are you in there?'

There was no reply. He looked questioningly at Jennifer, not wanting to take the initiative in her house, but wondering what she would do next.

'This was my mother's room,' she said. 'It's ours now. Mine and Joe's.'

She reached out and pushed the door open. It made a creaking sound, but Julia, who was standing on the far side of the room, paid it no attention. The room was not large, though probably the largest bedroom in the house. There was only one window, with the drapes not fully opened and still cutting off the light. Various articles of male clothing were scattered on the floor and over the backs of a couple of rickety-looking chairs. A row of women's clothes hung more neatly on a rail against one wall, with a curtain that could be pulled over them to create a makeshift closet. The only real piece of furniture was an old dressing table with a mirror. On it were various articles of make-up, skin creams, tissues and so on – plus two or three photographs in old-fashioned frames. It was one of these that Julia was holding in her hand and gazing at intently.

After a moment she turned to look at her parents, untroubled by their presence; in fact there was a smile on her face as though she was glad to see them, anxious to show them what she'd found. She held up the photograph so they could see it.

'My mommy,' she said triumphantly.

Tom glanced at Jennifer, who did not object as he took the picture from Julia's outstretched hand. He felt Clare press against him to get a closer look. The picture was poor quality, a patchwork of opaque shadow and brilliant sunlight. It was taken outside the house

101

they were in. Tom recognized a swing-seat he had noticed on their arrival, rusting now, but in the picture adorned with a yellow-and-white striped cover and cushions. On it sat a woman in young middle age with her arm around a girl about Julia's age. The woman had dark hair cut short, a pleasant face with a kind smile, but oddly deep-set eyes – an effect enhanced by the poor quality of the photograph. All the same, there was something troubled and troubling in those eyes, as though they had been gouged by years of worry and weeping. They were too old for the face they were in.

'Who is this?' Clare asked, pointing to the girl who was with the woman. She knew who it was, of course, just as Tom did; but they needed to hear it from Julia.

'It's me,' she said, as though they were teasing her by pretending not to recognize her.

But there was no resemblance between the girl in the picture and Julia. For one thing, the girl in the picture had dark hair. The face was more square and the features stronger; or perhaps it was just the expression she wore that made them seem so. She was unsmiling, almost glowering at the camera. It was not the face of a child whose life was filled with fun and laughter. Not the face of a child like Julia.

Tom turned to Jennifer for confirmation. She nodded once, her own eyes fixed on Julia in wonder mixed with growing fear.

'It's true,' she said. 'That's Melanie, my sister.'

20

Jennifer's married name was Sawyer. Her maiden name had been Hagan. Her sister's full name had been Melanie Hagan.

'What was your middle name?' she had asked Julia.

'Anne,' was the unhesitating answer, in a tone of voice that wondered why anyone should ask such an obvious, silly question.

They sat on the stairs – Jennifer, Tom and Clare – while Julia sorted through some old stuff of Melanie's that she'd spotted in the junk room. Jennifer had offered to make coffee downstairs, but it seemed somehow wrong, even impossible, to treat this thing as a social occasion. Besides, Tom and Clare wanted to know exactly where Julia was every second of the time. As long as they were there, on the stairs, she wasn't going to slip past them and out of the house as easily as she had slipped in.

'My mother never got over Melanie disappearing the way she did,' Jennifer said. 'She was always sure something terrible had happened to her. She used to wake up screaming from nightmares that she would never talk about.'

'Why *did* your sister run away?' Clare asked.

Jennifer shrugged. 'Kids.' It served both as an explanation and an admission that some things remained for ever beyond human understanding.

'But surely,' Clare insisted, 'there must have been a search. A child can't just disappear. She might have been abducted, injured – anything.'

'She bought a ticket for Buffalo at the bus station. We were told there was a couple who remembered giving her a ride east, just past Rochester. After that the trail ran out.'

'Did she have much money with her?' Tom asked.

'She took our mom's housekeeping money for the week, plus about twenty dollars that were in my purse. She wasn't abducted. She ran away. There was no question about that.'

'And you think your mother died because of that?' Clare said.

Jennifer shrugged again. 'Heart failure, they said, seven, nearly eight years ago. That's all they tell you – heart failure.'

There was a pause which none of them knew quite how to fill. In the distance they could hear Julia sifting through stuff, opening boxes, pushing things around. 'It's all right,' Jennifer had said, 'it's all my stuff in there, none of it's Joe's. She can go through anything she wants.'

'Was Joe living here?' Tom said. 'Before Melanie left?'

'Yeah – the four of us. Me, Joe, my mom and Melanie.'

'And your father?'

'My dad had left long since. Melanie couldn't have been more than four when he went. He was a drunk. Nobody missed him, least of all my mom. I don't even know if he's alive or dead.'

Tom thought back to the dolls Julia had played with in Hunt's office five years ago, remembering how she had kept her 'other daddy' always at a distance, never quite one of the family.

'So,' Jennifer said after another moment's silence, 'what do we do now?'

'I wish I knew,' Tom said. 'As I told you, we don't know how or why, but our daughter seems to have been born with some memories that belonged to your sister. Apparently – and this is something I only found out last night – apparently it's a phenomenon that happens amazingly often.'

She listened closely as he told her about Julia's sessions with Hunt. 'Did she talk about me?' she asked when he'd finished.

'Not so far as I know,' he said, looking to Clare for confirmation.

She shook her head. 'I don't believe so.'

'It seems that the memories are patchy at best,' Tom continued. 'She's never said anything about leaving home or what happened to her. She didn't even say where she came from. It's just by chance that we're here. At least we thought it was by chance. To be honest, I'm beginning to wonder.' He spread his hands in a gesture of helplessness. 'I don't know what to think.'

At the sound of Julia's footsteps they all turned. She emerged from the room she'd been in with an armload of CDs, videos, and a few magazines.

'These are all mine,' she said. 'Can I keep them, Mommy?'

She had asked the question of Clare, who looked momentarily startled by it; then, Tom saw, reassured.

'You'd better ask Jennifer,' she said.

Julia turned to put the question, but Jennifer forestalled her. 'Help yourself to whatever's in there, honey,' she said, 'as long as it's all right with your mom.'

She very pointedly made the reference to Clare. Tom decided he liked this woman more than he'd thought he was going to, despite her husband. He saw the warmth in Clare's response as she flashed Jennifer a quick smile of thanks, then got to her feet and held out her arms towards Julia. 'Of course you can keep them, darling. Let me help you carry them out to the car.'

The three of them walked out together. Jennifer watched as Julia carefully loaded her new-found 'possessions' into the back seat. 'You know,' she said to Tom in a quiet aside that Julia wouldn't overhear, 'it's true – every one of those things she picked out belonged to my sister.'

It was if some kind of fever had broken in Julia. She

was entirely herself again – sweet- natured, well behaved, Tom and Clare's own child. She raised no objection to returning to the hotel, and said goodbye to Jennifer politely, hardly as one might to a long-lost sister, rather a new acquaintance one has made that afternoon.

But her parents asked no questions and raised no obstacles. They were grateful for the calm that seemed to have descended on her.

'I think we're going to have to be in touch,' Tom said to Jennifer before they drove off. 'I'm sorry if that's going to be a problem for your husband.'

'Don't worry,' she said, 'he's a decent man, basically. Joe just doesn't trust what he doesn't understand.'

'You can hardly blame him for that,' Tom said, getting behind the wheel and starting the car. Jennifer stood by the roadside and waved them goodbye. Julia waved back through the rear window, like the end of a family visit anywhere in the world.

On the drive back nobody spoke more than a few words. Tom said they'd missed their flight, but he would try for a later one. Julia continued to raise no objection. There was a feeling that something was behind them, and that fact gave both Tom and Clare an immense sense of relief.

They tried not to think about what might still lie ahead.

21

Brendan Hunt clasped his hands behind his head and sat back. 'I can only come at this from the way I've been trained,' he said. 'There are various forms of clinical fabulation described in the textbooks, and this is a classic example.'

'Then how do you account for what happened to us at Niagara Falls?' Tom said.

Hunt unclasped his hands and spread them wide in a gesture of surrender. 'I can't. And I don't dismiss it lightly. In fact, I don't dismiss it at all. I accept that everything you've told me actually happened, and I have no explanation. If I want one, I have to fall back on concepts like ESP, the ability of the mind to pick up information through channels that we haven't yet fully understood. Maybe in time we will understand them. Maybe eventually we'll all read each other's thoughts instead of having to talk to each other. Maybe what happened to Julia is just a glimpse of the kind of thing the mind may one day treat as routine. I don't know.'

It was the day after the family had returned from Niagara Falls. Julia had spent an hour with the psychiatrist, then returned home with her mother. Tom had stayed behind to hear what he thought.

'So in your view this reincarnation idea is nuts?' Tom had told him on the phone what Pam had said, and what he himself had discovered on the Web. Hunt had even taken a look for himself before his session with Julia that morning.

'To be frank, most of it strikes me as strictly wacko. On the other hand, some of it seems remarkably persuasive.'

'Did you come across that Dr Lewis page?'

'Oliver Lewis – yeah, I'd heard of him. He's no fool, and he's clearly sincere.'

'So you know he has hundreds of case histories where he's proved beyond doubt that children have been born with memories of other people's past lives – people from families with whom they have no connection whatever?'

'Well, be careful before you say "proved beyond doubt". That's a big claim, and I'd need to examine some of the evidence myself.'

'You've got Julia,' Tom said.

Hunt looked at him for a moment, weighing him up thoughtfully. 'Do you really buy into all that?'

'I'm just trying to keep an open mind. After what I've witnessed at first hand, that's the least I can do.'

'What about your wife?'

'Clare thinks pretty much the same. She's ordered a

couple of books she read about on the Web. She even suggested we get in touch with this man Lewis himself.'

Hunt tipped his head in a way that suggested this was a course of action he would neither encourage nor oppose. 'As I said, Oliver Lewis seems like a good man. He was head of psychology at UBMA till he retired. He must be seventy by now.'

'But can you treat her – Julia? I mean, if this thing's not just a psychological condition, but something more? What are we supposed to do?'

Hunt leaned forward, sliding his elbows across the polished surface of his desk, his brow furrowing as he tried to find a way through the dilemma he could see the man across from him was in.

'Look, Tom,' he began, 'I hope I'm the last person in the world just to dismiss out of hand anything that doesn't fit into the framework within which I normally work. Any psychiatrist gets people coming in with stories about being abducted by aliens, living in a parallel universe, or being the reborn spirit of some Egyptian goddess. And you always have to have some little place at the back of your mind that says, "OK, if this is not a condition that responds to standard methods of treatment, is it possible that something is happening here that is beyond the limits of what I have been trained to understand?" It's not for nothing there are different schools of thought on almost everything, including the human mind. Freud, Jung, Adler, Lacan and all the rest – all looking at the same mystery from a slightly different perspective. And the human mind *is* a mystery in the end, one that I suspect we'll never get to the bottom of.'

'So what you're saying is . . .' Tom stopped, because he wasn't quite sure what Hunt was saying. Hunt finished the sentence for him.

'I'm saying we should not close any doors. At the same time, we need to be aware that a lot of them lead nowhere. On this question of reincarnation, it's an idea as old as time itself. It's accepted without question by many Eastern religions, specifically Buddhism. But it has no place in the West. Now why is that? I don't know. Is it because we are wrong in the West? Or is it just a cultural thing? In the West we talk about the inextinguishable spirit of man as a kind of metaphor, in the East they mean it as a literal truth. And not just spirit but personality. What does it mean? I don't know.' He sat back with a sigh. 'I'm sorry,' he said, 'I'm just thinking out loud, which isn't much help to you.'

'On the contrary, it's reassuring to meet an expert who's honest enough to admit he's baffled.'

Hunt gave a thin smile. 'You know what I think? I think that even if some kids do pick up, by whatever mechanism, on the past lives of others . . . I don't think it matters. If it did, it would have amounted to something more than it has by now. But from what I've read, even in the East, it doesn't change the way people live and what they do all that much. In general these memories, whatever they are and wherever they come from, and even if they've been verified as literally true, tend to fade away when the child gets into its teens. Ultimately it makes no difference. It's a loose end. Life is full of loose ends.'

'And we shouldn't pull on them? Is that what you're saying?'

'I think I'm saying pull on them by all means, but don't expect them to lead you anywhere much. You're not going to unravel the whole ball of wool, you're just going to wind up with longer loose ends – you know what I mean?'

'Yeah, I know what you mean.' Tom sighed. 'All the same . . .'

'You want to get to the bottom of this thing. I understand.'

'Will you continue to treat her, even if we do contact this guy Lewis?'

'Of course I will,' Hunt said, almost shocked that Tom had put the question at all. 'I've told you, I don't regard Oliver Lewis as any kind of charlatan, though there are plenty of those out there. On the contrary, I'll be interested to meet him.'

'The thing that worries me, both of us, Clare too, is that we're getting Julia involved in some kind of weird world – you know, spook-hunters, fortune-tellers, seances in the front room. Do we have the right to do that to her?'

'I don't believe you'll be doing that. You know what struck me this morning? The fact that Julia herself shows no signs of being disturbed, yet the girl she claims to remember having been was clearly disturbed. I think that's a good sign, that detachment, and it's something I want to help her hold on to.'

He was right, of course, though Tom hadn't actually thought of it in those terms. 'I get the impression that sometimes she "becomes" Melanie more than others,' he said. 'But most of the time she remembers in, as you say, a detached sort of way, like it's just a story she's read.'

'That was certainly how she sounded this morning. Tom, if you're agreeable, I think I should see her a couple of times a week for the time being. But don't think of it as "treatment", because that's not the way I want *her* to think of it. I'm just someone she can talk to, outside the loop as it were – a point of reference. And a lightning rod, if she needs one.'

They shook hands as Tom left, reassured by what he'd heard and less afraid than he had been. He called Clare on his cellphone from the car. They decided to take the plunge and do what they had been hesitating over. They decided to get in touch with Dr Oliver Lewis.

22

'Strictly speaking,' said the dry, rather careful voice on the telephone, 'you're a contaminated case, therefore of no real value for research purposes.'

'Contaminated?'

'Forgive me, it's an offensive-sounding word, but not intended as such. It means simply that you have already made contact with the family from which these memories of your daughter's seem to arise. Therefore I would be coming in after the fact, not before. Which means I cannot rule out an element of collaboration between the two sides.'

'Dr Lewis, I assure you—'

He cut off Tom's protests with an understanding laugh.

'No, no, please don't think I'm accusing you of dishonesty, Mr Freeman. I'm quite sure from everything you've told me that you have nothing to gain by inventing such a story. The other family, however . . . well, I would have to meet them before I made up my mind.'

'All right,' Tom said, 'I see your point. From an academic point of view, you're right. But my wife and I are just trying to understand this thing that's happened to us, and frankly we're looking for some help.'

'I'm not sure I can give you the kind of help you're looking for,' he said. 'If you want explanations, I don't have any.'

'I think my wife and I need to find out as much about this as we can.'

There was a pause. Tom wondered what the other man was thinking. Was there a warning in that pause? Was this something they should avoid knowing too much about?

'I must say, it sounds like a sufficiently interesting case to be worth taking a look,' Lewis said eventually. 'Give me till tomorrow to rearrange my schedule. I'll be in touch.'

Clare, meanwhile, had made a point of having a conversation with Julia's teacher, Betty Kaye. She and Tom had decided it was better she be aware of the situation than not. She was a little taken aback, Clare told Tom afterwards, but listened carefully and seemed to understand. She too had heard of such things. 'Actually, it's amazing how many people have,' Clare said, 'when you start to talk about it. Heard of, but never come into contact with it. Or if they have, they've simply explained it away as a child's over-active imagination.'

Which was exactly what he and Clare would have done, Tom knew, until now. The same thought passed through Clare's mind. She was silent a moment before saying, 'Anyway, it doesn't appear to be a problem. Julia's behaving perfectly normally, working well, doing just fine. Betty Kaye says she'll keep an eye open – in case.'

Tom nodded. One more item ticked off on the checklist, one less immediate problem. But he could not shake off the feeling that there was more to come. That thought hung over both of them, unspoken. It was like having someone you love seriously ill but in remission. You know it could all start up again at any moment.

As promised, Dr Lewis called the following afternoon. He said he would fly up from Taos in New Mexico, where he lived, in a couple of days. He politely refused both Tom's offer of hospitality and any help in finding somewhere to stay, preferring always to make such arrangements for himself, he said. He intended no discourtesy: it was merely a part of the independence he needed to maintain of the people and events he was investigating. They didn't hear from him again until early evening on the day of his arrival. He said he would like to see Tom and Clare before meeting with Julia. They told him she was staying over at a friend's house, so he took a cab and was with them in fifteen minutes.

There was a photograph of Lewis on his Web site that made him look rather solemn and forbidding. Tom recognized him at once from it, but found him animated by a much livelier spirit than he had imagined. There was a humour in his eyes and a directness in his manner that created a sense of immediate contact. But the voice remained as dry as on the phone, careful in its choice of words and sparing in their use.

Tom offered him a drink, but he accepted only water. As they sat down, Tom became aware that the older man was watching the two of them closely, though discreetly. He must have sensed their unease, and began at once to reassure them that nothing he would be proposing would be likely to cause any disruption in their lives, or Julia's. He was there purely to gather evidence, not even to assess it; that would come later. Above all, they should not think of him as offering any kind of therapy. He knew the child was in treatment with Dr Hunt and had no wish to interfere with that; he would be seeing Dr Hunt to make this clear to him.

'You know there's a certain irony I've come to see from those books I've been reading,' Tom said. 'In the East, reincarnation is so widely accepted as a fact that there seems little point in gathering further evidence to prove it. Whereas in the West, it's so contrary to everything we believe that almost no amount of evidence will ever be sufficient to convince us.'

What he was trying to tell Lewis was that, even though this stuff was new to him, he had made an intelligent stab at understanding it. Lewis smiled thinly in acknowledgement of the effort.

'You're right, there is quite a difference there,' he said. 'Of course Western sceptics dismiss all Eastern mysticism as, to quote one of the most prominent of their number, "no more than a device for reconciling people to a perfectly dreadful earthly life".'

'But surely the evidence we have, including what you've gathered yourself,' Clare said, 'can't just be dismissed out of hand. It has to be explained somehow.'

'Or explained *away*,' Lewis said, with a hint of the weariness that comes with too long an acquaintance with the closed-mindedness of his fellow men. 'The sceptics like to point out that even in the East, or *especially* in the East, a poor family giving birth to a deceased member of a wealthy one may have a lot to gain by the association.'

'But surely they can't claim every case is a fraud,' Clare said with a note of exasperation in her voice. 'That's just absurd. *We* don't know what's going on with Julia, or how or why; but we do know for a fact that it's not fraud.'

Lewis nodded sympathetically. 'Of course you do. Personally, in all the hundreds of cases I have investigated, there have been only a handful where fraud was even a possibility.'

'So what is the sceptics' answer to that?'

'There's a very useful word they have for occasions when they can't explain something away either as fraud, unconscious bias, flawed procedures, or downright stupidity. The word is "anomaly". Anything that cannot be accommodated within what we already know and believe is simply labelled an anomaly and left to one side – until, hopefully, we forget about it.'

'Or,' Tom said, 'until what we know and believe expands sufficiently to include it.'

'Which can take an awfully long time.'

'I've been reading about birthmarks in one of those books,' Clare said. 'I don't see how anyone can ignore the evidence for that.'

'Well, their first line of attack is usually coincidence,' Lewis said. 'And, of course, the fact that a child is born with a birthmark that resembles the gunshot or knife wound that killed the person he remembers having been in a previous life . . . well, it *could* be a coincidence. Almost anything *could* be a coincidence. But you have to ask yourself which explanation stretches credulity further: that degree of coincidence, or the acceptance of reincarnation?'

'And the sceptics prefer coincidence?' Tom asked.

'Yes. In their perverse way, they think it makes more sense. Just as some of them end up claiming that memories of past lives, for which they grudgingly admit the evidence is considerable, is really just ESP.'

Tom remembered what Brendan Hunt had said about the possibility that remembered lives might well be some form of telepathy or ESP that we didn't understand yet. But somehow, from the way Lewis had put it, he found something very strange about that idea now.

'*Just* ESP?' Tom echoed, with a deliberate note of disbelief in his voice. 'An ordinary, everyday thing like ESP?'

Lewis seemed pleased that Tom had picked up on

the absurdity of the idea. 'They argue,' he said, 'that since there is at least some experimental evidence, however slight, for ESP, but absolutely none for the existence of a soul independent of the body, then ESP must be accepted as the likelier explanation.'

'But they spend half their time proving that ESP doesn't exist,' said Clare. 'They can't have it both ways.'

'I'm afraid they can, and most of the time they do. Not that I'm *against* sceptics or scepticism. In fact, I've always been something of a sceptic myself. Otherwise, one is liable to be a gullible fool – an accusation I have spent quite a number of years attempting to refute.'

There was a silence, which Tom broke with the only question he could think of.

'So what's your own belief, Dr Lewis, assuming you have one? What do you, with all your experience of this kind of thing, think it adds up to?'

Lewis settled further back in his chair and gave a cryptic smile. 'If I knew that,' he said, 'I wouldn't still be gathering evidence and cataloguing case histories. And, frankly, I have to face the fact that perhaps it doesn't add up to anything. I have no theories.'

Tom thought back to what Brendan Hunt had said about loose ends, and how pulling on them didn't guarantee you would unravel the whole ball of wool. It crossed his mind that Brendan Hunt and Oliver Lewis might share more common ground than he had thought they would. He found that somehow reassuring.

23

He had been there many times, he told himself. It was a dream he knew by heart.

Yet still it made no sense to him. Each time it began in that same cellar. Each time he sensed the hand of death close by. Each time he closed his eyes, then opened them to see her – that girl's lifeless body. Each time panic overwhelmed him, and he began the breathless, stumbling sprint down twisting passages, towards the broken wooden door with the jagged halo of light around it.

The next thing he knew, he was scrambling and slipping through the tangled, muddy undergrowth, cutting himself on stones and thorns. Each time he fell and looked back at the strange, half-ruined house with its mock-Gothic turret. It sat, as always, on the far side of the scooped-out hollow that had once been a garden; as always, it made him think of a worn tooth in a decaying gum, as though the whole bleak landscape was grinning at him evilly.

And then the thought occurred to him, and each time it seemed it was occurring for the first time, that maybe this was not a dream at all. This was too real to be a dream. He could feel the earth, cold and coarse, beneath his hands as he slipped and fell. He could hear the hum of tyres on the damp road surface that he could not see from where he was, but down which he knew he was about to run.

Time does not flow, he told himself. It is a landscape that we move through, something fixed and preordained. Free will is a lie. The things we do were always there, awaiting our arrival, as this moment had awaited him. He had not dreamt it in the past; he had merely glimpsed what lay around the corner. If there was any dream at all, it was the dream of his happiness with Clare and Julia. Now he had woken to reality.

This living hell was his real life . . .

Tom awoke, as always, with a cry of terror. He was breathless and perspiring, sheets and blankets tangled around him.

He reached for the light by his bed, remembering as he did so where he was: in the hotel in Niagara Falls that he and Oliver Lewis had checked into the previous day. He looked at his watch. It was 4:20 in the morning.

For a while he lay still, trying to calm himself, trying to throw off the feeling that he was a fugitive in fear of discovery. Then, as his terror began to fade, he swung his feet to the floor and crossed the room to get a fresh bottle of water from the mini-fridge. He sank into an armchair and put the bottle to his lips.

What did it mean, this hideous repeated dream? Was that supposed to be Melanie Hagan in that house? And why had he cast himself as her murderer? He knew enough about dreams to know they were not literally true. They worked obliquely, using symbols that you had to decipher.

But what was the meaning of *these* symbols? The dead girl had not been part of the dream at all when it began. First, there had been only the house, and the sense of dread that sent him running from it. It was only on that recent night in New Orleans, just before Clare's phone call from Niagara Falls, that he had dreamt of the girl for the first time. There was some significance in that connection, the phone call and the dream. There had to be.

Was Melanie reaching out to him from wherever she was? Just as she was reaching out to Julia? Or was this whole phenomenon, as Lewis had suggested and Hunt obviously agreed, without any purpose or hidden meaning or pattern of any kind? Nothing more strange than a car radio picking up interference from overlapping signals?

Tom and Clare had talked into the night about whether or not he should pursue further research into the life of Melanie Hagan. The first thing on which they both agreed was that if he did so, then Julia must not be directly involved in any way. All that mattered was for her to get well under Brendan Hunt's care. Their job, as parents, was to help that process.

As Lewis had pointed out, the most remarkable thing about most of the cases he had investigated was the *lack* of connection between the dead person and the child who had inherited their memories. So why investigate the life of Melanie Hagan at all? Lewis wasn't pushing for it, but he was willing to help if Tom wanted him to. So what did Tom hope to achieve? In many ways it was a hard question to answer. Finally, the most he could say was that he felt he had no choice. Whichever way he looked at the situation, and however much he made an effort to avoid the word 'possession', with its chilling overtones of devilry and witchcraft, the fact was that the consciousness of another child, disappeared and possibly dead, had somehow returned through the mind of his own child. That alone sent a shudder down his spine that he could not ignore. It was at the very least an extraordinary invasion, a frightening brush with something it was hard to define as anything other than the supernatural. However much he told himself that he was not a superstitious man, he could not just pretend this wasn't happening, or treat it as something neutral and wait for it to go away. He felt the need to understand.

Perhaps that was the meaning of his dream – the house he was running from was the secret he was after. He was running from it in the dream because he was afraid of what he might discover – 'strange forces' that human beings should not tangle with, and so on and so forth. And the body of the girl inside, the body of Melanie Hagan, if that was who she was – was she the dark secret at the heart of the mystery? If so, why? And how?

A glance at his watch told him it was past five. Outside it was still dark, but he knew he would get no more sleep that night. He had been slumped in an arm-chair for the past forty minutes, facing a television screen that flickered into life only now as he pressed the remote. He watched for a while, flicking through channels, but it was hard to concentrate. In the end he gave up and got dressed.

It was becoming light as he left his hotel and stepped into the chill morning air. He walked for an hour through the sunless grey streets with their rich green foliage and trimmed hedges. The traffic had been just stirring when he set out; now it was a constant steady buzz. He turned around and started back for the hotel, where he and Lewis had arranged to meet for breakfast at eight. The previous day he had spoken with Jennifer Sawyer on the phone and arranged for her to be at the hotel at nine thirty, after her husband had left for work.

Joe Sawyer's hostility to these enquiries worried him. It wasn't simply that Sawyer posed a threat, though he undoubtedly did; more importantly, Tom was anxious to understand why. He could not free himself from the feeling that Sawyer knew something that the rest of them didn't, and which he was anxious they should not discover. Tom was aware that he had no real reason for thinking this, just instinct; by and large, he had always found, people who are disproportionately angry about something usually have something to hide, if only their own fear.

Tom had his suspicions about what Sawyer was hiding. The problem was going to be finding proof.

24

Oliver Lewis's room at the hotel had a sitting area separate from the bedroom, and it was there that he put his detailed questions to Jennifer Sawyer and got her answers down on tape. He asked if she minded him taking a photograph as a record of the session. She had no objection, and he produced a miniature camera from his jacket and snapped off a couple of shots.

Tom sat in on the session, putting questions of his own from time to time. It was not what Lewis described as a 'scientific' process. Ideally, he should have collected each family's side of the story separately; but as this was already a 'contaminated' case, he was relaxing the rules. For his part, all Tom cared about was getting as much information as he could as fast as possible. The more he could learn about Melanie Hagan's disappearance, the more he felt he might understand about her mysterious intrusion into their lives.

'Frankly, the impression I got was the cops don't give a damn when some teenage girl disappears – unless she's the daughter of a senator, or some family with enough money to hire lawyers and private investigators.' Jennifer's voice was bitter as she recalled that traumatic time. 'All they did after tracing her somewhere east of Rochester was put her name and photograph on a database, and wait to see if anyone responded.'

'And did anyone?' asked Lewis.

She shrugged defeatedly. 'Some. None of the leads they got led anywhere.'

'What about your father?' Tom asked. 'You said he walked out when Melanie was four. Did anyone check if she'd made contact with him?'

'The cops tracked him down somewhere in Ohio through his social security records. They said he knew nothing, and cared less.'

'Did you yourself deal with the police, or your mother?' Lewis asked.

'My mom was a basket case. It was Joe who did most of it, talking to them, checking out what they'd got and so on.'

'Were Joe and your sister close?' Tom asked.

She shook her head. 'Not close, no. He was good to her and did his best, but she always resented him being in the house. She'd kind of got used to it being just her, me and our mom after our dad left. The last thing she wanted was another man in the house, running things.'

'Was he doing that – running things?'

'You've met Joe,' she said, 'so you know how he is.'

There was a note of resignation in her voice, but also, Tom thought, a certain dry, if not grim, amusement.

'I don't know how he is at home,' he said, 'with the family.'

She gave another of those little shrugs of self-protective indifference that Tom was becoming accustomed to. 'He does the best he can, and back then my mom and I were both glad to have him around.'

'But your sister wasn't?' Tom suggested, pressing the point.

She sat in silence, as though the answer to his question had already been given and there was no need to say more.

'Did Melanie ever say to him what Julia said the other day?' he asked.

She looked at him with a puzzled frown.

'You remember,' he said, making it a challenge as much as a question. '"Fuck you, Joe!" Did Melanie ever say that to him?'

'She might have. She had a mouth on her, for a kid.'

'Did he ever hit her, the way he threatened to hit Julia?'

Jennifer avoided Tom's eyes. 'It happened a couple of times.'

'A couple?' Lewis was just watching now, leaving the questions to Tom. 'Was that why she ran away?' he said.

'It was her fault,' she said, her voice hardening with a note of defiance. 'She rode him till he lost it. He shouldn't have hit her. He knew that. He said so to my mom. He felt bad about it. He apologized.'

'Did he apologize to your sister?'

'I don't recall. I guess.'

Tom let a moment pass before he continued, trying to avoid the impression of browbeating her. Then he said, 'So why d'you think your husband is so hostile to the idea that we reopen this question of your sister's disappearance?'

She looked at him suddenly with almost the same degree of hostility he had sensed in her husband. 'Look,' she said, 'I know what you're getting at, but you're on the wrong track. Joe has a lot of faults, but they don't include putting his hand up little girls' skirts. That's not why she told him to fuck off, and it's not why he hit her. I hope that's plain enough for you. Because if it isn't, we can stop this whole thing right here.'

Lewis intervened, leaning forward in his armchair with a mollifying gesture. 'Mrs Sawyer, no one is making any accusations. Like you, we simply want to get to the bottom of this matter – which means sometimes asking the kind of questions we would rather not ask, though we have to all the same. We appreciate the clarity of your answer to this one.'

The thought ran through Tom's mind that Lewis had done this often before, and was therefore skilled in handling people and their touchy sensibilities – Jennifer Sawyer certainly seemed reassured by his manner. Tom left it to the older man to wind up the interview, getting such details as she could remember about the days and weeks leading up to Melanie's disappearance. There was little, so far as Tom could see, of any significance: nothing he hadn't known already.

'We shall need to talk with your husband,' Tom said as they were finishing. 'I hope that won't be a problem for you.'

She gave a weary sigh, as though such a thought was simply irrelevant to the realities of her life. 'Don't worry about me,' she said, 'just look out for yourself.'

25

Joe Sawyer worked in a paper mill only a couple of miles from where he and Jennifer lived. She gave his job description as supervisor. From what Tom gathered, it meant handling the guys who delivered and unloaded the raw material of massive logs, a job requiring little more than the ability and readiness to deck anyone who got persistently out of line. Sophisticated industrial relations did not, it seemed, play much of a role at this level of the paper-making business.

Tom decided to wait for Sawyer outside the gates when his shift ended at 5 p.m. He tried to dissuade Oliver Lewis from coming with him, seeing no reason to involve someone of his age in what could become an unpleasant confrontation. Lewis brushed aside his misgivings, observing that the best way to avoid trouble was to be in the company of an elderly person who could always clutch his heart and threaten to expire at the first sign of violence. Tom laughed; he was beginning to like Oliver Lewis quite a lot. All the same, he insisted that

David Ambrose

Lewis remain in the car Tom had rented while he waited
for Joe Sawyer on the sidewalk.

Sawyer emerged with a group of men, mostly tough-
looking customers like himself. He was chatting with
two of them when he saw Tom. The men followed
Sawyer's gaze as he stopped and glared in Tom's direction. He said something to them, and they moved off
towards a parking lot over to one side. One of them
stole a glance over his shoulder, curious about what was
about to happen, but followed Joe Sawyer's advice to
stay out of it.

Sawyer started towards Tom with deliberate slowness,
his arms hanging loose in the sleeves of the same leather
jacket he had been wearing that first time they had faced
each other at the family house. He let his gaze fall to
the ground as he walked, focusing on Tom again only
when he got right up to him, crowding him with his presence. Tom did not step back, which was obviously what
Sawyer wanted him to do; he was damned if he was
going to be intimidated by the kind of crude bullying
attitude that Sawyer was obviously a specialist in.

'You told me you didn't want me at your house, so I
came to where you work,' Tom said, taking the initiative. He stood with his hands casually in his trouser
pockets, looking up at Sawyer, who was a good two
inches taller.

'Did my wife send you down here?' Sawyer asked.

Tom had discussed with Jennifer what he would say
if this question came up.

'I asked her if she could put me in touch with any of the police officers who'd investigated her sister's disappearance. She said you were the one who'd liaised with them, not her.'

Suddenly Sawyer's gaze went past Tom and his eyes narrowed threateningly. 'What the fuck . . . ?' he spat out softly. Tom turned, and saw Oliver Lewis with his miniature camera taking a shot of the two of them together.

Lewis slipped the camera back into his pocket and strolled up to them, beaming amiably.

'Mr Sawyer, I imagine,' he said. 'Glad to make your acquaintance.'

'Who the fuck are you?' Sawyer growled.

Tom made the introductions; neither man offered to shake hands.

'If somebody takes my photograph, I like them to ask me first,' Sawyer said.

Lewis was unperturbed. 'My apologies, Mr Sawyer. I had no wish to offend and no intention to embarrass you. It's a picture merely for my personal records.'

'What personal records?' The muscles in Sawyer's jaw were still tight as he spoke.

'Dr Lewis has spent many years investigating the kind of phenomenon we saw the other day with my daughter at your house,' Tom said. 'It's something that happens all over the world – and something that I, for obvious reasons, would like to understand better. So would your wife. I'm sure you can understand that, Mr

Sawyer. As to what we want, I just told you. To talk to
the cops who were looking for Melanie. To see if there's
any stone been left unturned, any avenue of investiga-
tion that might tell us more.'

'You think I'm holding out on you? You think I have
something to hide? Is that what you're saying?'

'Mr Sawyer,' Lewis said, in that reassuring tone Tom
had already seen him use to good effect with Jennifer,
'we are simply trying to verify the extent to which Julia
Freeman's memories correspond with the events of
Melanie's life. Your wife has made it clear that neither
you nor she has anything to hide. We have no interest
in proving otherwise.'

Sawyer thought this over for a moment, then said, 'I
could use a drink. There's a bar over here.'

Without waiting for their response, he led the way to
a door alongside a darkened window on which the single
word 'Nick's' was written. The interior was fairly basic,
with a scattering of tables and a tarnished mirror behind
the bar. A handful of men sitting around the place probably came from the plant, because they looked up at his
entrance and acknowledged him with a nod. Tom asked
what he could get him, but Sawyer insisted it was his call.
Lewis and he had a beer, Tom had a mineral water. He
noticed a flicker of reaction in Sawyer's face to this choice,
but it was accompanied by no comment.

'OK,' Sawyer said, returning with their drinks, 'let's
get this over with. I don't know what this fucking baloney
is all about, and I don't care. You want to find Melanie

– go ahead and find her. My guess is she's working as a hooker out of some trailer park in Vegas or Reno, living with some pimp who knocks her around when he's had a few drinks. That'd be about her speed. Do what you have to, but leave me and my wife out of it – you hear what I'm saying?'

'You're talking as though you're sure she's alive,' Tom said. 'Have you any reason to think that?'

'I've no reason to think she's dead or alive. All I know is she's been gone a long time.'

'Was there a problem between yourself and Melanie?' Tom asked. 'Is that why she left?'

Sawyer looked at Tom as though he would have liked to smack him in the mouth, but he'd made his mind up to go along with this thing and was sticking with the decison – so far.

'Yeah, there was a problem. The problem was the kid was a bitch. Soon as her mom and her sister were out of the house, she'd be walking around near-naked, asking me if I liked what I saw. Or she'd come into my room when I was sleeping late after a night shift. You get the picture? When the cops started asking around after she disappeared, they found she had a reputation for giving the best blow job in the neighbourhood – when she was all of thirteen years old. It didn't surprise me, but I made sure none of that got back to her mother or her sister. They already had enough trouble.'

He leaned forward, sliding his arms across the table and tilting it slightly towards him with his weight.

'But nothing ever happened between the kid and me. I respected my wife, I respected my marriage. I still do. And I'm advising you to do the same and leave us out of this shit you're trying to dig up.'

Lewis was sitting comfortably, untroubled by the implied physical threat behind everything the man opposite him seemed to do or say. Tom gave a single nod, conveying that he had taken on board Sawyer's words without being unduly impressed by them.

'Did you ever hit her?' he asked.

Sawyer's gaze focused on him and hardened. 'My wife tell you that?'

'She didn't have to,' Tom said. 'I saw the way you reacted to my daughter the other day. "Fuck you, Joe," she said. And you were ready to kill her.'

Sawyer's big hand tightened around his glass until it seemed he might break it.

'I didn't kill her,' he said, not taking his eyes off Tom as he spoke, wanting to watch every word hit home and make its mark. 'I didn't fuck her either. Yeah, I hit her a couple times. She asked for it. And she was damn lucky that was as far as it went.'

'So,' Tom said, 'you admit that when she disappeared, you were glad to see the last of her.'

'I don't admit a damn thing. Don't try your fancy lawyer tricks on me.'

'I'm not a lawyer.'

'Then maybe you should get yourself one before you start making accusations you got no right to make.'

Sawyer lifted his glass and kept his eyes on Tom as he drank. Lewis broke the silence that followed with his soft, forensically dry voice.

'Your wife told us that you were the one who dealt with the police on the family's behalf. Do you think they did everything they could to find her?'

Sawyer did not even glance in Lewis's direction, as though he was of no importance and the question not worth answering.

'They traced her to some place east of Rochester. That's all I know.'

'And after that. . . ?'

He shrugged. 'I guess the trail went cold.'

There was a moment's silence, then Lewis asked: 'Do you remember the name of the officer in charge of the case?'

Only now did Sawyer look sharply at Lewis. 'What d'you take me for? The fucking memory man? It's been ten years, for Christ's sakes!'

He finished his drink and put his glass down with a finality that was underscored by the way he scraped back his chair and got to his feet in the same movement.

'Don't come around the house, and don't come around here any more. Either of you. Not even if you find her. Not even if she's married to a movie star and living in Beverly Hills. As far as I'm concerned she's history, and she can stay that way. That goes for my wife, too. You understand?'

137

He didn't wait for a response from either of them, just turned and walked out of the place. A couple of men at the bar glanced over with vague curiosity, but nobody was paying any serious attention.

'So? What d'you make of that?' Tom said to Lewis after the door had swung shut behind Sawyer.

He leaned back in his chair, cocked a speculative eyebrow and pursed his lips. 'Nasty piece of work. Capable of pretty much anything, I'd say.'

'You know what,' Tom said, 'we need to find the cop who was in charge of the case. If he's still alive, it shouldn't be impossible.'

26

'Detective Schenk?'

The heavyset man lifting fishing tackle and a cooler from the trunk of his car paused and turned in Tom's direction. 'Used to be. Who wants him?'

'The station gave us your address, said they'd call ahead.'

He grunted, slung a tackle bag over his shoulder, and slammed the trunk shut.

'Been out since dawn. My wife must've took the message.'

He glanced briefly at Oliver Lewis, who was standing by the car, then back to Tom.

'You want to see me about something?'

'We have an interest in a missing-person case I believe you worked on almost ten years ago. My name's Tom Freeman, this is Dr Oliver Lewis. We'd be grateful for a little of your time.'

Schenk, whose large head was covered in a mass of curly grey hair, weighed up both men through rimless glasses, decided they looked harmless enough to turn his back on them, and started up the gently sloping drive towards the modest but well-kept bungalow in which he lived.

'Come on in,' he said, 'time's something I got plenty of these days.'

The door was opened by a stocky but trim woman with short blonde hair and a bright smile. 'You must be the men they called about,' she said to Tom and Lewis. 'Murray, if you'd only remember to take your cellphone with you . . .'

The old cop handed her the cooler, saying something good-humoured about the privileges of retirement including no fire drills. Tom introduced himself and Lewis to her, and discovered her name was Evelyn. She asked if they would like some coffee. They accepted gratefully, then followed Schenk through to his den at the back of the house. It was wood-lined with a hand-ful of fishing trophies proudly on display along with pic-tures of his finest catches over the years. An elderly black German shepherd, half asleep on a beat-up leather sofa, gave a perfunctory bark as they entered. Schenk ruffled the dog's ears affectionately, then turfed him off to make a place for Lewis to sit. Tom took an equally beat-up armchair, while Schenk took the big chair behind his paper- and book-cluttered desk, hit the recline lever, and leaned back contentedly.

Evelyn Schenk brought in the coffee while Tom was in the midst of explaining what they wanted and giving the background to the whole story. Like the good cop's wife she must have always been, she gave no sign of even hearing what was being said, let alone having a response to it or offering any comment. She placed a plate of homemade cookies on the corner of her husband's desk and invited her guests to help themselves, then left the room and closed the door behind her.

Schenk listened to the story with furrowed-brow concentration. As a cop he must have heard a lot of weird things in his time, but Tom got the impression that this struck him as being in a class of its own. When Tom finished, Schenk didn't look up for a few moments. Then he reached for a cookie, crunched on it, and turned to Oliver Lewis.

'You say this happens a lot, Doc?'

Lewis nodded. 'More than you might imagine until you look into it.'

'Damnedest thing I ever heard.' He paused. There was a hint of scepticism in his voice as he asked, 'But you're the only one who's done what you might call scientific research into it?'

'Heavens, no,' Lewis said. 'Are you on the Internet?'

A computer was fixed to a hinged stand by the desk. Schenk reached out and pulled it towards him. 'Sure,' he said. 'What d'you want to check out?'

Under Lewis's direction, he typed the word 'reincarnation' into a search engine as Tom had done a few days earlier. Schenk's surprise at the extent of the response was as great as Tom's had been. Lewis guided him through a few of the sites, including briefly his own. When he'd seen enough, Schenk sat back and ran a hand over his chin, absorbing what he'd learnt. He looked over at Tom.

'So you believe your daughter is possessed by this Melanie Hagan, Tom?'

Like all the cops Tom had ever known, Schenk had the habit of addressing people by their first names right from the initial meeting.

'I'm not sure Dr Lewis would want to call it "possession",' he said, glancing in Lewis's direction, 'but frankly, in my view, I'd say there's an element of that to it.'

Lewis made a dubious face. '"Possession" usually refers to demonic possession,' he said. 'You know, *The Exorcist*, that kind of stuff. What we're dealing with here is something subtler, and not necessarily malevolent. In fact I haven't known any case that I would describe as outrightly malevolent. It's simply a question of unexplained memories lodged in minds where they have no reason to be.'

'But always children?'

'Almost invariably.'

Schenck thought a moment, then looked at Tom again.

'So tell me, Tom, why do you think this Melanie Hagan has chosen to come back – assuming she's dead – through your daughter?'

'That's something I've been asking myself,' Tom said, 'and I have no idea.'

'The point of this phenomenon seems almost to be that there's no point,' Lewis interjected. 'There's a whole subset of cases where a deceased individual's memories and personality traits appear to be reborn into younger members of their own family, but even there I've never come across a case of somebody returning with a specific purpose – you know, the will's in a tin box under the stairs, that kind of thing.'

Schenk grunted in response, and sat with his chin buried in his chest, gazing down at his well-rounded belly. Tom suspected he was thinking of many more questions that he would like to ask, but which he finally decided to ignore in favour of focusing on the immediate business his visitors were there for. He looked up with a brisk, faintly disdainful sniff, as though metaphysics was no subject for a cop to waste his time on.

'All right,' he said, 'I'll help you if I can. It's a long time ago, and I can't say I recall the case. But I'll dig out my notebooks and see what I can find. Why don't you fellows help yourselves to another cup of coffee?'

They did just that while Schenk rooted around on his hands and knees in the back of a deep drawer at the bottom of a large chest. Eventually he produced a handful of tattered flip-open notebooks, asked them the precise date, as near as they had it, of Melanie's disappearance, and then selected one of them. He skimmed through several pages, frowning, then began nodding his head.

'OK . . . I've got it now . . . yeah, I vaguely remember this guy . . . Sawyer, Joseph Anthony Sawyer . . . brother-in-law of the missing girl . . .'

He thumbed through a page or two, then back.

'I can't tell you much. She was picked up in Buffalo by a couple driving east. Looks like the trail went cold. I can't tell you if it's still officially an open case without checking records . . .'

'We know it's an open case,' Tom said. 'The girl was never found, so it has to be.'

Schenk flipped another page, then turned the notebook sideways to read something he'd scribbled in the margin. 'The officer who traced her out of Buffalo was Detective Jack Edwards. I know Jack, we've worked together. He's still on the force – Sergeant now. I'll be glad to call him for you, see if he can help at all.'

Tom and Lewis waited anxiously as Schenk dialled a number that he read off a Rolodex, and was put through almost immediately to his old colleague. They heard only Schenk's end of the conversation as they spent a few moments catching up on friends and families, and laughing over a couple of old in-jokes. Then he came to the point and explained why he was calling. He listened in silence a moment before covering the mouthpiece of the phone and turning to the two men with him.

'He doesn't remember any more than I do, but he's checking the computer.'

The three of them waited in silence. After a couple

of minutes Edwards came back on the line and said something that brought a puzzled frown to Schenk's face.

'Are you sure of that?' he asked. He listened some more. 'OK, thanks, Jack. I'll tell them. Yeah, you too. So long, pal.'

He hung up. 'According to the computer, the girl was reported back home and safe with her family – six days after she went missing.'

27

It was mid afternoon when Tom and Lewis reached Buffalo. Schenk had made another call to say that they were on their way, and Sergeant Jack Edwards came out to the station desk to meet them when they announced ourselves.

'We can go around the corner and get a cup of coffee,' he suggested. 'Or there's a bar that's pretty quiet this time of day.'

Tom and Lewis had drunk enough coffee and opted for the bar, which Tom suspected was also the preferred choice of Jack Edwards. If he thought for a moment that the peppermint he was sucking could disguise the smell of liquor on his breath from an old hand like Tom, he was very much mistaken. It came as no surprise when Edwards ordered a large vodka with a Miller Lite as chaser. Lewis settled for a straight Lite, but Tom noticed a flicker of almost hostile recognition in Edwards's eyes when he himself took his usual mineral water. The two men had never met before, but on a certain level they already knew each other only too well.

'OK,' Edwards said, 'Murray's filled me in on what you want. You're asking a lot, I hope you know that. But Murray and I have done each other a few favours over the years.'

He took a slug of his vodka and followed it with the beer.

'We're very grateful for your time, Sergeant Edwards,' Tom said. 'I know you're a busy man. All we want is anything you know about the search for Melanie Hagan.'

Edwards pulled a piece of paper from his shabby jacket and unfolded it. 'OK,' he said, 'I've got a print-out here of everything we have, and it's not much.'

He had a slight tremor in his hands which most of the time he disguised cleverly by keeping them moving or in his pockets. That was something else that Tom knew about. Holding on to something solid, even a glass, was no problem; in fact it was a help. But paper was always the giveaway, especially when you had to hold it long enough to read what was on it, which Edwards had just made the mistake of doing. He couldn't have been much more than fifty, if that. He was of medium build, balding, and with the waxy, sweating pallor of a man running on nervous energy and with no idea how close to exhausted his supply of it was.

'When exactly were you told that the girl had been found and was back home?' Tom asked.

'Date's right here. The fourteenth. Six days after she was first reported missing.'

'And who told you she was back home?'

'I don't have a record of that.'

'Who would normally make such a report?'

'Well, the family, of course. Or whoever had reported her missing.'

'Sergeant Edwards,' Lewis leaned forward slightly, inserting himself into the conversation in that discreet and diplomatic way he had, 'is there any routine procedure to verify that some missing person, especially a child, actually is back home when someone reports that they are?'

Edwards shrugged. 'Depends. Depends on a lot of things.'

'Such as?'

'Circumstances. If there are any suspicious circumstances, for example.'

'Which in this case there weren't?'

'None that went into the record –' Edwards tapped the paper, which he had set down on the table, with his knuckle – 'and none that I recall. Teenage girl takes a bus, then hitches a ride, doesn't cross a state line, isn't in the company of anyone of known bad character. If she turns around and the family reports her back home a week later – end of story.'

'Tell me,' Tom said, after taking a moment to absorb this information, 'did you yourself deal directly with any members of the family?'

'Yeah, the brother.' He checked the paper again. 'Sawyer.'

'Brother-in-law.'

'Right. Brother-in-law. That's the only name down here.'

'Do you happen to remember anything about him?'

Edwards gave the kind of weary smile that suggested he was dealing with people in a league he shouldn't even be wasting his time on.

'After ten years? Have you any idea how many people I see in a month, or even a week, let alone a year?'

'I'm sorry,' Tom said, 'that was a long shot, I know. But look, you know she took a bus to Buffalo, then hitched a ride to Rochester, which means you must know who she hitched that ride with.'

Edwards consulted the paper again, leaning over it where it lay on the table, avoiding picking it up again and exposing his unsteady hand.

'There are no details of that. Apparently some couple saw a picture of the girl in a local paper.'

They fell silent for a moment. Edwards took the opportunity to drain what was left in the two glasses before him, then pushed back his chair and got to his feet.

'Now, if you gentlemen have no further questions for me, I've got work piling up on my desk . . .'

They thanked him, exchanged a perfunctory handshake, then sat down again as he left, and looked at each other.

'He killed her,' Tom said. 'It's the only explanation. Sawyer murdered her.'

28

Sawyer was on the same shift, ending at five. Tom stood on the same spot where he had waited for him a few days earlier. This time, Sawyer emerged alone. When he saw Tom, he stopped, nodding slowly in acknowledgement of the implied challenge. Then he started forward with a grimly cold smile spreading over his face.

Tom didn't move as Sawyer approached, walking this time with the special swagger of a man who had delivered a fair warning and was now looking forward to showing that he had meant it. Tom took the initiative.

'This time let's skip the drink,' he said. 'Just tell me why you lied to the police about Melanie being back home.'

Sawyer froze and the blood drained from his face. 'Who told you that?'

'The police – who else?'

'You interfering son-of-a-fucking-bitch!'

His fists were balled, and Tom readied himself for the punch he knew was coming. It was more than a little crazy, but some part of him wanted to fight this man.

He knew, rationally, that he wasn't a physical match: Sawyer was bigger and more powerful than he was. And yet that crazy part at the back of his brain kept reminding him that madmen have the strength of ten, so provided you're mad enough you need not fear anyone. Tom was mad, deeply mad, at this man in front of him. He felt a kind of blind rage towards him for what he'd done to a defenceless girl and what he'd drawn his daughter and his whole family into. He wanted to show him that the world wasn't run by men like him. And he wanted to do it himself, with his own hands – as he'd been ready to do when Sawyer had threatened Julia.

Tom also had an advantage – one that Joe Sawyer didn't know about. It would have got him out of trouble if he'd started a fight that he wasn't winning. But it was an advantage that he didn't want to use.

'Look over there,' he said. Sawyer turned. 'See anyone you recognize?'

Sawyer's jaw dropped when he saw Murray Schenk leaning against an unmarked car. Standing on the far side, looking across the roof, was a young detective from Murray's old station with a Neanderthal forehead who weighed two-fifty pounds and all of it muscle.

'Let's get in the car and go talk at the station,' Tom said.

Schenk had set the whole thing up seamlessly. Although retired, it was obvious that he remained a popular figure on the force, and they had been glad to help him out. While Sawyer was being grilled by Schenk and Neanderthal man in one room, Jack Edwards, who had driven over from Rochester, watched the confrontation on closed-circuit television in another. Tom and Oliver Lewis were with him. It took a while, but eventually Edwards was sure he remembered Sawyer as the man he had talked to in connection with Melanie Hagan's disappearance, that he was the man who had later called him to report that she had returned safely home and the case could be closed.

Edwards went to join the men in the interview room while Tom and Lewis continued to watch on closed circuit. It was obvious the moment Sawyer saw him that he knew the game was up. Until then he'd been prevaricating, demanding to see a lawyer, asking whether he was under arrest, and making a big show of his willingness to cooperate voluntarily to clear up this 'misunderstanding'.

Even before he'd shut the door behind him, Edwards was cutting through the crap with practised 'bad cop' savagery.

'We don't need the body, Sawyer. This case will stand up without the body. Your only chance is if she walks into that courtroom to prove she's alive. Your second best chance is to make a confession – now. You've been tortured with guilt for ten years, you're full of remorse for what you did, maybe the judge'll go a little easier on you than he might. Or *she* might. Think about that, Sawyer. What if the judge is a woman? We can fix that, you know. A woman judge is going to like you even less than I do. So if I were you I'd think real hard. If you make us *nail* you for this, and we will, you are going to get *so fucked*. You know what they do in jail to guys like you who fuck little girls and then kill them . . .'

'I didn't kill her! I swear I didn't kill her!'

Sawyer wiped a hand across his face. He was white as a sheet and pouring with sweat. Tom noticed that Lewis had his camera in his hand again and was taking shots of the TV screen they were watching. He thought this would probably be disapproved of, if not actually illegal; but as there was no one around to see, he supposed it didn't matter.

'You fucked her, didn't you!' Schenk said, nailing Sawyer with a baleful gaze, no doubt perfected by years of experience, that seemed to drill right through the eyes of the frightened man in front of him.

'Sure he fucked her,' Edwards said, pushing his face closer to Sawyer's. Tom could imagine the smell of liquor and peppermint on his breath. 'He fucked her, got her pregnant, then he killed her.'

'She wasn't pregnant!'

Silence hit the room like a sledgehammer. Tom and Lewis looked at each other in front of the television screen, then turned back to watch the morbidly compelling spectacle as Sawyer began to come apart.

'I didn't kill her. She never said she was pregnant.'

'How many times did you fuck her?' Edwards's voice, cold and quiet now, dripped an almost tangible contempt.

'I don't know. Six, seven.'

Sawyer kept his head down, his shoulders hunched protectively as though to hide his face and avoid looking at any of them. His voice shook with fear.

'It wasn't my fault . . . I tried . . . She was coming on to me every chance she got . . . She told me if I didn't do it, if I didn't fuck her . . . She was going to tell her mother that I had . . . that I'd been . . . Oh, Christ! . . . I didn't kill her! I swear I didn't kill her!'

'Then why'd you tell me she was back home?'

'I just figured . . . I figured if she stayed away . . . if nobody was looking for her . . . that would be best . . .'

'But you made sure she was going to stay away, didn't you, Joe? By killing her and burying the body.'

'No, I didn't! I didn't do anything!'

'You just said you fucked her.'

'I didn't kill her.'

'You hit her, didn't you?'

'Yeah . . . a couple of times.'

'And she ran away.'

'Not just from me . . . from that place . . . home, the neighbourhood, everything . . .'

It went on. After a while, Tom turned to Lewis again. 'You know something? I'm starting to believe him.'

'Sawyer?'

'Yes.'

'Why?'

'Because if he killed her, why draw attention to himself by lying about her being back home?'

Lewis thought a moment, then answered: 'Maybe he just had to stop the police looking for her. Maybe he'd killed her but wasn't able to hide the body very well. Maybe there were a couple of leads that would take them straight to it if they kept on looking.'

'Too many maybes,' Tom said. 'He's a piece of shit and a fool, but I'm not convinced he's any more than that.'

It seemed that both Jack Edwards and Murray Schenk must have come to the same conclusion, because they let Sawyer go home after another half-hour, albeit it with all kinds of warnings not to leave town, and (this at Tom's suggestion) a special warning to not even think about taking any of it out on his wife, or they'd break his legs.

Schenk, Edwards, Tom and Lewis repaired to the local cops' bar around the corner from the station. They drank in silence for a while, each contemplating the table around which they were sitting.

'What now?' Tom said eventually.

Edwards clinked the ice in his glass restlessly, then took a drink before answering.

'The case stays open,' he said, 'but not much is going to change unless we get some kind of break. Even if we *are* looking for a body, and like you I'm not convinced we are, we haven't the first clue where to start.'

Tom could feel an idea taking shape at the back of his mind – a long shot, and perhaps his last.

'Jack,' he said, 'could you make a call for me?'

29

The call Tom asked Jack Edwards to make was to the local paper that had carried the picture of Melanie – the picture that Edwards had told them was recognized by a couple who had given her the ride into Rochester. The police had no record of who they were, but Tom thought there might be a slim chance that the paper itself still had something. A call from the police department, he reasoned, would focus their minds far better than a request from a private citizen.

As Edwards pointed out, knowing who brought her to Rochester wouldn't necessarily tell them what happened to her next, but he agreed it was worth a shot – especially when somebody else was doing the leg work.

The paper's young editor, who had only been in the job eighteen months, gave Tom all the cooperation he could hope for. The library was scoured, old notebooks examined, even phone records checked. The result was negative.

Oliver Lewis had flown out the day before, due in

Stockholm to deliver a public lecture. He promised Tom
he would say nothing and write nothing about Julia's
case for the time being. In return, Tom promised to keep
him informed of any developments. As there hadn't been
any, Tom thought he would wait until he got back home
to call him. Instead, he called Clare on his cellphone
while drinking a solitary coffee in the newspaper's canteen. He told her that he'd drawn a blank and would
be driving back to Niagara Falls and taking a plane out
the following morning.

'You know what?' she said, 'I'm glad you've drawn
a blank.'

'How so?' he said, not entirely surprised.

'You remember when Brendan Hunt called last week
and asked if we still had that stuff Julia brought back
from the Hagan house?'

Tom remembered it well. He had taken the call. Hunt
had asked what they had done, more importantly what
Julia had done, with the bundle of old magazines,
records and clothes that Jennifer Sawyer had let her pick
out from the stuff that Melanie had left behind.

'As far as I know, it's in the bottom of her closet,'
Tom had said. 'Why?'

'Does she play with it much, spend time sorting
through it, or anything?'

'Not that I've seen.'

Just to be sure, Tom had checked with Clare. She
confirmed his impression.

'That's good,' Hunt said. 'Here's what I want you to

do. Put it in a sack and hide it somewhere safe, but where you can get it back easily any time you might want to. But do that now, before she comes home.'

Julia hadn't noticed that the stuff was missing. Or if she had, she'd not mentioned it. Tom and Clare had spoken every day since then, and still she had said nothing.

'Brendan Hunt called again today,' Clare said, 'and told me we could throw the stuff out now. He said she's either forgotten about it, or wants to forget about it, and he'd rather there was no chance of her coming across it by accident. And he wants to see us both as soon as you're back.'

Neither of them dared say openly what they were both feeling – that this whole extraordinary and disturbing episode might be finally drawing to a close. Wherever it had all come from, whatever it had been about, Julia had come through it unharmed. Now, she was herself again. They had their daughter back.

'I'm leaving tomorrow, first thing,' Tom said. 'Make an appointment as soon as you like.'

He shook hands with the editor and thanked the members of her staff who had done everything they could to help him. It was as he was leaving the building that he heard a busy patter of feet behind him, as though someone was hurrying to catch up with him. He turned to see a slight figure, a woman he would have guessed was in her seventies. She was bustling, slightly stooped, but with an alert and lively face.

'Pardon me,' she said, 'it's Mr Freeman, isn't it?' She glanced right and left, as though anxious to be sure their conversation was not overheard. 'Did you find what you were looking for, Mr Freeman?'

'Well, no, as a matter of fact I didn't,' he answered, intrigued by her interest.

'Please don't think I am in the habit of eavesdropping – nothing could be further from my intention. But I work on the switchboard . . .'

She gestured to an open door, through which Tom could see the chair she had just vacated and the headset on the desk in front of it.

'Only two days a week now, but they've been very kind to keep me on. I've been here thirty-nine years . . .'

She rattled on, unable to come to the point even though obviously pressed for time: Tom could see lights flashing on the switchboard she had abandoned.

'I knew you were in the building today and yesterday, because I happened to overhear the call from Sergeant Edwards to say why you were coming. I would have spoken to you at once, but as I mentioned, I am here only two days a week, which means that I hardly know many of the newer members of staff . . . of course, when I was full time I—'

'Is there something you can tell me?' Tom interrupted, trying not to seem rude, but in an effort to head off the digression he felt was likely to continue indefinitely.

'Well, yes, indeed – indeed there is. That's what I'm saying. You see, none of these people, with very few exceptions, were even working here ten years ago. I myself, of course, am one of those exceptions, obviously, as I told you. Thirty-nine years I've been here. So I well remember the incident you're interested in.'

'You mean you know who recognized the photograph of that girl?'

'Well, of course I do. It was my cousin – Alice Macabee.'

Ten years or so older than her garrulous cousin, Alice Macabee was now living in sheltered accommodation in a pleasant suburb only a half-hour's drive from the newspaper office. She walked with the aid of a Zimmer frame, but was mentally alert and had a beguiling sense of humour.

'You've got to have tea or coffee,' she said as she hobbled into her kitchen annexe. 'It's the only exercise I get. They bring me all my meals, but I get to make my own tea and coffee.'

'All right,' Tom laughed. 'In that case I'll gladly have a cup of coffee.'

The switchboard operator, whose name he had discovered was Marion Walsh, had wanted to drive him over herself when she came off duty, but he had insisted that he did not have time to wait. In the end she had agreed to call her cousin, then reluctantly given him directions to find his own way there.

'I recall the child very well,' said Mrs Macabee, as they settled into armchairs by a long window that looked onto a communal garden. 'Howard, my late husband, who passed away two years ago, didn't want to stop for her at first. Howard didn't approve of hitch-hikers. But I could see she was only a child, and it was far better she ride with us than some of the people who might have picked her up.'

'Did she tell you her age?' Tom asked.

'She said she was seventeen. Of course I didn't believe her for an instant, but I was shocked when I read her real age in the newspaper a few days later. She certainly looked a good deal older than thirteen.'

'What was she like? Did she talk about herself, where she came from, where she was going?'

'She said she was going someplace, but I can't remember. She said her mother had given her money for the bus, but she had decided to keep it and hitch rides. We told her that was not a good idea, with the kind of people there were about. But of course you can't tell young people anything. Our own two were the same. They're in their forties now with children of their own, and they're going through all the worries and anxieties we had with them.' She gave a light, good-natured laugh. 'Well, you can't expect children to grow up just the way you want them to. That wouldn't be reasonable, would it?'

'You're sure you can't remember where she was going?'

'Somewhere further east. Where was it, now? Maybe the name will come to me if I don't think about it.'

'And nobody ever asked you about all this? The police, nobody?'

'Well, of course, by the time we saw her picture she was no longer missing. At least, that's what we were given to understand at the time. What you tell me now, of course, is very disturbing. You mean to say the poor child has not been heard of since?'

'I'm afraid not.'

'That makes me feel awful, quite awful. We should have done something more, at least made some effort to be sure she was safe.'

'It isn't your fault,' he said. 'You were very kind to her. No one could have done any more.'

They sat in silence for some moments. A palpable sadness had descended on Mrs Macabee as she thought back to the child she obviously remembered so well.

'Albany!'

The name burst from her suddenly, startling Tom. 'Albany?' he said. 'You mean she was headed for Albany?'

'That was it. I knew I'd remember if I gave myself time. She said there was a music festival somewhere near Albany.'

She was looking at Tom with a bright, half-smile of triumph. But she must have seen something in his face that she didn't expect: something which, from the sudden change in her expression, perhaps even alarmed her. 'Why, Mr Freeman, is anything the matter? You look quite strange.'

'No, it's nothing,' Tom said quickly. 'A coincidence, that's all.'

'A coincidence?'

'Just that—' He broke off. 'Nothing, really. Nothing at all. Thank you, Mrs Macabee, you've been a great help.'

30

'Tom! For heaven's sakes! Tom!'

Clare tried to hold his thrashing arms, but he threw her off with a violence that slammed her hard against the headboard of the bed. She gave a cry more of shock than pain.

Tom sprang from the bed and across the room, arms still flailing as though smashing invisible obstacles out of his way. His eyes were open, but he saw nothing. He had overturned a small table before he stumbled against a chair and fell to the floor with a crash that shook the house.

'Tom! Stop!'

If he heard her, he gave no sign of it. Clare ran to help him up, refusing to let go when he tried to push her away. A terrible wail started up from the back of his throat.

'Tom – wake up! Wake up!'

She shook him as hard as she could, but it was a while before his eyes began to clear and his gaze, still filled with fear, focused on her.

'It's all right,' she said. 'You were having a nightmare. It's over.'

He gave a puzzled frown. He looked around the room, as though he could not believe where he found himself or understand how he got there. A thread of spittle fell from the corner of his mouth, and he began muttering incoherently – for all the world, Clare thought with a chill of recognition, like a tortured, crouching figure in a picture of some nineteenth-century bedlam.

'It was your dream again,' she said. 'It's over. You're all right.'

She wrapped him in her arms. He seemed at last to come to himself, and clung to her, breathing hard. Then his eyes widened in response to some new and, she supposed, imaginary horror that he saw over her shoulder. She turned. Julia stood in the door, pale and frightened in her nightdress.

'Darling,' Clare said, 'it's all right. Daddy was having a bad dream, that's all.'

The child's gaze remained fixed on her father. What she saw frightened her even more than the noise and screaming that had awoken her in the middle of the night. This naked man with the haunted eyes staring out of a haggard face was some awful impostor, not the father she knew. After a moment she could stand the sight no more; she turned and ran.

'You'd better go to her,' Tom said, his voice thick and raw-sounding. 'Tell her I'm sorry . . . I'll come in a minute . . . when I've put some clothes on . . .'

David Ambrose

Clare hesitated to leave him, but she could see he was himself again, though badly shaken. She went quickly to her daughter's room. The child lay face down on her bed, sobbing, her whole body trembling from the shock that had exploded out of nowhere over them.

'Darling, it's all right . . . Daddy was just having a bad dream . . . It's over now . . .'

The child turned abruptly and clung to her as though for dear life. 'I'm frightened,' she said.

'I know. So was I. So was Daddy. You know how scary dreams can be. But it's all right now.'

She heard a movement behind her. Turning, she saw Tom standing in the door, framed against the light as he pulled the cord of his bathrobe tight around his waist. He seemed hesitant about entering, as though afraid he was not wanted there.

'Darling, look,' Clare said to Julia, 'Daddy's here. He's all right now. Everything's all right.'

The child looked past her mother's shoulder, fear still lingering in her eyes.

'I'm sorry,' Tom said lamely in a whisper. 'I'm so sorry, darling . . . I didn't mean to frighten you . . .'

He looked on miserably as his daughter clung all the harder to her mother in fear of him. But then, as though suddenly conscious of the pain her attitude was causing him, or perhaps simply thankful that her father was himself again, she impulsively held out her arms to him.

Tom ran to her, clasping her so tightly that he feared after a moment he might hurt her, so he relaxed his

166

grip. She did not relax hers. The feel of her small arms around him brought a comfort that he had not dared to hope for. He pressed his face into the soft blonde hair on the top of her head, and hid his tears in it.

Half an hour later, having got Julia settled back to sleep, Tom and Julia sat on kitchen stools in their bathrobes, sipping mild lemon tea.

'It's always the same, in every detail,' he was saying, 'except it's starting to change.'

'Change how?'

'It's starting earlier. First of all I was in this over-grown garden, then I was in the house itself – some kind of cellar. Now I'm in another part of the cellar.'

'And you still haven't seen whatever it is you're running from?'

He didn't answer at once. He hadn't told Clare about the girl in his dream. The day before he had told her about Mrs Macabee, because that was something factual that he would have felt dishonest and guilty about hiding from her.

'The fact that the girl was headed for Albany doesn't necessarily mean she got here,' had been Clare's first reaction.

'I know,' Tom had said, 'but it's quite a coincidence. Time and place.'

That conversation had also taken place in the kitchen. Clare was chopping vegetables, preparing dinner. She looked sideways at him, as though trying to assess whether he was attempting to tell her more than he wanted to say. 'What word would you use?' she asked.

He shrugged, trying to show her that he wasn't making too much of the point. 'It's a link, that's all. I mean it might explain . . . something.'

Clare turned her attention back to what she was doing. 'Have you told Oliver Lewis about it?'

'No. I haven't told anybody – except you.'

That was where they had left it. But now, alone and awake together in the middle of the night, with no distractions and no excuses, he knew he had to tell her the rest.

'There's something else,' he said. He was sitting hunched over his cup on the counter in front of him, not looking at her.

'Tell me,' she said.

'I know what it is I'm running from. In the dream.'

It took only moments to tell her about the girl, but the silence when he'd finished threatened to stretch out to infinity. Eventually, he began counting the seconds. Ten went by, and another ten, and still she had not spoken, looked at him, or reacted in any way.

'I need to know what you're thinking,' he said.

Her voice was flat. 'It's a dream, Tom. How can a dream mean anything?'

'I don't know. It just frightens me, that's all.'

She turned her gaze in his direction. He saw it had frightened her too. The colour had drained from her face.

'So what are you saying? That you killed that girl? Is that what you think?'

'All I'm saying is the timing's right, and the place . . .'

'What place?' There was anger in her voice now. She was going to fight this. 'Some crazy Gothic house – probably something you saw at a funfair when you were a child? It's not enough, Tom. You're obsessed with this Hagan girl because of what's happening to Julia. Of course you are! We both are! So now you're dreaming about her. That's not so hard to understand, is it? It's natural. It doesn't make you a murderer!'

'I was out of control back then. You didn't know me. I could have done anything without remembering.'

'Do you *believe* you killed that girl?'

'I don't know!'

'Well, I do. I *won't* believe it.'

She slipped off the stool she had been sitting on and started towards him. He too stood, and held out his arms to her. But instead of slipping into them as she normally would, she raised both fists and hammered them painfully against his chest. 'How can you say what you just said to me? How can you even think it? You . . . you . . . you fucker . . . you . . . I love you!'

Only when she had exhausted her rage did she fall towards him, wrapping her arms around him and pressing her face to his. 'I love you,' she repeated, in a whisper this time.

He could feel the wetness of her tears on his cheek. 'I love you too. And I'm sorry, but I couldn't not tell you.'

'I know.' She pulled away, drying her eyes with the back of her hand. 'So, you've told me. Now what do we do?'

'I don't know.' He shook his head. 'I don't know what to do, I don't know what to think.'

'Why not talk to somebody? I'm out of my depth with this. So are you.'

'Talk to who?'

'Oliver Lewis? Brendan Hunt?'

'Oliver's in Europe. And Brendan Hunt's a *child* psychiatrist.'

'What's the difference?' She gave a dry laugh. 'Grown-ups are just big kids. Besides, a shrink is a shrink. What's more, he's Julia's shrink, and this concerns her.'

'Maybe you're right. I'll call him tomorrow.'

As they stood holding each other in the centre of the kitchen, the distant chime of a church clock struck three in the still night air.

'Today,' she said. 'You can call him today.'

31

Murray Schenk was doing what came naturally to a cop, retired or not. He was making routine enquiries. It made a change from fly-fishing, a surprisingly welcome one. Once a cop and so on, he told himself. But it was more than that. These were too many loose ends about the Hagan case, and too many loose screws about the Freeman story. All of which left a heap of stuff for someone to get to the bottom of and, so far as Schenk could see, he himself was the only one ready to take a shot at doing just that.

There was also the lingering and uncomfortable suspicion that if he or Jack Edwards or someone in a position to do so had made a few more routine checks back then when it really counted, when the Hagan girl had first gone missing, then maybe things might have turned out better. Maybe it was too late to make a difference now, but Schenk did not feel he had any choice but to try.

He had started by making a thorough check of Oliver

171

Lewis on the Web and in a few reference books. There was no doubt that the man's ideas on previous lives were by most of his colleagues' standards out on a limb, but he was too distinguished to be dismissed as a crank. Tom Freeman, he also discovered, was highly thought of by his peers. Award-winning commercials had been followed by award-winning documentaries: a successful career change, but with, Schenk observed, something of a gap in the middle. He had already noticed that Tom Freeman did not drink, which suggested he might once have done so too enthusiastically. That, too, would require checking out.

Schenk had a journalist friend whose daughter worked for CBS in New York. She knew Tom Freeman only through his work, not personally, but she suggested someone who might be able to help. After a couple more calls, Schenk found himself sitting in a movie editing room with a man who'd been associate producer on a couple of Tom's projects. Schenk explained his interest in Tom by saying he had been retained by an unnamed media conglomerate who were thinking of offering him some big job. He suspected the man didn't believe him, but he didn't seem to care either way, and was happy to talk.

'It's no secret,' he said, talking about Tom's past problems with alcohol and drugs. 'Like a lot of people who've gone through that, he's perfectly open about it.'

'This problem – was it while he was still working in advertising, or after?'

'Both. It started while and continued after. Until one day he had to make some serious decisions about his life. That was about the time he met Clare.'

'That's his wife?'

'Yeah – great lady. And a very important part of his recovery – as he'd be the first to admit.'

'Was that how they met, in recovery?'

'Not in the sense that she was in the programme. She just happened to be visiting the hospital where he was after the accident.'

'Accident?'

'Oh, God, he was really broken up by all accounts. Clare said she found out later they hadn't expected him to live.'

'What happened?'

'Nobody knows. Least of all him. He must have been hit by a truck or something while he was stoned into orbit. Anyway, that was kind of what brought him to his senses.'

'So this must have been, what? About ten years ago?'

'Yeah, just over.'

'Do you know where it happened, this accident?'

'Somewhere outside Albany. I don't know exactly where. There was some music festival.'

It all added up, Schenk was forced to admit, to absolutely nothing. So why did he have this nagging feeling that there was more to it, more to find out?

Then he got a call from Jack Edwards.

'Murray, does the name Alice Macabee mean anything to you?'

'No. Should it?'

'I don't know. I just heard from a daffy-sounding old bird who says she's her cousin. The old bird works the switchboard of the paper I fixed for Tom Freeman to go talk with in Buffalo. She says her cousin gave Freeman some information about the Hagan kid, and wants to know if he's found out what happened to her yet. Apparently he left his phone number with this Macabee woman, but she's lost it. So she asked her cousin to try and track him down.'

Schenk took Alice Macabee's details, then called her.

32

Brendan Hunt listened without moving, his eyes down for much of the time, but glancing up whenever Tom hesitated or his voice faltered, encouraging him to carry on. Finally, when Tom was finished, Hunt drew a long breath and leant back. He reflected for some moments before he spoke.

'The first thing you have to understand,' he began, 'is that we don't dream our memories. Or, more accurately, we don't dream them *as* memories. We convert them into the language of dreams. So if you really had killed a girl in the cellar of some strange-looking house, you wouldn't be dreaming about killing a girl in the cellar of some strange-looking house. That might be what your dream was *about*, but it wouldn't be the dream you were having. In the trade jargon, it's the difference between manifest content and latent content.'

'I understand that. But this one is just so *real*. I can *feel* the walls when I touch them. I can feel the earth, cold and wet, when I fall in the garden. I mean, I was always told that if you pinch yourself and you don't feel it, that means you're dreaming.'

'Have you tried pinching yourself?'

Tom realized he had to think about this before answering. 'I don't think so. No, that's funny – I don't remember doing that.'

Hunt smiled. 'It's not an infallible test. Though with a little practice, some people find it's a trick they can use to wake themselves up. You might try it, but don't worry if it doesn't work.'

'But look, Brendan,' Tom said, leaning forward to impress his point more earnestly, 'supposing someone does something so terrible that they can't bear to think about it, they just want to forget it. They push it out of their mind. I mean, they push it out of their *conscious* mind and into the *unconscious*, which is the only place it can go. In that case, why couldn't they dream about it *exactly* as it happened, not necessarily in dream language?'

'Even when you're asleep, the mind still censors itself. The conscious mind, the part of you that can't accept the truth when you're awake and has therefore suppressed it—'

'With a lot of help from alcohol and some serious narcotics.'

'With all that. That same part of you is still there when you're dreaming. You still don't want to face up to what you've hidden from yourself.'

'What if another part of me wants to?'

'Perhaps part of you does. And when you're asleep,

your defences are down, it's not so easy to hide from your secrets any more. So you dress them up as something else. Dream images, which use visual and verbal puns and references instead of straightforward everyday language. It takes a long time to decipher what these things mean, if in fact you ever can finally.'

Tom thought about this, then said in a flat, defeated voice, 'Maybe some things are best left forgotten.'

Hunt inclined his head slightly, acknowledging the point. 'Of course,' he said, in the tone of a man who wanted to be fair to all sides, 'there are distinguished scientists and psychiatrists who would argue that dreams mean absolutely nothing, anyway. Just the rumblings of the mental digestive system.'

'I find it hard to believe that.'

'And I find it hard to believe that you are the man you are trying to accuse yourself of being. I think you're adding two and two together and making five. I really do. I'm speaking as your friend, not as your therapist, which anyway I'm not.'

Tom looked at him for a while, then said, 'So you don't buy the Jekyll and Hyde thing.'

'No. Not in your case. Not even with the help of a lot of drugs and alcohol.'

'But the girl was *there*. Right there in Albany, at the festival. And so was I.'

'So were a lot of other men, Tom.'

Tom sighed and sat back, wearied by the effort of searching for answers in this complex morass of memory and guesswork, but determined to go on. 'But *why*? What is the *kind* of reason I might be having this dream?'

'It may be that there's some deep-seated thing that's bothering you and you're trying to come to terms with it. If you really want to find out what it is, you could get into analysis or some other form of treatment – not necessarily with me, but I can name a number of excellent people you could see.'

'All I want to know for now,' Tom persisted, 'is what can it mean to dream repeatedly that you've murdered someone?'

'Well, the most obvious interpretation is that you're harbouring repressed anger. It may mean that you're on the edge of violence and only just managing to contain it. But I don't think that's your problem – although I don't have to tell you how much anger there can be associated with addictive behaviour, which is still there and has to be dealt with even after the addiction itself has been controlled.'

'All right,' Tom said, 'I can see that. Is that the only thing this dream can mean?'

'Lord, no. It can mean a lot of things – dreams often can. For example, it can arise out of an unconscious feeling that you're freeing yourself from something. Adolescents often dream of killing their parents around the time they start wanting to become independent, but all they're doing is killing their feelings of dependence, as part of personal growth.'

'But what does it mean to dream you've killed a *child*?'

'Like I said, if you really want to get to the bottom of it, you may need to see somebody over a period of time. Anything I say now isn't much more than a shot in the dark.'

'That's OK – keep shooting.'

Hunt regarded him a moment, making a decision about whether to go on. 'Well, I'd say that you're afraid of failure, of falling back into your old ways, when you were controlled by your addictions. To you, that's what failure means – falling back. That's the fear that you're running from in your dream, which you see as this decaying, forbidding old house. And now you've made the house even more frightening by filling it with the worst thing you can imagine – for example, the idea that you've killed a child.'

Tom nodded. 'That's logical. Except why would I necessarily pick on the idea of killing a child? There are plenty of other things that scare me.'

'You picked up on it because of what's been happening with Julia, and the fact that it's thrown up the story of this missing girl. Remember, you'd learned about Melanie Hagan before she started popping up in your dream.'

'But why,' Tom persisted, slapping the back of one hand into the palm of the other, 'why was I dreaming about the house *before* that?'

Hunt's professional, easygoing calmness soothed and absorbed the frustration Tom felt. 'You said the first time you had this dream was around the time of Julia's birth.'

'I was running out of the house, but I didn't know why. I didn't know there was a dead girl in there . . .' He stopped and ran a hand over his face. It was a gesture of extreme weariness, of a man nearing the end of his tether. 'Or maybe I did . . . I just didn't remember until Melanie Hagan came back into my life – through my own daughter.'

Hunt was silent, letting Tom's words settle in the air between them, giving them the weight and the reflection they deserved. Finally he said, 'I don't believe anyone can explain why your daughter has these memories, Tom, so you shouldn't jump to conclusions. You're trying to find reasons and logical sense where maybe there isn't any. As Oliver Lewis admits himself, sometimes we just have to accept that there are no explanations.'

33

Murray Schenk gave a last wave to Alice Macabee and got into his car. She watched him through the window of her living room, as he turned his key in the ignition, checked his mirror, and pulled out. He would drive around for a while — it always helped him clarify his thoughts, and right now he needed to think over what he had just learned.

It was obvious from the way she had talked about him that Alice Macabee had liked Tom Freeman too. There was no reason why she shouldn't: he was a charming, good-looking, courteous man. What she didn't know was a fact that Murray Schenk had just discovered: that Melanie Hagan had disappeared at exactly the time and in exactly the place where Tom Freeman had been on his last drink- and coke-fuelled binge.

Tom knew it, too. He had known it since his own visit to Alice Macabee. So far, he had kept the information to himself.

Schenk decided it was time to put him to the test.

* * *

The phone in Tom's office at the back of the house had rung several times during the morning, but he had let his machine pick up the calls. When he checked it later there were messages from his business manager, a couple of TV executives, and a researcher who was working on a new idea for a series. The two last callers had left no message. He wondered if they had his cellphone number – and as though in response to his thought, it rang in his pocket. He recognized Murray Schenk's gruff tones at once.

After they had got the pleasantries out of the way, Schenk said, 'I just wondered if you came up with anything at that newspaper office last week, anything that might help us?'

Tom couldn't be sure if he was imagining it, or whether there really was a hint of suspicion in Schenk's voice. Surely a cop would know better than most people how to disguise his feelings? But there was something in the deliberate casualness of his tone that suggested a trap. It was perfectly possible that Schenk had traced his footsteps and spoken to Mrs Macabee himself. Tom thought fast, and saw he had no choice. Either Schenk knew the truth already, or he would find it out soon enough.

'As a matter of fact I did, Murray.' He tried to sound relaxed, but his voice was tight and he had to clear his throat. 'I found out something, but I decided I wasn't going to do anything about it. The reason is that I'm trying to protect my daughter. She seems to be getting over this . . . this "thing" that's happened to her, and that's the way my wife and I want to keep it.'

There was silence on the line. Tom waited.

'What did you find out, Tom?' Schenk said eventually.

Tom wondered how to play this, how much to say, how much to hold back. It troubled him that he was thinking like a guilty man. Since his conversation with Hunt he had clung to the thought that maybe he really was putting two and two together and making five. More importantly, so had Clare. It wasn't much of a lifeline, but it was all they had.

And now here was this cop trying to hook them on it.

Of course the thing that Schenk could not possibly know about was the dream. Tom was sure that Hunt would keep that confidential.

All right – strategic disclosure. That was the way to play it.

'I guess you've spoken to Mrs Macabee yourself, Murray. Am I right?'

'You're absolutely right, Tom,' Schenk said. His tone was neutral, no acknowledgement that he had been testing the other man; but both were on their guard now.

'I'm sure you can understand our point of view,' Tom said. 'My wife and I feel that this has gone far enough. If our daughter, through some psychic fluke or whatever you want to call it, has picked up on something that happened before she was even born . . . Well, let me put it this way, Murray: I was the one who started to unravel this whole thing because I wanted to find out what was happening to Julia. Frankly, I think I've found out all I want, and I've gone far enough. My only concern now is to see my daughter get well, which she is doing. And that's something I don't intend to jeopardize.'

'I understand what you're saying, Tom, and I'd feel exactly the same in your place. But from where I stand, things look a little different.'

'How d'you mean?'

'I mean that if I and a few of my colleagues had done our jobs better ten years ago, then that girl might have been found. Or at least we might've found out what happened to her.'

'Have you spoken to Jack Edwards? Is he pursuing this?'

'Jack has enough to pursue with what's happening now. More than enough. Like I told you before, I have nothing but time.'

Tom realized he was being made to understand that Schenk was not going away. 'You're retired, Murray. Are you making some kind of personal crusade out of this?'

'I intend to try and find out the truth.'

'Well, I respect that. But you're not going to involve our daughter in any of it. I want to make that clear right now.'

'I'm not planning to involve your daughter. I doubt if there's much more she can tell us, anyway. But don't you think we owe it at least to Jennifer Sawyer to tell her whatever we know about her sister?'

'Perhaps. But it's not much, is it? I mean, it's hardly a solution to the mystery.'

Schenk was silent a while, then he repeated Tom's words. 'No, it's hardly a solution to the mystery.'

Tom was unsure whether he heard resignation in his tone, or something else. A veiled threat, perhaps? Certainly an acknowledgement that the story was not over but was, as Tom's childhood comic books used to say, 'to be continued'.

'Well, Murray, 'you must do what you think is right. But I'm through – for the reasons I've given you.'

'I understand. I'll call you if anything new comes up.'

'OK, Murray – do that.'

34

Murray Schenk hung up the phone and wondered about calling Jennifer Sawyer. In fact he did feel, as he had said to Tom, a genuine obligation to keep her informed. And he would do so. But for the moment it could wait. Right now he had further enquiries to follow up, other lines of thought to explore. He dialled the number he had been given for Dr Brendan Hunt in Saracen Springs.

The following day, just after 12:30 p.m., Brendan Hunt made the ten-minute drive from his office to the Citadel Motor Lodge on Scarsbrooke Avenue, where Schenk had checked in that morning. It would be better to meet there, Schenk had said, because it minimized the risk of running into the Freemans, or anyone who knew them.

Hunt drove slowly past the freshly painted cabins in the bright midday light until he came to the number Schenk had given him. He knocked at the door, and took his first look at the man who opened it for him.

'Good of you to find the time,' Schenk said. 'Come on in.'

The room was characterless even by the standards of an average motel: bed, TV, bar, and a couple of large but oddly uncomfortable armchairs. Hunt refused either coffee or a drink. Schenk flipped the top off a beer, then the two men sat opposite one another, Schenk with his hands resting on his ample stomach, contemplating his visitor with Buddha-like inscrutability.

'What exactly is it you want to talk to me about, Mr Schenk?' Hunt said, taking the initiative to get the conversation started. 'You were somewhat cryptic on the phone.'

'You have to be these days. Never know who's listening.'

'That's true. But if I can be of any help . . .'

'It's Tom Freeman,' Schenk said, and took a sip of his beer. 'I know you're the girl's psychiatrist, so there's a limit to what you can tell me about her. But it's her father that interests me.'

'Well, to an extent the parents are covered by the same confidentiality, but I'll do what I can.'

Schenk fixed him with a relaxed but concentrated gaze that was, Hunt suspected, a routine technique in his bag of interrogatory tricks.

'I'm going to tell you a couple of things about Tom Freeman that you maybe don't know,' Schenk began, 'and I'd like you to tell me what you think. Evaluate them, so to speak, in professional terms.'

'Go ahead.'

Schenk outlined what he had learnt of Tom's drink and drugs days, and of the final episode that had landed him in the hospital ten years ago. Hunt nodded thoughtfully as he listened, and then said that Tom had in fact told him the story himself.

'If you're asking whether he's fully recovered, in so far as we use the term "recover" for addictive problems, I'd say without question. He hasn't so much as touched a drink or smoked a joint since he woke up that day in the hospital.'

'OK,' Schenk continued, 'I accept that. Now I'm going to tell you something else, which maybe you don't know.'

'If it's about that girl disappearing at the same time, right there at the festival . . .' His tone was polite, but conveyed an impression that he didn't have time to waste hashing over old news.

'So he's told you about that, too?'

Hunt nodded. 'I don't believe he's making any secret of it. Besides, all we know is she was headed for Albany. We don't know for sure that she got there.'

'True, but . . . let's suppose she did.'

'What I assume you're asking me, Mr Schenk, is whether I think it possible that Tom killed Melanie Hagan in a state of temporary fugue – drug- and alcohol-induced amnesia. Is that your question?'

Schenk nodded. 'That's my question.'

'Well, my answer would be – it's possible. Remotely possible. But highly unlikely.'

'You don't think he has it in him, is that what you're saying?'

'You could put it that way, if you like.' Hunt shrugged. 'I'm not his psychiatrist, and so I can't claim it as a clinical evaluation. But it's a strong instinct.'

'So what we're dealing with here is coincidence, pure and simple. The girl's disappearance, Tom's blackout . . . and his daughter being born with the missing girl's memories. Pure coincidence.'

Hunt drew a deep breath, then let it out slowly. 'Obviously there's something more than coincidence going on here. But if you ask me what it is, I have no idea, Mr Schenk.'

'Call me Murray, please.'

'Murray.'

A silence hung between the two men. Schenk took another pull on his beer, then smacked his lips reflectively. 'D'you think maybe she's trying to tell us where she's buried? Wouldn't that make sense, Brendan? Couldn't that be what's going on?'

Hunt, whose gaze had wandered over to the wind-ruffled trees he could see beyond the half-open Venetian blind over the window, focused once again on Schenk.

'So you're assuming she's dead, Murray.'

'Oh, yes. She's dead all right.'

35

Julia went up to bed at nine, asking that her father come and kiss her goodnight as he always did. When Tom entered her bedroom, she was lying with her eyes closed, breathing steadily. He did not know whether she was really asleep or just pretending, lying in wait to take him by surprise as she sometimes did. Whatever, he would play the game her way. He tiptoed across the room so softly that even if she were awake she would not hear him, and he would be the one to surprise her. He got right up to her bed and leant over it. Still she did not react: no flickering of the eyelids or telltale twitching of the mouth as she fought to suppress her laughter. Maybe, he decided, she really was asleep. He bent down and kissed her gently on the forhead, just below the hairline.

'Goodnight, my darling,' he whispered, and switched off the lamp at her bedside. He paused at the door, turning back for one last glance. She had not moved. He started out, pulling the door partially shut behind him.

'How long you gonna wait, cocksucker!'

He whirled around. Julia lay exactly as she had been, breathing steadily and deeply, not moving. Yet the voice had been hers, or almost hers. Not the tone. The tone made all the difference.

'Darling?' he said, his voice catching in his throat, nearly making him gag. 'Julia?'

She did not stir.

Could he have imagined it? Was the voice in his head, not in the room? It was possible. Anything was possible. That was the one thing of which he was sure by now. After all that had happened, the fact that he should start hearing voices was hardly a surprise. He started out of the room once again.

'Come back here, you fucking jack-off!'

Again he spun around. This time there was no doubt. Those words had been spat across the room at him, not something he'd imagined. Nor was the sight that met his eyes imaginary.

Julia sat facing him on the edge of her bed. But this girl was no longer his daughter. There was a smile on her lips that was more like a sneer – an expression of mockery and teasing, fearless superiority. As he watched she leant back on her hands, shifting her weight so that her pelvis was thrust towards him in a way that was blatantly and lewdly sexual.

'What's happening?' he demanded, his voice unsteady. 'Julia?'

The girl on the bed laughed at him. 'Forget the kid, big boy. You're talking to me.'

191

He took a step towards her. 'Get out. Get out of my daughter. Get out.'

The girl looked up at him and sniggered. 'What's the matter, Pops? Upset that I got into your daughter before you did?'

Without realizing it, he had raised his hand and was on the point of smashing it across her face. She showed no fear, did not even flinch. Something in the cold, detached amusement of her gaze brought him back from the edge. He remembered Joe Sawyer that first day at Niagara Falls. He'd had exactly the same reaction when Melanie had spoken to him through Julia. Slowly, Tom lowered his hand, trembling, to his side.

'Get out, you bitch,' he said, his voice low, his lips stretched tight over his teeth. 'Go back to hell, where you belong.'

Her eyes did not leave his, but she gave no sign of even hearing his words, let alone heeding them.

'You need a drink, baby. That's your problem – you know that? You're not going to remember anything without a drink.'

'What am I supposed to remember?'

'Why, *everything*, of course.'

She contrived to give 'everything' a suggestive edge, with a lift of the voice and a mock-innocent widening of the eyes.

'Just tell me what you want, damn you. Tell me what you want me to do.'

'Remember that night.'

Her sarcastic gaze was unflinching and unafraid, and there was no doubt what night she was referring to. He felt defeated and powerless. When he spoke, his voice was hollow.

'I don't remember anything about that night.'

'River and Pike – remember?'

'I don't know what you're—'

'You need a drink. Then you'll understand a lot of things. Now fuck off out of here.'

He watched, dumbfounded and yet horribly fascinated, as she swung her feet up on the bed, settled back, and pulled the quilt demurely to her chin. Keeping her gaze on him, but without expression, she closed her eyes. A moment later, the still form of his daughter lay there, sleeping as she had been when he first came into the room.

Tom stood for some time, paralysed by indecision. Part of him wanted to wake Julia up and challenge her with what had just happened; another part of him felt sure she would remember nothing. If he were to go downstairs right now and tell Clare, she would believe him, of course, but believe *what* – that he'd hallucinated? Probably not: she had more confidence in his mental stability than that. But what would she make of the suggestion that he take a drink?

A drink? Was that even conceivably the answer? The only way to reconnect with what he had forgotten?

Remember that night. River and Pike. What did it mean? It rang a bell – but what bell, where from? He was still turning the words over in his mind when he found himself already halfway downstairs. He had left Julia's room without being conscious of doing so. What now? To his right he could see the light on in the small room that Clare worked in at home. She was preparing some figures for a meeting the next morning. She had told him she would be busy for about an hour, so he decided not to disturb her. He would think this thing through by himself. He headed for his own office at the back of the house.

36

It was more than an hour before Clare finished her work and came out to join him. When she didn't find him in the living room or kitchen, she headed for his office. She smelt the liquor even before she entered the room, and pushed open the door unable to believe her senses. Tom was seated behind his desk, with an almost empty whisky bottle in front of him and a glass in his hand.

'For God's sake don't look like that,' he said. 'It's not the end of the world. Nothing to get into a state about. I'm doing this for a reason.'

'Why? What reason?'

She watched in disbelief as he took another sip of the neat whisky. She noticed how he held his glass, as though afraid of losing it, defying anyone to part him from it. His words were not slurred and his eyes seemed to focus on her easily enough; nonetheless, he was a different man from the one she had left earlier that evening. A switch had been thrown somewhere inside him. There was a defiance in his eyes, challenging her to say all the things he knew she would be bound to say.

Instead she just looked at him sadly, tears welling in her eyes. 'I can't help you, Tom, not if you do this.'

'I know you can't help me,' he said. 'I'm not asking you to. I'm trying to help myself.'

'Not like this.'

'Yes – like this.'

With a gesture that spoke volumes about the rage she could sense building inside him, and which he was struggling to contain, he snatched up the bottle and topped up his glass.

'Just tell me what you're trying to do.'

'I'm trying to remember who I was when I was drinking.'

'Why?'

'Why the hell d'you think?'

She saw his hand tighten on the glass, and feared that he was either going to break it or fling it across the room.

'Just tell me what's happened,' she said, 'what's happened in the last hour. Something must have.'

He took another drink, greedily, like a man who just had to get the stuff inside him.

'Tom, stop. Just stop. Getting drunk won't help anything. You know it can only make things worse.'

'Try to understand. I have to do this.'

He finished his drink, put down his glass, and pushed himself to his feet, sending his chair skimming back on

its rollers until it hit the wall. He swayed slightly, steadying himself with the knuckles of one hand on the edge
of his desk.

'It's all right,' he said, fending off with a forbidding
palm the attempt she made to help him, 'the old skills
are still there – like riding a bike. I'm fine.'

He took a deep breath, then straightened up with the
stiff determination of an old soldier preparing to go on
parade one more time and started for the door.

'Where are you going?'

'Out.'

'No, don't go out, Tom.' She moved to head him off,
but he pushed past her.

'If you go out, I'm coming with you.'

He ignored her.

'Is all of this just an excuse to drink?'

She had hurled the question at his retreating back,
surprising herself at the harshness of it, and the bitter-
ness of its tone.

He turned to look at her, but only to acknowledge he'd
heard her. He continued into the hall and reached for
his car keys on the table where he always left them. She
moved quickly to get between him and the front door.
He wasn't going to push her aside so easily this time.

'You're not driving! If you go out of here with those
car keys, I'm calling the police.'

He hesitated. Then his gaze went past her to the
stairs. She followed it. Julia stood at the top, wiping her
eyes sleepily.

David Ambrose

'Daddy . . . you didn't come up and say goodnight to me.'

Was that really his daughter, he asked himself? Or someone else pretending to be his daughter?

'Yes, I did, honey. You were asleep.'

She looked at him uncertainly. He dropped the keys he had just picked up back down on the table. 'I'm sorry,' he said quietly to Clare. Then he opened the front door and went out into the night.

'Where is Daddy going?'

Clare turned. 'Don't worry, darling. There's something he has to do. He'll be back later.' She started up the stairs. 'Come on, now – off to bed, you.'

37

It only hit him as he pulled the door of the house shut behind him. Perhaps it was a reaction of the night air on the bottle of Scotch he had consumed. Anyway, it proved that the ghostly presence he had faced an hour ago was right – the alcohol might well have dislodged things in his memory that nothing else would. 'River and Pike' suddenly did more than ring a distant bell. It started to sound familiar.

He walked for over fifteen minutes, but still could not place the reference exactly. Eventually, when he felt the exercise beginning to clear his head, he stopped in a liquor store and bought himself a half-bottle of Scotch. He brown-bagged it and sipped at it discreetly as he walked some more.

Then he got it. A doctor had sat on the edge of his bed and told him he was going to die if he didn't change his ways. In passing, he had told him that he had been pulled out of a ditch at some place called River and Pike. The reference had even featured on his medical discharge. As a location, it still meant no more to Tom than it had then. He recalled that he'd thought vaguely about visiting the place where he had almost died, but he had never got around to it. He had met Clare by then. Drink and drugs were part of his past. The future was Clare. He had planned to make a fresh start with a clean slate, and he had done so.

Clean slate? He shuddered at the implications of those two words. True, he had indulged himself in the fantasy of starting over, free of the past. For a time he thought he had succeeded. But you can never be wholly free of the past and of the things you've done there. The past is always with you. There was nothing for him to do but face it. He had gone too far to hide his head in the sand again. One step at a time. Just like getting sober. Now he was getting drunk again, and visiting his past – one step at a time.

He needed a cab, but he had to walk another few minutes before he saw one with its light on. He knew from experience that cab drivers did not stop for guys drinking from bottles, bagged or otherwise, so he slipped it in the pocket of his jacket. Luckily, he still had the trick of looking sober even when he was far from it, and getting in the back before the driver smelled his breath and heard his slurred speech.

'Where to?'

'River and Pike.'

He saw the driver screw up his face in the mirror. 'River and Pike? Where the hell's that?'

'I was kind of hoping you'd know. Don't you have a map or something?'

If the driver had one, he didn't seem to want to use it. He just scratched his chin, deep in thought. 'Wait a minute,' he said, 'I know it. Outside of Albany. Death Valley, right?'

'Death Valley's out in California, for God's sake.'

'No – it's just what people started calling it when they shut the mills down in the fifties. Used to be Grover's Town. Still is, except nobody around there calls it that.'

He slipped the car into gear and pulled out into the light traffic.

'Is that where they had a music festival ten years ago?' Tom asked.

'Yeah, that was the place. Plenty of space and not too many neighbours to worry about the noise. They had some good bands. Pity they never did that again. Were you there?'

Tom gave a sour laugh. 'So I'm told.' He felt in his pocket for the bottle and took a swig. He caught the driver glancing at him warily in his rear-view mirror a couple of times. He knew that look of old.

'Are you OK?'

'I'm fine,' Tom said, and this time emptied the bottle. He thought about telling the driver to stop at the next liquor store, but suspected that if he did he would lose him.

'You're not going to get sick and throw up back there, are you?'

'Depends on your driving,' Tom said.

'I don't like people to throw up in my cab.'

'Can't blame you for that, friend. I'll try to keep a grip.'

They drove in silence. Tom watched the night pass by, only vaguely conscious of where they were. It interested him that there was a coke quality to this high. Memory, he supposed. It was always alcohol and coke back then, one cleaning up after the other, then more of the other taking you on to some new place. The association was still there.

'How far the hell is it?' he heard himself saying after a while. 'Seems like we're taking a long time getting there.'

'Hey, if you're accusing me of taking advantage of you being half—'

'I'm not accusing you of—'

'Because the sooner you're out of my cab the happier I'll be.'

'All right, I'm sorry, I didn't mean to offend you.' He peered out of the window into unbroken blackness. 'Where the fuck are we?'

'Nearly there.'

The driver swung the cab left, bouncing over what felt like rough ground pitted with holes, and came to an abrupt stop. Tom could see neither lights nor movement outside the cab windows. He wondered briefly if he'd been lured into a trap and was going to be mugged by some confederates of the driver waiting there.

'That's thirteen-fifty.'

It took an effort for Tom to make his eyes focus on the clock, but it looked about right. He pushed open the cab door.

'Hey!'

'Wait there. I want to take a look around.'

'And I want thirteen-fifty.'

All Tom could see were the low, dark outlines of what he took to be abandoned warehouses. Further over, a line of yellow sodium lights on concrete posts wound away into the darkness, their trail visible far beyond any illumination they may have shed. The view in this direction seemed almost equally desolate, though more lights were grouped in the distance in a way that suggested signs of life.

'Are you sure this is River and Pike?'

'We're on River Drive. The lights you see up there, that's Pike Way.'

'Jesus . . . it's a total wasteland.'

'There's talk of yuppies moving in some parts, but Beacon Hill it ain't. Is there something special you're looking for?'

'I don't know . . . I just want to look around . . .'

'Did you hear me? I said thirteen-fifty.'

'For God's sake!' Irritated, Tom reached into his back pocket, rocking unsteadily with the movement so that he had to shuffle his feet clumsily to keep his balance. Using the reflection of the cab's headlights, he fished out a twenty-dollar bill and thrust it into the driver's outstretched hand. 'Now just wait here while . . .'

Too late, he realized his mistake. The driver floored his accelerator and roared off into the night, oblivious of Tom's angry obscenities. Moments later, he still stood on the same spot, swaying gently in the sudden silence. He seemed to be standing in some faint penumbra of light, though he couldn't make out where it was coming from. He looked up at the sky, which was covered by the same thick blanket of cloud that had been there all day.

Ahead of him, River Drive, far from running alongside any river, rose out of the darkness alongside a disused railway track, from which the rails and sleepers had long since been removed. In their place now was scuffed gravel and wild grass. A light wind was little more than a restless presence, occasionally gathering enough strength to whip a scrap of paper or a plastic bag across Tom's path. He glimpsed a furtive movement out of the corner of his eye, but, when he turned, saw nothing. It could have been a dog or cat, or some less domesticated creature.

He began to wonder what exactly it was he'd been hoping to achieve. Clearly, he was not about to make any remarkable discoveries, and nothing he could see around him triggered even the vaguest memory. He wondered where exactly he had been found, not that he any longer thought the knowledge would do him any good.

A noise behind him, like the creak of some ghostly carriage wheel, made him spin around – which made him lose his balance and fall. From this position, propped up on one elbow, he saw a lamp suspended from a cable stretched over the street. It was the source of the dingy light he had been standing in. Another breath of wind rocked it again, and he heard the same sound that had alarmed him.

He struggled back to his feet, brushing himself down and discovering a slight graze on his right hand. He took out a handkerchief and wiped it clean, then took stock of his surroundings once again. Looking up what the cab driver had said was Pike Way, he found he could see buildings behind the lights now. Most of them were two storeys, maybe three here and there. It was impossible to know which were abandoned and which were simply closed for the night. Then he saw one that might, conceivably, be a bar. He started towards it.

38

It was a one-level brick-box affair which looked as though it had been thrown together in a couple of days to occupy a vacant corner lot. There was a neon beer sign in the window and a dim light above the door. No one left or entered as he approached. He half expected to find the door locked and the lights left on only to deter theft, but the latch pressed down smoothly and it opened without trouble.

There was a pink glow to the interior that made him think for a moment that he had wandered into a cheap brothel. In fact it was nothing of the sort; a couple of red-shaded lamps on a shelf behind the bar, with another in a corner, created the impression. A second glance revealed a decor of spartan simplicity. A lone drinker sat at the bar nursing a beer, while the barman washed a couple of glasses and didn't even glance up to see who his new customer was. Two men at a table, one with a beard and ponytail, the other bald and wearing wire-rimmed glasses, broke off an intense conversation to look indignantly in Tom's direction, as though he had interrupted them. Then, having decided that he was neither a threat nor of interest to them, they continued talking in hushed tones punctuated by earnest hand gestures over their drinks. A young couple in their twenties, pale and washed-out looking, sat at another table, not talking, gazing blankly into space.

Tom took a seat at the bar and ordered a large scotch with ice. The barman served him without either looking at him or speaking a word. The closest he came to any human response was when the twenty-dollar bill Tom asked him to break caused a surly downturn of his mouth. Tom sat there drinking and wondering what he was doing in that place. He told himself he should call Clare and let her know he was all right – but, later, not right now. For now he needed to concentrate on what he had come here for – to trigger his memory into yielding up what it was so far determined to suppress.

Unless, of course, there were no memories to trigger.

But the evidence so far . . .

He ordered another drink, and asked the barman where he might find a cab around here. The man jerked a thumb over his shoulder. 'Head on up. You sometimes find one at the top.'

This didn't sound too promising, so he fumbled for his cellphone and asked the barman if he could give him a local cab number. He shook his head. 'They won't pick up down here.'

Before Tom could ask why not, the man moved away to serve the drinker at the far end of the bar. Tom hit the memory button on his phone, thinking ironically how much more reliable it was than his own memory, and called up the cab company he habitually used. There was no problem till they asked where he was. He called out to the barman for the address, which he gave as 405 Pike Way. 'It's in Grover's Town,' he said.

The reply came back, 'Sorry, we have nothing in that area. We can't pick up there.'

Before Tom could even protest, they hung up. He thought he caught the barman glancing at him with a smirk of satisfaction on being proved right. Tom said nothing – except to order another drink.

He had no idea how long he had been there, or how many drinks he finally had. He was aware of dropping his wallet at one point and seeing the wad of dollars he was carrying spill out onto the floor. Somehow he managed to gather it all up without falling over, which required quite a balancing act, and no one offered to help. He noticed that the man with the ponytail and his friend with the glasses interrupted their conversation once again to watch him. Or maybe he only remembered that later, thinking back in the light of what happened afterwards.

'Like I said, walk up the road. You'll find one.'

He'd asked the barman again about calling a cab. The barman had announced that he was closing down and started turning out the lights. The couple in the corner had left some time ago, as had the lone drinker at the far end of the bar. Others had drifted in and out during the evening. Tom had no idea what time it was. He looked at his watch, but it didn't make much sense; either it or his head was moving around so much that it was impossible to focus.

'OK, that's it, folks, let's go.'

The barman wanted them out of there. Ponytail and his friend finished their drinks and departed into the night. Now Tom felt the barman's hand on his arm, steering him in the same direction. He was too far gone to argue, though he still made some incoherent effort to insist on calling a cab and saying that he'd have another drink while he waited. He was still talking when he found himself alone outside in the dark, with the door firmly bolted behind him. A moment later the neon beer sign went out.

He started in the direction he had been told to take. At least, he thought it was the right direction – he was far from sure. He headed towards lights, where he could see an occasional passing car in the distance. It was absolutely clear to him that he was on the wrong side of the tracks, in a part of town where cautious people did not venture at night. Too late for caution now, he told himself, stumbling awkwardly as he tried to walk faster out of there.

Had Clare been right? he wondered. Was all he wanted an excuse to drink? Or did he need to drink because somewhere he knew that the horror he was hiding from was true? Was he drinking to forget, or to remember? He wasn't sure he knew the difference any more.

They stepped out from nowhere. Two men. At the same time he felt a blow in the stomach that stopped his breath and, he thought, his heart. He curled around the pain like a ball and fell to the ground. As he went down, he took another blow on the side of the head. He was barely conscious as he felt them going through his pockets. They didn't speak, neither to each other nor to him. As fast as they had appeared, they disappeared.

He didn't really feel like moving, but a voice inside him kept telling him he had to. It was a mistake. As he struggled to get to his feet, the contents of his stomach gushed up into his mouth. He pitched forward and landed in a heap of retching, foul-tasting helplessness. After a while he found a handkerchief and cleaned himself up as best he could. He took several long, reviving breaths of air, sitting with his back against a wall. The lights he had been heading for looked not far away now, not as far as he had thought. He had almost reached safety. But not quite.

The corner of his mouth started to hurt, and he could taste blood. He put his hand up to feel the damage. It didn't seem serious, just bruising and a bitten inner lip. He started once again to push himself to his feet, and felt something under his hand. It was his wallet, emptied of cash and credit cards, of course. All the same, he slipped it carefully back into his hip pocket. He suddenly wondered yet again what the time was, and pulled back the sleeve of his jacket – to find that his watch had also gone. Of course. Why had he not expected that? He realized how slow he was, how damaged and fragmented his thought processes. He reminded himself that he had come to this place to look for the truth, however painful, and all he had done was get drunk. A wave of self-loathing swept over him, followed by another of self-pity. He recognized the reaction. He remembered it from way back. Nothing ever really changes, he told himself.

Another thought came into his mind: he should call for help. But when he reached for his cellphone, he discovered it too had gone. He struggled to his feet and prepared to head for the lights. He didn't know whether he overestimated his strength or underestimated the amount he had drunk. All he knew was that after a couple of steps his legs buckled under him and he felt himself staggering helplessly sideways. He didn't know where he fell or on what, only that a curtain of blackness descended over him.

For all he knew, it could have been the final curtain of death. And at that moment, he would not have cared.

39

Tom opened his eyes to a strip of grey, cold sky framed between two black walls. Perhaps it was the light that woke him; or, more likely, the painful dryness in his mouth and throat. He had no idea where he was, or why he was lying amidst a pile of plastic garbage bags and cardboard boxes. He seemed to be in an alley between two buildings, and from the smell around him one was a cheap burger joint: the air was thick with the stench of stale cooking fat and ketchup.

The smell made him nauseous. He retched, but threw up only thin spittles of sour bile. The effort brought with it a crucifying rhythm of hammer blows inside his skull, beating time with the pumping of his heart.

He took his time before trying to stand up. Even then, it was hard work. The main obstacles were stiffness and that thundering headache which got worse with each move he made. But he knew about those kind of headaches. He remembered them well. They wore off eventually, and, like the memory of all pain, became

212

unreal – until the next time. There had always been a next time. And then for all those years, no next time. Until now.

The alley as well as the garbage sacks and cardboard boxes had protected him against the worst of the cold, but he still felt as though the night air had penetrated right to his bones. He needed a drink.

Amazing how the craving returned so quickly, he thought. You think it's gone away, but it never does. You can pretend all you like, avoid the sight, taste or smell of the stuff. But one sip is all it takes to start you off again. That's why the most you'll ever be is a recovering alcoholic, never a recovered one.

His head began to clear slightly as he walked and his circulation started up. Aside from craving alcohol, he needed water. He was parched and dehydrated. He approached a road junction around which were clustered a handful of buildings, each one oddly separate from its neighbour. It was obviously the kind of place where land was cheap and there was plenty of it to waste – which, come to think of it, was pretty much what his cab driver had said. A ghost town since the fifties. The whole place had a bleak, utilitarian look. A couple of·general stores, a cheap hotel, an ugly apartment block. The traffic remained as thin as it had looked the previous night, not a cab in sight.

He stood on the edge of the sidewalk and wondered what he was going to do. In his trouser pocket he found two dollars twenty-five in small change, which his attackers had apparently missed. He went into one of the stores that was just opening up and bought a bottle of water, which he opened even before the haggard-looking man at the checkout desk had taken his money. The man gave Tom a curious look, but made no comment. Tom asked if there was a phone he could use. The man pointed to a pay phone on the wall. He went over to it and started dialling. He wanted to tell Clare he was all right, then figure out how to get home.

'Where are we? What's the address here?' he called over to the man on the desk.

'Corner of River Drive and Pike Way,' came the reply.

Tom froze. 'Wait a minute,' he said, 'I was dropped off at River Drive and Pike Way last night – down there.' He pointed in the direction he had come from. The man looked puzzled for a moment, then understanding dawned.

'Down there? No way. You're talking about Pike Way and *Waterside*.' He gave a brief, grim laugh. 'That's a bad place, man. You don't want to go down there. River Drive's right here. You're looking out at it now.'

Tom turned his gaze through the window. His mouth fell open and his head started spinning even worse than before. He stopped dialling and hung up the phone. He could not imagine how he had missed what he was looking at – except that when he had arrived at the store it must have been behind him, at an angle. Now he was looking at it full on.

Directly across from where he stood, on the far side of a scooped-out piece of ground that he remembered as though he had been there a dozen or more times, as in a strange way he had, was the house in his nightmare.

His hangover was forgotten as he hurried along the suddenly familiar road. He saw the house now from the angle of his dream, except that in his dream he was running away from it, and now he was running towards it. In the distance a grey horizon was streaked with the same sunrise that he recalled so well.

Yet there was a difference. The tangle of undergrowth and trees had been cleared away, leaving short grass, rough-textured and dry, but tidily kept. The hedge that separated the formerly overgrown garden from the road had also gone, and in its place was a wire fence with a security firm's name prominently displayed. He looked through the fence and down to the basement area in search of that half-rotten door he remembered so well. In its place was a wide, sturdy-looking steel door, painted black – probably a garage. In front of it was a turning space, concreted over, with a path leading around a corner and up one side of the house to the road beyond.

He stood rooted to the spot, needing time to absorb what he was actually seeing as opposed to what he'd been expecting to see, what his brain had told him he must see. There was no question it was the same house, and the same landscape. But with differences – differences which, he realized, could be accounted for by the normal passage of time. Say about ten years.

The words of his cab driver from the previous night came back to him again: the yuppies were moving in and starting to transform the neighbourhood. Maybe that was what had happened here. There were no longer any broken or boarded-up windows in the house. The brickwork had been cleaned, the roof fixed, paint applied where it was needed. The run-wild vegetation, through which he stumbled in his dream, no longer existed; nor did the old gate that he remembered making such a distinctive creaking noise as he passed through it to the road.

It was proof that his nightmare was more than a dream. It was a memory, repeating itself as he slept, the heartbeat of his guilt, which would never go away.

What had he done? He feared he knew only too well. But conscience – he could not think what else to call it – was forcing him to face up to and acknowledge his crime. That was the process he was going through, and it was nearing some sort of a close. The thought of what that close might be made his blood run colder than at any time during the whole awful night he had just spent.

He started around towards the far side of the house. It struck him that he had never seen it from that side in his dream, so he had no idea what to expect. It turned out to look very like he would have imagined – a once grand house fallen on hard times, and latterly converted into apartments. He could see plants and various decorations in some of the four bay windows and in the tower windows higher up. The place looked comfortably spacious, though not fashionable or chic; but then, he reflected, rents could not be high in this neighbourhood, even though the house was just outside the worst part of it.

There was a single front door up several steps. Next to it was a vertical line of doorbells. He counted seven of them, with names written alongside. He went up to take a closer look. Benson, Garrett, Sizemore, Webber, Morrissey, Gordon, St Leonard. None of them meant anything to him.

Even from where he was standing on the top step at the front door, he could not see into either of the angular bay windows on each side of it: they had been built fractionally too high for that. He wondered about ringing one of the bells – but what would he say? What *could* he say? To *anybody*?

40

Aside from Clare, the only person who knew about the dream was Brendan Hunt. Obviously Tom would tell Clare about his discovery, but he could not bring himself to do it at that moment. He did not know how to. He needed to absorb it first, to think about what he must do.

He called Brendan Hunt from the store where he'd bought his bottle of water. He needed an opinion – unemotional, uninvolved, but from someone who knew everything about the whole story: someone who was neither as determined to put a noose around his neck as he feared Murray Schenk would be, nor as intent on denying he was a murderer, no matter what the evidence, as Clare would be.

'I'm sorry to call so early,' he said, 'you're probably asleep.'

Even as he spoke, he felt the absurdity of his words. He was in the most desperate situation of his life, and he was apologizing for needing help.

'On the contrary. I'm in my car, I have an early meeting. What can I do for you?'

'I've found the house – the house I told you about, in my dream. It actually exists.'

There was a momentary silence on the line. Then Hunt, calm and professional as ever, asked him to recount what had happened. Tom filled him in on the bare details.

'All right,' Hunt said, 'I'll be right there. Just tell me where you are.'

They arranged to meet on the corner of River and Pike. Hunt said he'd find it.

Tom called Clare. She picked up on the first ring, and stifled a sob of relief when she heard his voice.

'I'm sorry,' he said. It was all he could think of to begin with. 'I'm all right. I've just called Brendan Hunt, he's coming to pick me up.'

'Where are you?'

'Outside Albany. Grover's Town.'

'What are you doing out there?'

'I'll tell you about it when I'm home. I can't now.'

'Why didn't you call me, not Brendan Hunt? I would have come for you.'

'I know you would. But I have to talk to him about something. I'll tell you when I'm home.'

'Soon?'

'I promise – soon.'

Forty minutes later Hunt's car pulled up, and Tom got in the passenger side. Hunt looked him up and down

– not critically, but letting him see that his unkempt appearance had been noted.

'I've been drinking,' Tom said. 'I passed out and slept rough.'

'Did something trigger it? The drinking?'

It was a shrewd question, to which Hunt already, Tom suspected, knew the answer.

'Julia. Except it wasn't Julia. It was her – Melanie.'

'What happened?'

'She reminded me of something. The place where I was pulled out of a ditch ten years ago. She sent me back here. Then I found it – the house.'

'Where?'

'Drive over there, and stop on the far side.'

Hunt followed Tom's directions. They sat looking down through the wire fence at the strange, now-renovated house.

'In my dream it looks the way it might have a few years ago. Ten, say. About the time Melanie Hagan disappeared.'

Hunt was silent a moment, then said, 'And the door down into the cellar? Where was that?'

'It wasn't really a cellar. You would have had to go down to it from the house, but from this side, it was ground level. The door was where that garage is now.'

Again Hunt was silent, as he thought about what he was hearing. 'All right – so what's your own interpretation of all this? I assume you have one.'

Tom was a little taken aback, but he answered the

question as best he could. 'Obviously I remember the place because of something that happened here. Something I've been suppressing from conscious memory but recalling in the dream. It's hard to get away from that, isn't it?'

'And what is it exactly that you've been recalling in this dream?'

'You know what I'm talking about,' Tom said, impatient with what he took as Hunt's evasiveness. 'I'm talking about killing that girl!'

Another pause. Hunt looked down to where his hands rested in his lap beneath the steering wheel. 'Cases of people doing what you're talking about – committing murder, then forgetting all about it – are extremely rare.' He turned to look at Tom, making sure that his words were sinking in. 'I'm inclined to seek some other explanation before accepting something as unlikely as that.'

'But it's possible, isn't it? I mean, there have been cases.'

'I don't deny it. I'm just saying such cases are rare.'

Now it was Tom's turn to fall silent, frustrated by Hunt's refusal to see things his way – the only possible way, however painful. 'I'm going to have to get this house opened up somehow,' he said suddenly. 'I have to find out who owns it, and get permission to dig up that cellar.'

'Nobody's going to let you do that on the basis of a dream, Tom.'

'It's more than a dream,' Tom exploded. 'The house exists. It's in front of you – look at it!'

Hunt remained calm, his voice quiet and professionally reassuring. 'I can see the house. And I grant you it looks very like the house you described – but I have only your word that it really is the same house.'

'For Christ's sake, this is the corner where I was found that night – River Drive and Pike Way. The reason I dreamed about this house and recognize it now is because I saw it that night. I was running away from what I'd done, and I got hit by some truck . . .'

Hunt opened his hands in a gesture that suggested an attempt to appeal to reason and common sense. 'Tom, wait, listen to me. All right, let's say you saw the house that night. That was probably the worst night of your life. Not necessarily because you went crazy and killed somebody, but because you nearly killed yourself. After that night you pulled yourself together, you became the man you've been for the last ten years. That night, when you saw this house through whatever miasma of drink and drugs you were in, maybe it was the last thing you saw before you were knocked down, so of course you remember it. It symbolizes something – because that night was the dividing line between your old life and your new. Remember what I told you, a dream about committing murder can actually be signifying change or growth. In reality, it was yourself that you murdered that night – your old self. You finally killed that old self off and started a new life.'

Tom felt angry and even insulted by Hunt's rationalizations. This was not what he had wanted from him. He needed someone to validate his guilt, to give him a good reason for feeling as bad as he did. 'Oh, for fuck's sake! You just won't face up to what's under your nose!'

Hunt ignored his outburst. 'Tom, the most obvious explanation – of anything – is very rarely the right one. Try to remember that. For Clare's sake as much as your own. And Julia's.'

41

They drove most of the way in silence. When they turned into the street where Tom and Clare lived, Hunt pulled over just short of the house and stopped the engine. Tom reached for the door handle, but Hunt laid a gently restraining hand on his arm.

'Tom, before you go, just one thing.' As though he had been reflecting for some time, he said, 'I think it's important you say nothing about this for the time being. To anyone.'

Tom looked at him. 'You mean Schenk? Or Oliver Lewis?'

'Anyone,' Hunt repeated, with a quiet emphasis that made Tom realize he meant more.

'Not even Clare?' His voice echoed the surprise he felt.

'I think it's better. For now.'

'Why?'

'For all the reasons we've been discussing. Why frighten her with something you can't be sure of yet?'

'But I *am* sure.'

'No, you're not. You can't be. Remember what I told you – this may be a long way from what you think.'

Tom sighed and leant back in his seat, unsure whether he felt more frustrated or relieved by this advice. Hunt watched him, knowing what must be going through his mind.

'At least sleep on it,' he said. 'Let's talk again before you do anything you can't undo.'

'That might have been good advice ten years ago,' Tom said, with the gloomy resignation of a man who had already accepted defeat.

'It's good advice now, Tom. Please take it.'

'So what do I tell her happened?'

'Tell her the truth. You got drunk, you got mugged, and you woke up in a pile of garbage. Just leave out the bit about the house.'

Tom looked uneasy. 'I'm not sure I can do that.'

'Because you're afraid you'd be lying to her?'

'I've been open with her so far. How can I stop now?'

Hunt was silent, weighing Tom's objection against the advice he was trying to give him. He went on in the tone of a man who found himself obliged to say more than he had intended. 'Tom, telling her about the house could be more of a lie than saying nothing.'

'I don't understand. What d'you mean?'

Hunt looked momentarily uneasy. It was not a response Tom was accustomed to seeing in him; the effect was both unsettling and oddly compelling. He awaited the answer to his question with suddenly sharpened attention.

David Ambrose

'I suppose what I'm saying,' Hunt began, picking his words with very deliberate care, 'is that I feel there's something just so *wrong* here, that we are a long, long way from understanding what's really going on.'

'Wrong? In what way?'

Again, Hunt thought before answering. 'To be honest, I'm not sure. It is, if you like, a gut feeling. I need to think about it some more. But from what I know about you, from what I know about this whole set-up . . .' He shrugged. 'There's something wrong, Tom. It's too obvious, it's too . . . tidy. There's more behind it than meets the eye.'

Tom digested what he was hearing. 'Set-up? Do you mean I'm being set up? I don't see how that can be, it doesn't make sense. How could anyone possibly . . . ?'

Hunt raised his hand. 'As I say, I need to think about it some more. For the moment there's something I'm missing. I suspect it's just under my nose, though I can't see it. Why don't you go home and get some rest? I'll call you later.'

Tom wanted to know more, much more. And he wanted to know it right then. But he was too tired to argue, and his head was starting to spin all over again. 'All right,' he said, 'if that's what you think, OK. I'll wait for your call.'

He got out of the car and walked the remaining few yards to his house. Clare had the door open before he was halfway up the path. They faced each other without speaking, as though neither of them could find the

right words for this moment in their lives. Then, perhaps because there were none, Tom was seized by such
a confusion of emotions – remorse, love, fear, and a
painful sense of loss – that he began to weep like a child.
Clare gathered him into her arms and brought him
inside, pushing the door shut behind him, locking out
the world.

'I'm sorry, I'm so sorry about . . . about . . .'

'It's all right,' she said, holding him, 'it's all right,
you're home now.'

They stood like that for some moments, he trying to
sob out some kind of broken apology, she calming and
soothing him and telling him there was no need.

'But . . . you know . . . what I . . . what I wanted,'
he said, gasping for air between the words.

'Shhh . . . it's all right . . .'

'I was . . . trying to . . . remember . . . that was why
I started drinking . . . to remember . . .'

She stepped back a little and her eyes searched his
face.

'And did you?'

He returned her gaze, wiping his eyes with one hand
while fumbling for a handkerchief with the other. He
was acutely aware that this was the moment when he
had to choose between keeping his promise to Hunt or
confessing everything to Clare. But Hunt's words were
reverberating strongly in his mind. They had opened
up possibilities he neither understood nor, so far, dared
to believe in. They had both confused him and given

him hope, a combination he did not know how to describe. Hunt had left him in the end, with no choice but to say nothing. He shook his head, and was grateful when she did not press the question further.

'Why don't you take a shower,' she said, 'get some rest? I'll bring you something to eat.'

He was exhausted, and the prospect of oblivion in the comfort of his bed was appealing, though he was far from sure he could sleep in his present state of mind. Ten minutes later, he stepped out of the shower and began towelling himself down. Through the door into the bedroom he saw Clare appear with a tray of sandwiches and one of the herbal teas she was always urging him to drink. He pulled on a robe and went through. She caught his fleeting look of distrust as he sniffed the clear green liquid.

'It'll help you sleep,' she said.

'I don't want to sleep.'

'All right – but come and lie on the bed with me.'

She put down the tray and punched up some pillows for him. He stretched out and leaned back. Clare climbed up alongside him, curling her legs up beneath her.

'Try the tea.'

Obediently, he reached for the cup and drank. Like all herbal teas in his experience, it tasted odd but not unpleasant. The sandwiches were chicken and grilled peppers, a combination she knew he loved. It was only when he bit into one that he realized how hungry he was. Clare stroked his face with the backs of her fingers as he ate.

'I thought about it while you were out,' she said. 'In fact I thought about it all night . . .'

'I'm sorry,' he mumbled thickly. 'I should have called, I tried—'

'It's all right, really. Don't talk about it any more. I'm just trying to tell you that I thought about it, and I simply don't believe that you've ever harmed anybody, or ever would. I just don't believe it. I can't.'

He wanted to tell her about the house. But he wanted even more to believe that Hunt was right, and that there would finally be some other explanation. 'I know,' was all he said. He looked up at her. 'I love you.'

She slid her arm around his shoulders and rested her head on top of his. 'I love you too.'

Again they fell silent. Suddenly he didn't feel like eating the second half of his sandwich. He told himself that he was clinging to a hope that might be nonexistent. And if that was so, then this moment might prove to be the last good one of their lives together – his and Clare's.

And Julia's.

And . . . ?

And that other disembodied life that had taken sinister possession of her? A life that had returned literally from beyond the grave to smash their futures? Because of him? Of what he'd done? In, if only metaphorically, another life?

David Ambrose

'We're going to be all right,' Clare said softly, and her words startled him because they sounded like an answer to his thoughts. But he knew that she was simply offering him her strength. Her belief in him. Enough to bolster up his own.

'Yes, of course,' he murmured in response. 'Of course we are.'

42

He had fallen asleep without knowing it. When he awoke, he saw that the curtains were partially drawn to shield him from the sun and there was a late afternoon light falling across the room. Also, he was in the bed now, not just on it. Clare had somehow got his robe off and arranged everything without disturbing him.

Suddenly he sensed an extra presence close by, and turned sharply. Julia was standing in the door, watching him with solemn concentration. He sat up, recoiling as he did so from the terrible sensation of reacting to the sight of his own child with fear.

But was this his child? Or the other one, come back to haunt him?

'Sorry, Daddy, I didn't mean to wake you.'

The voice was Julia's. He realized he had been holding his breath. He swallowed.

'You didn't. Come in, darling.'

'Mommy said I wasn't to. She said you were very tired.'

David Ambrose

'That's all right – I'm fine.'

Tom pushed himself up in the bed and made room on the edge for her. She hopped on it, put her arms around his neck and gave him a kiss. Then she looked up at him, frowning from the weight of some preoccupation on her mind.

'Daddy?'

'What is it, darling?'

'Where did you go last night?'

He hoped she didn't see his hesitation. 'Didn't Mommy tell you?'

'She said you had to go and see somebody. Who did you have to see?'

'Oh, nobody very interesting. Just somebody I might be working with and who had to . . . had to catch a plane.'

'Somebody for one of your films?'

'Yes. So . . . how was school today?'

'It was OK, I guess.'

'You don't sound too sure.'

'Mrs Simmons is sick, and I don't like Mr Dawber who took us for English instead.'

'What don't you like about him?'

She screwed up her face. 'He gets real crabby over nothing, just some little mistake. And kind of sarcastic.'

'Oh dear, that doesn't sound too good.'

'No.'

They chatted on for a while, until Clare called up to say that Sarah had arrived for Julia's piano lesson. She had been learning on and off for the past two years: off when she briefly decided she might prefer the clarinet, and on again when she decided it was the piano for her after all. She gave her daddy a hug and went on down.

Tom went back into the bathroom and contemplated his reflection in the mirror. He needed a shave, but decided he could leave it for today. Then, on second thoughts, he decided to take care of it. He smeared foam, ran a basin of hot water, and reached for his razor. As he did so, the sound of halting and repeated piano chords began to float up from downstairs. His eyes clouded abruptly with tears. The contrast between the quiet house, broken only by those innocent sounds from downstairs, and the horror that still lurked in his mind, was too much to bear. Suddenly he needed a drink so badly that he was almost sick from the thought of having to fight the craving.

But then, he told himself, what did it matter? Why shouldn't he stay drunk till this whole thing was over? Who would blame him?

Or just the occasional drink, to get him through it. The occasional drink is quite possible, even for the problem drinker. You may drink within reason for weeks before going off the deep end again. Maybe weeks would be enough time before . . . what?

What indeed? He had no idea. All he knew was how much he wanted a drink. He had to fight it, and he was going to need help.

He saw in the mirror that Clare had come into the bedroom and was watching him. She stood perfectly still, her eyes on the reflection of his own, following the struggle he was having with himself. He spoke to her without turning.

'It's going to be all right,' he said. 'I'll get on top of it. Whatever happens, I swear to you I'll deal with this thing sober.'

She came up behind him, slipped her arms around his chest and hooked her hands back over his shoulders. 'We have forty minutes till that music lesson ends.'

Sexual desire, even if it had crossed his mind, would have been the last thing he would have thought himself capable of. But now, with her soft warmth pressed against his back, he wanted nothing more than to lose himself in the flesh of their two bodies, to repay her love with his need of it. He turned to kiss her, but she laughed and held him off, reaching for a towel to wipe the white foam from his face.

Later, lying in each other's arms, they listened to the broken chords and simple tunes come to a sudden halt downstairs. Clare said, 'Whoops! Better get this show back on the road.'

She swung her feet to the carpet and quickly pulled on her clothes. He watched her with a mix of wonder, disbelief, and sated but rapidly reviving lust. 'You know something?' he said. 'The way you're handling all this, you must be as crazy as I am.'

'I hope so,' she said, flashing him a sidelong grin. 'If

it turns out we're incompatible after all these years, I'm going to be really pissed.' She planted a quick kiss on the tip of his nose, and disappeared downstairs.

Tom ran a hand over his chin and reminded himself that he still hadn't finished shaving. He pushed himself up from the bed and headed for the bathroom. This time he finished the job before he once again became aware of a figure in the mirror watching him. But it was Julia this time, not Clare.

'Hi, darling,' he said, drying off his face and addressing her reflection. 'That sounded like a pretty good music lesson. You've been making real progress with—'

He stopped as her eyes held his, with a strangely adult confidence, in the glass. He knew at once, just as he had the previous night, that this was not his daughter.

'OK,' she said, 'now you've found the place, what are you going to do about it?'

He didn't move. He didn't trust himself to turn and face her. Whether from fear of her, or of what he might do to her, he did not know.

'What do you want me to do?' he asked, his voice catching in his suddenly dry throat.

'Do what the shrink says,' she said in a flat, metallic tone – almost like a robot, he thought, and for a moment wondered whether she'd been hypnotized.

'I've done that,' he said, and realized that his own words were spoken in the same flat tone. Was he too hypnotized? Or was he dreaming? Hunt's words about pinching himself crossed his mind, but he didn't try it;

the gesture in the face of that grave, unblinking presence would have been too absurd.

'I know you have,' she said. 'Go on doing it. Go with the shrink. You'll get out of this.'

He watched her reflection as it turned and walked out of the room. 'Wait!' He spun around and started after her, his hand already out to seize her by the shoulder and pull her about to face him. He did not know what good it would do, and some part of him said that it would be dangerously akin to waking a sleep-walker.

But it was not his doubts that made him hesitate. It was the ringing of his cellphone on the bedside table. Automatically, and relieved to have his action dictated by reflex and not choice, he picked it up.

'Hello?'

'I'm not waking you, I hope.' It was Brendan Hunt.

'No. I slept a while – three hours, more.'

'How are you feeling?'

'Not too bad. Better.'

'That's good. Sleep was what you needed. Listen, Tom, you and I need to talk. I take it you've said nothing to Clare – about what we discussed.'

'No.'

'I think we should meet in the morning. I see that Julia has a session at eleven thirty. Why don't you bring her in yourself? I don't need more than ten minutes with her, we're practically through. We can send her back to school in a cab, which will leave you and me some time together. I have more to tell you than I could this afternoon.'

236

'OK,' Tom said, and wondered whether to tell Hunt what had happened only seconds earlier with Julia. Could it be merely coincidence that Hunt's call had followed on so swiftly? Surely not.

Something, he told himself, was taking its course. But what?

'All right,' he said, 'we'll be there. Eleven thirty.'

When he went downstairs ten minutes later, Julia was on the phone, talking perfectly normally to a friend, planning some outing for the weekend. Clare was starting to put supper together in the kitchen. 'Brendan Hunt just called,' Tom said, managing, though he did not know how, to sound casual. 'He suggested I take Julia in for her session tomorrow – so we can talk.'

'Fine,' was all Clare said, then added: 'You'll be able to take her back to school afterwards, won't you?'

'I'll call her a cab.'

Clare continued preparing supper. Tom hesitated, feeling a little strange about what he was about to say next; then he felt stupid for feeling strange.

'Listen,' he said, 'I think I should go to a meeting.'

The meeting in question was, of course, an AA meeting. Alcoholics Anonymous. He hadn't attended regularly for several years. Perhaps he had become overconfident: if so, he was now having to face the fact of how brittle his self-discipline had been. Recovery, even after one slip, is an uphill road.

Clare took the announcement in her stride. 'OK,

we'll eat when you get back.' They kissed, with a tenderness that reflected the memory of what had happened upstairs.

'I love you,' Tom whispered in her ear. They held each other in silence for a while. Then without another word, he turned and left the house.

43

He had made a call to check out where the nearest meeting was at that hour. It was only a half-dozen blocks or so; he remembered the location well. He set out on foot – partly because he felt like the exercise, but also because he was afraid there might still be enough alcohol in his system to make driving a bad idea.

The meeting was in part of a school building. He hadn't been there for at least four years, but as he approached he saw at once that nothing had changed: through the iron gate and into the empty playground, towards two large lighted windows through which he would see fifteen or twenty men and women already gathered in the incongruous surroundings of bookshelves and brightly coloured children's drawings, desks pushed aside to make room for several rows of folding chairs. Mugs of poisonously well-stewed coffee were, as always, being dispensed to everyone. He felt like a traveller returning home after a long absence, to find everything unchanged and instantly absorbing him as though he had never been away.

As he stood there, outside looking in, he felt an over-whelming urge to turn his back and walk away. What he really needed was a drink, not an hour or more of 'I'm Bob – Frank – Joan – George, and I'm an alco-holic.' Not those bland slogans he could see stuck up on the walls: 'One Day at a Time'; 'Take it Easy'.

'Hi, Tom! Good to see you.'

He turned in the direction of the voice – a man in his fifties, tall, well-built, with thick white hair. He remembered him well, but not his name. The man offered his hand, Tom shook it automatically.

'John,' he said. The name had come back to him from some dark recess of memory.

'Are you coming in?'

'Sure,' Tom said. They walked in together.

There was a guest speaker that night, a woman called Joyce, who opened the meeting by telling her own story. She was thirtysomething, attractive and well dressed, who described how, only a few years ago, she had wound up sleeping on the streets and stealing bottles of Listerine for its alcohol content. She made the room laugh at the madness of the things an alcoholic will do for a drink, and wince in recognition of the lies they all told themselves about their problem.

When she finished, the meeting was thrown open to the floor. There were, as always, a couple of good per-formers exorcizing their demons with practised skill and wit – as entertaining as any stand-up comic. As always, there were others who had trouble finding the right words, but whose need to speak out was palpable, and who were thanked as warmly for their contribution to the meeting as the best of speakers had been, perhaps even more so.

Suddenly Tom realized how badly he needed to speak himself: how desperately he wanted to tell those people in that room the reason he'd got drunk last night. But to what end? His was more than a story of alcohol addiction. It was a story he had no right to make this group, or anyone, share with him.

He was not just two people in the way that they all were – the drinking and non-drinking versions of themselves. In him there was a far more terrible division: between the man who loved his wife and child and lived a happy, decent life; and the murderous madman whose brain had been so ruined by alcohol that he no longer had knowledge or control or memory of who or what he was, or of what unspeakable things he might have done. His was a hell without forgiveness or respite.

Slowly he became aware of a curious pain in his hands, and realized that his fists were balled so tight that the nails were digging into the palms. He opened them up and saw he had drawn blood in two places. He took out a handkerchief and crumpled it between his hands. Except for the fear of calling unwanted attention to himself, he would have got up and left right then.

But to go where? The nearest bar? He realized with a shiver of alarm how much he still wanted a drink. The floodgates had been opened, and were not about to shut again without a struggle. It was going to be his struggle, and he would have to fight it alone. Ironically, this place he had come to for help in that fight had only reinforced his sense of hopeless isolation.

It took an effort of will to sit through the rest of the meeting. The different voices with their oft-told stories and their well-worn jokes echoed meaninglessly in his head. He was on the edge of panic. He felt beads of perspiration forming on his forehead and upper lip, and used his handkerchief to wipe them discreetly away. No one paid attention. No one looked twice. He was dealing with his own personal hell, as they all were with theirs.

At the end, he left quickly, avoiding conversation or even eye contact with anyone, and started walking briskly home. Clare would have supper ready, Julia would be waiting for him to go up and say goodnight. He was a lucky man to have that welcome waiting for him. He kept on telling himself how lucky.

Without being aware of it, he found he'd stopped on a corner. Straight ahead lay home. To his left was a road leading towards a collection of neighbourhood shops and restaurants – and bars. He could see one as he stood there, its illuminated sign so clear and vibrant that he could almost hear the electricity buzzing through the neon. He could hear too, or at least imagined that he could, the sound of ice clinking in a glass, and the warming taste of the liquid that would work its magic and stop the screaming in his skull that he didn't know how to stop any other way.

Just one, perhaps? Just one drink to fend off the horrors? Just one, and then home?

He stood where he was, looking one way, then the other. He knew it was more than a question of simply making a decision. That was already made someplace in his head that he did not have access to. All he was waiting for now was to find out what it was.

All he was waiting for was to find out what he was going to do – by doing it.

He started for home.

44

They arrived a little before eleven thirty the following morning, but Hunt was ready for them.

'I hope you parked in my garage, Tom, like I told you,' he said.

'Sure. That's a big help.'

Both Tom and Clare had suffered parking problems in the past, whether bringing Julia to her sessions or picking her up after them. Clare had arrived flustered and apologetic one day after taking an age to park. After that, Hunt had given her the code to his private garage, which had room for two cars.

'Julia,' Hunt said, 'why don't you go talk to Sally for a moment while I have a word with your father.'

The child headed off happily to the office of Hunt's receptionist, whom she liked. Hunt steered Tom into the waiting room.

'So how are you feeling this morning?' he asked. 'You certainly look better.'

Tom gave a thin smile of acknowledgement. 'I went

to an AA meeting last night. I managed to get home without stopping for a drink.' He gave a quick self-deprecating laugh. 'I'd forgotten how bad it could be.'

'You made it, that's all that matters.'

'I wouldn't quite say *all*,' Tom said. 'I mean, where exactly are we now? What is it you said you have to tell me?'

'Just give me ten minutes with Julia, that's all I need. Then I'll have Sally get her back to school. After that, I'll be right with you.'

Tom took a chair and picked up a newspaper. He was too distracted to read with any concentration, but it was something to do. Hunt closed the waiting-room door and started down the corridor to where he could already hear Julia chattering happily with Sally Young.

'Hello, Julia. How are you today?'

Big smile. 'I'm fine, Dr Hunt, thank you.'

He told Sally to go over to the hospital and check out some records he wanted, and then go straight to lunch.

'Okay, Dr Hunt,' she said, happy to have an extra hour to herself. 'I'll see you this afternoon. 'Bye, Julia.'

''Bye, Sally.'

Hunt held open the door to his private office. 'Come on in, Julia,' he said. As always, she walked ahead of him and settled in her usual place, then turned to look up at him brightly, ready to begin. And, as always, it was only when the door closed, with the muted click of its latch, that the transformation took place. The voice changed, along with the whole posture of her body. The innocent nine-year-old was instantly replaced by the precocious, foul-mouthed and foul-minded adolescent of fourteen.

'OK, big boy, what's it gonna be? Blow-job? Ass-fuck? Whatever does it for you.'

'Stop it, Melanie,' he said wearily, as he so often had. 'You know nothing like that is going to happen here. How could it?'

She smiled knowingly, enjoying the power she was so sure she wielded over him.

'You're gonna have to kill her in the end,' she said. 'That's the only way you're ever going to silence me, you know. You're going to have to kill the brat. That fucking Julia.'

PART TWO

'Confession'

45

Nature or nurture? Are we born hard-wired, or are we manufactured by experience?

It is not enough to say something of both. That is an evasion, not an answer. It does nothing to explain how the balance works, or the real difference between them.

Introspection is no help. It can tell us something about *what* we are, but not *why*. I remember well the day I discovered what I am, but despite a lifetime's asking myself why, I am no nearer.

The discovery happened in Colorado. It had been my father's idea. White-water rafting: an adventure for all the family, the brochure said. I don't remember much of it in detail. It's all something of a blur. Except for what happened to my sister.

Cassie, at fourteen, was four years older than me. She had brought her best friend Naomi along. In fairness, our parents had given me the chance of also bringing somebody along, but I had chosen not to. The fact was,

David Ambrose

I didn't have many friends. Certainly no one close enough to invite along on a vacation. I also knew that I would take so much razzing from the girls that I preferred to endure my humiliation with no witness of my own age and sex.

As it turned out, however, things didn't go as badly as they might have done: the girls had each other's company to take their mind off me, and anyway there was a limit to the tricks they could get up to in front of my parents.

I enjoyed the rafting. We had a guide, of course, and although he promised us we were all perfectly safe so long as we followed the rules, it was exciting – like a fairground ride, where you know you're securely strapped into your seat but still feel you might be smashed into oblivion any second.

And, of course, accidents can happen.

What happened to Cassie was an accident. Well, basically. There was a certain amount of stupidity involved. And other things. It didn't happen on the water. It was one morning, after we'd camped overnight in the two tents that came as part of the trip. They were incredibly comfortable, with inflatable beds and even a heater if you needed it. We had food in tins, along with fruit and vegetables in special coolers. All the comforts of home in the wilds of nature.

All the same, that's where we were: the wilds of nature. And you needed to take care. Normally our parents, or Charlie, our guide, kept a close eye on the girls

250

and me wherever we were. But on this particular morning they must not have been paying as much attention as usual, because suddenly, as we were packing up and getting ready to move on, my mother looked around and said, 'Where are the girls?'

Everybody started looking around, and we realized there was no sign of them. There was no immediate panic: somehow, I had always noticed, grown-ups worried less about two or more kids disappearing or getting into trouble than they did about one. Safety in numbers, my mother said. We called their names for a while, but it was only after a couple of minutes with no response that my parents started to look concerned. At first they were angry, thinking it was just some stupid prank, or simply thoughtlessness. I confess I was looking forward to the prospect of my sister getting the kind of ass-chewing that was normally reserved for me, but as we all fanned out and started looking for them, calling their names, I began to sense that something was definitely wrong.

The terrain we were on, aside from the level patch by the water's edge where we had spent the night, was wooded and rocky. Wherever you went you were either climbing up or slithering down a steep slope. I was following my father down into some trees, but he turned and ordered me back to the camp. 'Wait there in case they show up,' he said, 'then call us. Remember that emergency whistle Charlie showed us on the life-jackets? Use that – we'll hear you.'

I felt a little aggrieved to be left out of the search party, but when you're ten years old you spend a lot of time feeling aggrieved – especially if you have a sister like Cassie who has friends like Naomi. I sat on a small canvas stool and waited, keeping my eyes and my ears peeled. The calls of my parents and Charlie quickly faded into the distance, though occasionally a voice reached me faintly, like an echo. For a moment I was frightened by the thought that they might all disappear, spirited away by some strange evil force in this mysterious landscape – or simply get lost, eventually falling to their deaths in deep crevasses and swirling torrents. Night would come and I would find myself alone, with no chance of ever getting out of there. In time they would send out search parties and helicopters, but I would be dead by then. Or half-starved and insane. I had read about such things, seen them on television.

In fact I didn't sit there for much more than ten minutes by my watch before I heard Naomi's voice from a totally unexpected direction. It seemed to be coming from along the river bank, where neither of my parents nor Charlie had been headed. And she sounded distressed.

I sprang to my feet and started running. She stumbled towards me through some dense and prickly undergrowth, oblivious to the scratches on her hands and face. 'It's Cassie,' she said as soon as she saw me. 'She fell. I think she's hurt.'

'Where is she?'

Naomi pointed back the way she had come. 'We walked along the river, then climbed up a track. Cassie went first, and when she got to the top she stopped and turned to take a shot of me climbing up after her. I don't know what happened – something gave way beneath her feet. A piece of rock must have come loose. She just screamed and disappeared down the other side. When I got to where she'd been standing, I couldn't see anything, but I could hear her shouting, "Help me! Get help!"'

She looked around, as though realizing only now that she was talking to me alone, and asked desperately, 'Where are your parents? Where's Charlie?'

'They're looking for both of you,' I said. 'They went off in that direction.' I pointed. 'Charlie went over there.'

'You've got to get them,' she said. 'Get them – quickly!'

'No – you go. Shout – they'll hear you. I'll try to help Cassie.'

'It's dangerous. Be careful.'

'Where's the track you went up?'

'Just along there. Not far. You'll see it.'

I set off at a run. The dense bushes tore at my flesh as they had Naomi's. I could imagine the girls, when they were setting out on this adventure, only a half-hour or so earlier, picking their way fastidiously through all these branches and thorns. But minor discomforts didn't matter now.

Naomi was right: I had no trouble finding the track. It was, as she had said, steep, but an easy climb. About halfway up, I found Cassie's video camera lying smashed on a rock. It must have flown from her hands when she fell, coming down on this side while she slipped down the other.

I looked up and continued climbing, breathless now, perspiring, my hands and knees (I was wearing shorts) cut and bleeding. But I was anaesthetized against all pain, feeling nothing as I scrambled on up, but a blind panic that I wouldn't get there in time.

The girls had climbed surprisingly high. It was unlike them to be so physically adventurous, but I supposed they had been lured by the prospect of the spectacular view. When I got there, I saw it was indeed dramatic; and so was the rock face that slid away down the far side at a thirty-degree angle, ending in a jagged over-hang above a deep crevasse, with the sound of torrential waters smashing against rocks below.

'Cassie Cassie!'

I called her name at the top of my lungs. At first there was no reply, then I heard her voice faintly over the rushing water.

'Help me!'

She must have been somewhere beyond that rim of rock I could see, on a ledge perhaps, maybe injured, unable to climb.

'We're coming!' I shouted back.

There was still no sign of Naomi with my parents

and Charlie. Perhaps she hadn't found them yet, but surely she must soon: they couldn't have strayed that far from the camp. All the same, I was alone. I had to act.

I could see that the sloping rock surface offered hand- and toe-holds for someone descending with great care and who didn't weigh too much. An adult would most likely slip and fall. But somebody my size and weight, a ten-year-old boy and not big for my age, could maybe risk it. I took a deep breath, and started down.

Like all kids, I knew how to climb; and, luckily, I wasn't scared of heights. I felt my way with the toes of my trainers, looking down before each move, then up as I shifted my hands. I could hear Cassie still calling.

'Help! Help me!'

Inch by inch I reached the edge. It took less time than I thought it would – no more than two minutes. I managed to twist around, keeping my feet where they were but shifting my hands. That was when I saw her.

She was hanging on to a lip of rock with her finger- tips, about three feet below the edge that had been visible from above. Her feet must have been resting on some- thing. 'What are you standing on?' I asked. I still had to shout to be heard above the water, its roar amplified now as it smashed and echoed off the rock walls.

'I don't know. I can't look down.'

She was paralysed with fear – that was the only thing keeping her there. If she moved, she would certainly fall. When I managed to peer down over the edge I was now stretched out along, I saw that her toes were on a lip of rock even smaller than the one she was gripping with her fingers.

I looked up again. Still no sign of help. Where *were* they? They *must* be here soon.

'All right,' I said, 'don't move. I'll try to pull you up.'

'No – don't! You can't! Where's Daddy? Get Daddy!'

'They're coming. Naomi's gone to find them.'

I swivelled around further, so that I was able to lower my feet and plant them, one behind the other, on the lip of rock that she was clinging to.

'No,' she said again, 'don't touch me! You're not strong enough. Leave me alone.'

I looked up again. Still nobody.

'Oh, yes I am,' I said. 'I'm quite strong enough.'

I lifted my right foot with slow deliberation – and stamped on her fingers with all my force. She screamed, but didn't let go. I stamped again. There was blood now, but still she clung on, staring up at me with a look of utter horror and incomprehension.

'What are you doing?' she wailed. 'You're mad! You're going to kill me!'

Still there was no break on the skyline above, no movement, no silhouetted figures looking down as witnesses to what was happening.

I stamped again, but my trainers were too soft, and she was hanging on with the preternatural strength of someone fighting for her life. And she was screaming. 'No! Stop it! Stop! Help!'

Her voice was still mostly drowned by the roaring

water below, but I had to silence her. I looked around desperately. There was a piece of rock close by. I had to work it back and forth several times until I got it free. It was heavy, but small enough for me to hold in one hand while I clung on to safety with the other.

She couldn't stop screaming now. No words, no pleas for help or mercy any more – just raw shrieks torn from her throat as though from some invisible claw.

One last glance back. Still no sign of anyone. This had to be my last chance.

I smashed the rock down on her upturned face. She fell as gracefully as an acrobatic diver executing a back-flip from the high board of a swimming pool – except she didn't complete the somersault she had so skilfully begun. She smashed, flat on her back, against a sharp-edged rock, bounced once, and slithered down into the churning water, disappearing from sight.

'Brendan!'

I whirled round with a gasp. My father was outlined against the sky above me, his hands cupped to his mouth to form a megaphone.

'Be careful! Can you see her?'

I shook my head.

'Stay where you are! Charlie's coming with a rope.'

I realized I still had the murder weapon, the lump of rock, in my hand. It was bloodstained now, but below my father's line of vision. I opened my fingers and let it fall to the depths below. There were also traces of blood by my feet where Cassie had clung on so desperately; but I was bleeding myself, so they wouldn't look suspicious.

'Hang on, Brendan. Charlie's here.'

I looked up and saw Charlie with a coil of rope. He was tying some sort of loop in one end.

'OK, Brendan,' he called out, 'slip this over your head and around your waist, then your father and I will pull you up.'

He swung the rope around his head like a cowboy lassoing a steer, then sent it snaking expertly out so that it fell right alongside me. I slipped it on as he had said, and tightened it, then let them pull me up to safety. I made the climb look harder and more dangerous than it was, pretending to slip once or twice in order to exaggerate the bravery of my having crawled down there in the first place.

But really, it was a breeze.

46

Frankly, I have no idea whether I would ever have actually killed my sister if the perfect opportunity had not presented itself. Would my life have been very different if I hadn't killed her? Who knows? To ask the question is to concede that the die is cast.

The fact is, my sister was born a bitch. I'm not saying she was born evil: she grew into that, though she sure as hell started life with a talent for it. I partly blame my parents. I mean, if you give a child a ridiculous name like Cassandra, you have to expect trouble. The very sound of it exudes a kind of preening narcissism. Of course, from birth she was known as Cassie, but there is a condescending quality even in the shortened version of the name, contriving as it does to remind you of how privileged you are to be on such casual terms with a familiar of the gods.

And then of course they spoilt her, appallingly, for four years – until I was born. Not that they *stopped* spoiling her after my arrival; they went on as they always had. The only difference was that she didn't have it all to herself any more. She pretended outwardly to share their love with me, but in her own mind she retained the divine right to be an only child, a position of which I had robbed her, and for which she decided I would be made to pay.

My father was a corporate lawyer, a partner in a large, important firm, and therefore relatively wealthy. For Cassie's third birthday there were carousels and clowns and pony rides in the garden of our house in Chicago. I wasn't there, of course – I wasn't even conceived by then, at least not quite – but I saw the photographs and movies later. In fairness to my parents, they did the same for me when I was three; but my sister, who was by then seven, contrived to spoil the day by faking pains that kept her in the Emergency Room all afternoon, with my parents dancing terrified attendance and leaving me to get on with my party alone. Well, there was the housekeeper and her husband, of course, along with the entertainers and a handful of visiting parents. I had a good enough time, but it wasn't the same as if my mom and dad had been there. And of course by the evening, when it was all over, Cassie was fine. Her indisposition was put down to food poisoning or some minor passing virus. She was brought home and put to bed with much fuss and ceremony, then brought cake and diet ice-cream on trays while she watched television. Her only acknowledgement of me was to stick out her tongue when I looked in her door to see how she was feeling. Her triumph was complete.

Needless to say, it doesn't take a rocket scientist to recognize the familiar stresses and strains of sibling rivalry here. What made this case somewhat special was the lengths to which my sister was prepared to go. The lies she told, and the humiliations that she heaped on me, often with the collaboration of her giggling girlfriends, strike me now when I look back as almost unimaginable in their viciousness. Much of it, of course, was pretty trivial, though nonetheless unpleasant: toys broken, clothes hidden, minor crimes around the house committed in ways that framed baby brother as the guilty party. The harder I protested my innocence, the more I became regarded as a habitual liar – a view confirmed by my sister's terrified screams one night when she found her bed infested by a mass of crawling worms and frogs. Who but a horrible boy of six, as I was by then, could have conceived of such a thing? When I dared to suggest that my sister herself might have staged the whole episode in order to incriminate me, I received for the first time a slap across the face from my normally tolerant father, who told me that he had had enough of my dishonesty, and if I went on like this I would be sent to military academy, where they knew how to deal with boys like me.

The threat of military academy was enough to ensure that I suffered in silence from then on. Whenever, through my sister's scheming, I was wrongly accused of some offence, I simply admitted my guilt. I became regarded as not so much a problem child as a stupid one: who but a fool, the reasoning went, could so consistently and trivially offend, screw up and goof off without being somewhat less bright than my poor parents had hoped their only son would be? My grades at school were indifferent, I was lacklustre at sports, and the few friends I had gradually fell away until I had none at all.

What nobody realized was that I was living through a full-blown depression brought about by my sister's increasingly sadistic behaviour towards me. It seems odd, looking back, that my parents had no sense of what was happening. They were sophisticated people: my father was a well-read man, and my mother an active patron of the arts. You might have expected them to be alert to such things. Perhaps today they would have been, but we forget how attitudes have changed in a single generation: a kid who is 'disturbed' now was just a pain in the ass back then.

Cassie saw she had me on the ropes, and fully intended to pummel me into senselessness. I believe her ultimate ambition was to drive me to suicide, and she might well have succeeded but for the intervention of fate – in the shape of that 'accident' in Colorado.

From the age of eight and until I was ten, my sister used the weapon of sex mercilessly against me. She was just beginning to develop a female body, and there was no denying she was an attractive girl. I saw the way boys looked at her with lust, and more than a few grown men too, including friends of my parents who thought nobody had noticed them stealing that extra little glance when she was bending over, or when the strap fell off her shoulder at the pool and the whole costume started to come 'innocently' adrift. My sister never did anything innocently.

In my case, she hooked my natural curiosity about the female body by making sure I saw enough of hers while pretending she didn't even know that I was there. Then, when she was ready, she would turn on me and accuse me of spying on her. Sometimes her tantrum would be kept just between the two of us; more often than not, it would be staged so that its angry ripples alerted the whole household to the fact that Cassie's stainless modesty had been threatened by the dirty, underhanded, sneaky prurience of her sex-obsessed little brother. I felt myself increasingly regarded, as a result of these tactics, as the kind of thing that people, my parents included, scraped off their shoe while wrinkling their noses in distaste.

The fact that all of this was happening during the early days of my own sexual awakening was particularly painful, though no doubt part of her plan. One morning I woke up with the most tremendous erection, which just refused to go away. I tried everything I could think of, to no avail. I had not expected my sister to come bursting into the bathroom, where she found me doubled over in a hasty attempt to conceal the problem in my pyjamas. To begin with she merely laughed cruelly at my embarrassment, then abruptly changed tack and ran out screaming that I had forced her to look at

David Ambrose

my 'thing', and even wanted her to 'touch it'. It was, at that time, the worst lie she had ever told about me, and one that I knew I would never forgive. Our parents, too embarrassed to tackle the problem directly, said nothing that I remember in any detail, aside from suggesting that I might take the precaution of locking the door in future. But I recall the sidelong, wounded glances, the clearing of throats and quick changes of conversation when I entered a room, the inescapable feeling that I was something alien, unwanted and ugly.

Then came the incident with Naomi. Naomi Chase, as well as being my sister's best friend, was also a remarkable lookalike. They were invariably taken for sisters, and sometimes even twins, though not identical. In their mean, nasty and hateful natures, however, they were absolutely identical. Just how much so, I found out one day when Naomi suggested that she and I get together alone, without my sister. She said it casually: why didn't I come over the next afternoon? Not to her parents' house, but to a boat house they had by the lake. She wanted to show me something, but wouldn't say what it was. If I would go there, all would be revealed tomorrow.

From the way she said it there was no doubt what she was talking about. I was nine, she was just thirteen. It was an offer neither I nor any normal red-blooded boy could have refused and retained a shred of self-respect.

It was a warm afternoon. High summer. I found Naomi waiting for me alone. She kissed me first, then

264

asked me if I'd ever seen a naked girl. I'd seen my sister, of course – half-naked, never totally. Sisters don't count, she said. You couldn't do the things with sisters that you could with other girls. Then she told me to remove my clothes. We were going to do things, she promised, that we would both enjoy.

Like a fool, I believed her. I was out of my clothes in seconds flat, waiting for her to do the same. That was when I heard the first muffled giggles from somewhere overhead. I looked up. The boat house had a high vaulted roof, an inverted V-shape. There was an area, a kind of mezzanine, that was used for storage – sails, oars, and various bits of sailing equipment. My sister and two more of her friends were there. It was a set-up, though I didn't realize how bad a one till I saw Naomi sprinting out of the door with my clothes under her arm and my shoes in her hand. The others clattered down some wooden steps and joined her in the bright sunlight outside, shrieking with laughter, their voices fading into the distance.

I got home wrapped in a piece of ripped tarpaulin I found in a corner. When my parents asked me what had happened, I told them I had gone swimming with some boys who had played a trick on me. My sister was hovering at the top of the stairs, trying to overhear what was being said. I knew she would brand me a liar if I told the truth, and she would be backed up by her friends. They would claim I had 'interfered' with Naomi in some way, and they had all come running to my rescue. I knew how their minds worked. I decided I would rather be punished for swimming without adult supervision than for the offence they would accuse me of.

They were strangers to the truth, all of them. There was no bridge between us.

Later, I came to realize there are no bridges between anyone. Just illusion, and sometimes disillusion.

But the truth as something to be shared and held in common?

Don't make me laugh.

47

Naomi's murder, almost two years after my sister's death, was never solved. She had been babysitting as a favour to one of her cousins. She was alone in the house from seven fifteen onwards – alone, that is, except for a three-year-old who remained fast asleep upstairs throughout.

The killer had apparently entered by breaking a conservatory window, then forcing a door into the house itself. Naomi had been taken by surprise and, after a brief struggle, strangled. Fibres found on her throat suggested that some item of silk had been used, possibly a scarf. It was never found. Nor was the fine gold chain she had been wearing. Murderers, the police said, especially serial sex murderers which was what they suspected they were dealing with in this case, frequently kept some personal object belonging to their victim as a memento of their crime – a habit which sometimes led to their discovery and arrest.

But not in this case, because the chain in question

was at the bottom of the river where I had thrown it on leaving the house.

My knowledge of the behaviour of serial sex and other murderers was gleaned from a couple of paperbacks I had picked up in a local bookshop. These books had enabled me to simulate perfectly the scene of a typical sex crime. The victim had been stripped naked after death and sexually abused, though the perpetrator had left behind no trace of saliva, semen, blood or any other substance that might have been helpful in identifying him.

I have to make a confession here – a confession in addition to the one I have just made. I had intended only that Naomi's death should *look* like a sex crime. It had never occurred to me that it should actually *be* one. But such was my limited self-knowledge at that age – twelve, going on thirteen – that the intensity of my sexual feelings towards this young female, this lookalike for my sister, took me by surprise.

As she lay there lifeless on the floor, I became immensely sexually excited. My first orgasm was spontaneous, and astonishingly voluminous – unlike anything I had experienced before, even with the aid of my wildest fantasies. I cleaned myself up with the silk scarf I removed from her neck (which was one of my mother's and which I later burned; she never even noticed it was gone). Even so, I was forced to relieve myself twice more by masturbation (silk scarf again, and, luckily, spare handkerchief).

Looking back, of course, it was inevitable that a sexual element should have been part of what was happening. But things that are obvious to us in our maturity are less so in childhood and youth.

The crime was never solved. A couple of known sex offenders were pulled in and questioned, but released for lack of evidence. I myself never even came into the frame. Had I done so, my alibi would have been that I was home the whole evening with my mother. She had started to drink after my sister's death, becoming withdrawn and increasingly uninterested in the world outside our front door. My father was frequently away on business, and it turned out later that he had been having an affair for some time. My mother doted on me as her only remaining child, and I did all I could to repay that affection – including the discreet disposal of her empty vodka bottles so that neither the housekeeper, gardener nor my father had any idea how much she was actually getting through. On occasion I even put her to bed when she fell asleep at the table as we had supper together, just the two of us. I had grown into a strong boy (hence more than a match for Naomi despite our age difference) and was quite able to help or even drag her upstairs when necessary.

On the night of Naomi's death, my mother and I were alone in the house. Our housekeeper was visiting family in the suburbs, and my father was, as usual, away. I had mixed her earlier martinis a little more strongly than usual and kept her glass carefully topped up.

It was not hard to persuade her to let me bring a tray up to her room with something to eat while she settled in bed to watch television. Thereafter, her evening passed in an alcoholic haze. Even if she had noticed that I was absent for almost two hours, she would not have remembered the morning after; and the unspoken pact that existed between us meant that no mention of her alcoholism would have been permitted to cloud her clear recollection of my presence at home with her that whole evening.

I was saddened when my parents divorced the following year, though to be honest the atmosphere between them had long since become unbearable. It was my sister's last poisonous bequest to our family. First she had driven me to distraction; now, after the death she had brought upon herself, she had driven my mother to drink and my father from home.

As I said before, my sister was born a bitch, but grew triumphantly into evil over time.

48

After the divorce, in which my parents were awarded joint custody of me, I was sent away to boarding school. It was not the military academy I had once been threatened with, but a civilized enough place where I found I could fit in without too much trouble. There was discipline, plenty of it; but I liked that. I followed enough of the rules to keep the authorities happy, while rebelling just sufficiently to keep in with my fellow students. I became good at sports, taking up boxing and karate. Altogether, I was growing into a clean-cut, good-looking and personable young man: a credit, I used to hear people say, to my parents.

Most of my vacations were spent with my mother, despite the joint custody arrangement. My father had moved to Los Angeles and was married to his former mistress. They had a new baby. Whenever I went to stay they made me welcome, and my father always ensured that I had whatever I needed in material terms. But I didn't much take to life in LA, preferring my old home and the city I'd grown up in.

271

My mother stopped drinking when I was fifteen. Frankly, it came as a shock to me. I got home from a school trip to Europe in the summer and found this stranger waiting for me. Well, not exactly a stranger: more like the mother I'd known when Cassie was alive. For a jarring moment it was like stepping back into the past; I felt a shiver down my spine. I don't know if anything in particular had brought on this new sobriety, some incident in which she had hit rock bottom in the way that alcoholics are supposed to before they can recover. If so, she never spoke of it to me. However, she had checked herself into a clinic after Easter, and was now resuming her social life and involvement with the museum boards and charity committees that she had spent so much time cultivating in the past.

I have to say that in some ways this was bad timing for me. I don't mean this selfishly. I was delighted for her, glad to see her back on her feet (literally) and finally getting over the trauma of my sister's death and my father's departure. It was just that on that trip to Europe, something had happened that had left me shaken and in need of drawing into myself – 'cocooning' – for a while. Instead, here was this brisk, sharp, witty and intelligent woman engaging me in conversation of a kind that had not taken place between us in ages. It was as though she felt obliged to show an interest in my life that she had not been able to recently. Which meant, inevitably, that she asked a lot of questions – and actually listened to the answers, so that I had to be very careful what I said.

There was no problem with talking about my life at school. The trouble started when she began to cross-examine me about the European trip. That was what I didn't want to talk about. That was where the raw spot, the difficulty, was. I was still coming to terms with what had happened and did not want to be consciously reminded of it – at least not until I had fully absorbed its significance. The fact was that I had been brought face to face with an inescapable truth about myself. One that I could not talk about. One that I would never be able to talk about.

Our group had spent two nights in Hamburg. The first day and most of the second we were marched through all the usual museums and sites of historical interest. Then, the night before we left, we were allowed a little time to ourselves. We were organized in groups of six, with an older boy in charge of each one. Visits to cafés and places of respectable amusement were permitted, bars and strip clubs ruled out. So, obviously, that was where we all immediately headed. We broke up into smaller groups of threes and twos, fixing a rendezvous for 9:45 so that we could all go back to the hotel together. The kid I was with, Lenny Rearden, started out in search of a porno shop, but got briefly side-tracked into an elaborate amusement arcade, where we quickly lost each other. It didn't matter, because we both knew where we all had to meet.

Then I met this girl. She was called Hannah. I hadn't even noticed her when I heard this voice: 'Are you American?'

I turned, and caught my breath. If my sister and Naomi had been almost twins, this one would have made them triplets. It wasn't just a physical resemblance; it was something from within, a look in the eyes, a physical self-confidence, an attitude.

'Sure, I'm American,' I said, flexing the muscles in my throat to stop my voice from rising to the squeaky pitch I'd felt it was about to. 'What can I do for you?'

She was maybe a year younger than me, but she looked as though she knew her way around the city, and quite possibly the world. Her English was good. We talked a while about how she wanted to visit America, maybe live there. I could see she liked me. Either that, or she thought I might somehow help her get there.

Her self-assurance made me nervous. My stomach was churning and my heart beating fast, but I think I managed to hide it. At any rate, after talking for a while, she asked me if I wanted to come with her to her sister's place. There was nobody there, she said; she had it to herself till the weekend.

It was an offer I knew I would never forgive myself for refusing. Looking across the arcade, I saw that Lenny was engrossed in some game with flashing lights and explosions. He wouldn't think twice if I disappeared, and would simply expect to see me at the rendezvous. Which gave me over an hour and a half.

Her sister's apartment was up three flights of stairs. It was tiny, with clothing and magazines and cushions scattered everywhere. She asked me if I wanted a drink, and I had a beer which she got from a fridge in an alcove where there was also a sink and small stove. She put on a CD and said it was an American band. I had never heard of them but I pretended I had, and we began to dance.

After a while, we started to fool around. She didn't object when I slipped my hand under her shirt. She moaned and squirmed a little, then took my hand and guided it down between her legs. The next thing I knew, she had her hand on me in the same place. But she stopped suddenly when she realized that I didn't have an erection.

'Brendan . . . ?'

I snapped out of my reverie at the sound of my mother's voice. We were sitting opposite each other in our drawing room in Chicago. I had been telling her about my European trip, but my mind had been on the one aspect of it that I could not talk about. Now she had asked me a question, and I had no idea what it was.

'I'm sorry?'

'You were miles away suddenly. Are you all right?'

'Yes, fine. I'm sorry, I think I've still got a touch of jet lag.'

We talked about the boat trip that we'd taken down the Rhine, the visit to Cologne Cathedral, then on to Paris. But all the time my mind stayed focused on that night in Hamburg, almost as though by keeping it in the forefront of my consciousness I was somehow

guarding against any word of it slipping out of my
mouth.

Hannah had said it was all right, it didn't matter that
I couldn't perform. I could tell she was disappointed
and somewhat contemptuous of me. I wasn't what she'd
thought and hoped I was: I was just a boy on a school
trip going home to his mother. She didn't say any of
this, but I knew it was what she was thinking. She
stopped the music and looked at her watch, and said
we should go now; she had to meet someone.

'Who d'you have to meet?' I said.

She shrugged. It was none of my business.

'A boyfriend?'

This time she looked at me, a kind of upward flick
of the eyes, as though I was some kind of curiosity that
had just walked in and she was going to make a joke of
later with her girlfriends. The way Naomi and my sister would have.

'Come on,' she said, 'why don't we just go?'

She took my arm to steer me to the door. I pulled
free and turned to face her, blocking her way out.

'Tell me,' I said. 'You've got some guy? Is that who
you're going to see?'

Her face tightened with anger. 'I've got a *man*,' she
said, giving the word an emphasis that made perfectly
clear what she meant. 'So why don't you get out of my
fucking way before you get in fucking trouble – kid!'

She pronounced it 'fockink', which sounded funny
and almost made me laugh. But her English was good,

I had to admit that. Fluent, colloquial. I had already been impressed by how many foreigners in Europe spoke English.

'You're not going anywhere,' I said. 'We're not through here yet.'

'Oh, yes, we fockink are!'

With that, she gave me a shove in the chest that startled me. It was a self-defence move; she had obviously learned how to take care of herself. Somebody else might have been intimidated by a blow like that, and she probably had other moves to follow it up. But I was already a brown belt in karate. I delivered two blows to her stomach and neck that sent her flying across the room. She landed in a corner. I watched as she struggled to clear her head and get to her feet. She wasn't sure what had happened. She was stunned. But she was getting ready to fight back. Suddenly she was reaching for something concealed beneath the bed – a knife or even a gun, I guessed. I sprang on her before she got there, and my hands tightened around her throat.

That was how it happened. But only then, after the event, did I realize that was what I'd needed all along: I just hadn't admitted it to myself. I had even suppressed the fact that all of the erotic images I had been furiously conjuring up in my mind in order to get a hard-on had been of Naomi, and of the night I had gone over to the house where she was babysitting.

Suddenly, it was as though that whole thing was happening again. A perfect replay. I realized that not only was that what I needed: it was what I wanted. I was rock hard . . . and I went to work . . .

I must have left traces of myself everywhere . . . I lost all control, yet . . .

It was as though part of me remained detached from the whole thing, outside my own frenzy, looking on calmly, neither endorsing nor condemning what I observed. Even the pleasure being derived from the acts performed was somehow not mine. It was gratification at one remove, like having sex in a dream. It was odd, that sense of disconnection from oneself.

Only when it was over did the two parts of myself come back together, like the images in a stereoscopic viewer. And only then did I come to terms with the fact that this was my fate, and my future. This was as close as I would ever get to satisfaction. I would, through this other self who would periodically emerge from my being like some comic-book superhero, occasionally touch perfection; but I would become fully aware of it – sense, taste, touch and everything – only by absorbing that alter ego back into myself, making his experience and memories all mine.

My mother was looking at her watch. She had a meeting of the orchestra board at three. There would be friends for dinner – she hoped that was all right with me. Meanwhile, why didn't I rest, get over my tiredness after the flight?

She kissed me on the cheek and left. My face, thank God, was dry; but my hands, clasped in my lap, were wet with perspiration. I ran to the small bathroom by the main stairs and washed them furiously, fearing that their clammy moisture would give away, to anyone who noticed it, the things of which I could not speak.

49

It was hardly surprising that I didn't sleep that last night in Hamburg. The following morning I hunted through the German newspapers we were encouraged to read as part of our study of the language. Sure enough, there she was. There was even a photograph in one of the papers – not of the corpse, but of her, I would have guessed, about a year earlier.

Needless to say, I didn't sleep for several nights; I wasn't entirely faking it when I told my mother I had a bad case of jet lag. True, I felt a huge sense of relief to be back on American soil, but I knew perfectly well that I was not yet free and clear. DNA profiling at that time wasn't as precise as it is now, but if they ever connected that girl's death with the fact that an American school tour had been in the city that night, and if they came after us to take blood samples or whatever, which they could conceivably do, then I would have a problem.

But as the days and weeks went by, I started to relax. I began to tell myself I'd got away with it. I felt as though some great weight had been lifted off me and I had been given a second chance at life. I swore to myself I would not waste it. I would put death behind me. I would go on as though Cassie, Naomi and Hannah had never happened. I realized how much I wanted to lead a normal life, and I made up my mind that I would try.

A few weeks later I met a girl called Karen. It was at a friend's house, playing tennis. She was the one who took the initiative, making an excuse to leave at the same time as me so that we could walk home together. She told me she'd heard I was a hero. I didn't understand at first. For a moment I thought she was making fun of me, then the penny dropped: she was talking about my sister. That of course was the version of events that the world had accepted: that I had almost lost my own life in bravely trying to save my sister's. I shrugged the story off modestly, saying it was no more than anybody would have done. But she said she didn't believe that; she thought I was special. She used the word twice. Special. Perhaps more than twice. By the time we parted, I had made a date with her for the weekend – by admitting I had been invited to a dance she would be at, and not objecting when she suggested we go together.

I was flattered and excited. She had soft blonde hair falling to her shoulders, and a way of moving and talking that was both demure and full of breathy sexual promise. Physically, she could not have been less like my sister, or Naomi, or Hannah. At the same time I was afraid. What if I couldn't manage the thing she was hoping

for from me? Would I humiliate myself again? Worse –
would I get angry and do what I had done in Hamburg?

There was no question about it: I could not go on as
I was. I had to change, and I persuaded myself that I
could. The problem was that like most boys of my age –
sixteen, soon to be seventeen – my sexual experience was
almost entirely confined to fantasy. Because, I supposed,
of my unusual history, my imagination was dominated by
memories of Naomi and the German girl and what I had
found myself doing after their deaths. Even the memory
of my sister and that look of utter disbelief and terror on
her face as I stamped on her hands and she fell to her
death could give me an extra charge sometimes. It was
obvious to me that I needed a new and different experience in order to vary and enrich my inner life.

But that was where I found myself caught in a vicious
circle. I began having sex with Karen in the way most
teenagers do – necking, heavy petting, oral stimulation;
and eventually, as confidence builds, cautious and protected penetration. She wasn't a virgin, so the last part
wasn't so difficult; and frankly, her experience, limited
though it was, proved a great help to me.

The problem was, however, that in order to achieve
and maintain an erection I found myself having to concentrate on those images from my past with even more
ferocious effort than ever before. The result was that,
instead of replacing my fantasies, I was reinforcing
them. And by reinforcing them, I knew even then that
I risked goading myself into repeating them.

Which I did not want to do.

Believe me.

If Karen had known what was going on in my head during our sessions together, she would have run a mile in terror. But as our relationship progressed I became more relaxed about my double life – inner and outer. I functioned. Actually, I functioned pretty well. We made a nice couple. To the world we were as normal as apple pie. To Karen herself we were as normal as apple pie. Only I knew what lay beneath the surface.

Karen and I broke up after a few months, but we remained friends. I used to see her around with other boys. I had a couple more relationships myself: I had the trick of it now; it was relatively easy.

But still it wasn't what I wanted. I knew what I wanted, though I wished I did not want it. I knew only that I was driven by some overwhelming force that I could neither define nor analyse, a force that propelled me in a direction that both terrified and excited me. To try and understand myself, I started reading books about human behaviour, graduating pretty quickly to psychology textbooks. I discovered that the kind of sexual crime upon which I had become fixated was essentially about possession: total power over another human being. I grew familiar with terms like 'necrophilia', and 'sexual sadist' – described somewhere as 'the great white shark of sexual predators'. That gave me an odd thrill, though I would hate to claim I was proud of it.

I felt alternately empowered and diminished. What

I was learning about myself was unthinkable. Except I did not have to think it. I had only to recall it. I had already *lived* it.

Once, years earlier, I had asked my father what morality meant. He told me that morality was what you did when nobody was watching. I smiled about that, thinking back, as I read about the id, the ego and the superego, the internalization of parental authority, and adaptation to social convention. That, I discovered, was what psychology was finally all about: striking a balance between personal fulfilment and the ability to function acceptably within society. Right and wrong did not come into it. That was for philosophy to worry about; and it too came to no firm conclusion. Altruism, the notion that we were capable of acting out of any motive other than selfishness and the search for self-gratification, was at best unproven. If you believed in it, that was because you wanted to believe in it. And if you didn't, it was because you didn't.

By the time I went to college, I knew what I wanted to be. Of course, I had to pretend to learn over again a lot of things I knew already because of my extensive reading in the subject. But that wasn't hard. And to be honest, I learned quite a few things I hadn't known already. Among them was the realization that knowledge changes very little. It will get you to the moon, or give you a nonstick frying pan, but it does not help with the great mysteries. It is powerless before them.

One of the things I knew, part of my 'knowledge',

was that I would never change. But, I discovered, I could function. It was pointless to fight what I was: I could only hide it. Just as we all hide something.

While in Boston, I published a couple of articles and received an offer to write a book. I was making a name for myself, and I was proud of doing well. I enjoyed the recognition and the respect with which a successful professional man is treated. I was also fascinated by the work itself, tinkering with young minds until they functioned in the way that was required of them. If I had to compare myself to anyone it would be an engineer – someone working with the finest and most sophisticated machines in the world. I could diagnose their problems and fine tune them to . . . if not perfection, functionality.

Marriage was something that colleagues and acquaintances occasionally hinted about. Why wasn't I . . . ? Was I thinking about . . . ? Had I met so-and-so's sister . . . ? Would I make up a four at a restaurant? I was sociable, within reason, though I worked hard. And I usually managed to have some woman in my life on a more or less regular basis, though I never lived with anyone. These relationships usually lasted from six months to a couple of years; I managed to wind them down amicably as it became obvious to the women involved that they were not going to culminate in marriage.

There were no more incidents after the German girl. Until Melanie Hagan entered my life.

50

I moved to Saracen Springs for several reasons. For one thing, it was small and it was beautiful, and I expected it to provide me with a quieter life, leaving more time for reflection and writing. Also, it was close enough to Albany and its surrounding communities to provide me with a big enough practice to earn a decent living; it wasn't as though I was burying myself in the middle of nowhere.

Shortly after I settled there, I was invited to deliver a paper at a convention in Toronto. I decided to drive there, taking a couple of days to relax and be alone. I stayed a night longer than I had intended, seeing a couple of old friends. It meant I had to drive back nonstop, which was not a problem if I started early, though it meant arriving home in the middle of the night.

I picked up Melanie near Utica. More accurately, she picked me up. I had stopped for something to eat at a burger place. It was about ten at night. As I was leaving, she approached me in the parking lot. She asked where I was heading. I told her Saracen Springs.

'Where's Saracen Springs?' she asked.

'Not far from Albany,' I said.

'Great,' she said, getting in the car without even asking. 'Albany's where I'm going. You can drop me off.'

She started talking about a couple of bands that were playing at a festival I didn't even know was happening there. She said she'd come from Niagara Falls, hitched a ride with an old couple as far as Rochester, then a woman with two screaming kids had taken her to Utica.

'You planning to stay long in Albany?'

She shrugged. 'Depends.'

'On what?'

'On what happens,' she said. 'Maybe I'll get a job or something.'

Frankly, I had not been aware until that moment of the resemblance she bore to my sister and to Naomi, as well as to the girl in Germany – though, of course, it must have registered subliminally. In fact, the physical resemblance was not all that remarkable. It was only when she started to talk that I realized just what it was I had with me in my car that night. The same knowing look behind the eyes, the same suggestive subtext in the language she used, the same sly hints of what was so far an unspoken promise; and the same conviction that she could do with me whatever she chose.

In a sense, she was right. Fatally so.

'Have you got any money?' I asked her.

'Not much,' she said.

I looked over at her. She was gazing out of the car

window with deliberate casualness, but fully aware that my eyes were on her.

'Got any ideas?' she said. It was obvious that she had taken my question as the opening move in a process of negotiation.

I let a few moments pass in silence, creating the impression that I was thinking this over. As indeed I was. Because I knew with absolute certainty what would happen if I took one more step in the direction things were going.

She took it for me. As the silence lengthened, she turned to me and said, 'You want to help me out?'

It was my last chance. I could have stopped the car there and then and thrown her out. But that would have risked provoking the trailer-park vindictiveness I was already quite sure she had in her. There would have been nothing to stop her noting down my licence plate and filing a complaint that I had tried to molest her, or worse. The embarrassment, considering my position, would have been considerable. As everyone knows, even if nothing is eventually proved, mud sticks. There was, I realized, no last chance. A line had been crossed. It was already too late.

'Well,' I said, 'maybe we can talk about that.'

'Sounds good.'

She gave me a smile of such sunny innocence that for a moment I was almost ready to believe I had misjudged her. Then I noticed that her thighs had parted slightly under the briefest of short skirts that she was wearing. I almost laughed aloud at my own naivety.

'Just to establish a spirit of goodwill,' I said, fishing out my wallet with one hand, 'why don't I give you fifty dollars on account?'

Her eyes widened greedily at this unexpected windfall, and her hand was already out there waiting as I pressed the bills into it. 'Hey, thanks,' she said. 'Great!' I watched her fold the money carefully into her purse.

'Now all we've got to do,' I said, 'is figure out where to go.'

'Go?'

I looked at her. 'You know what I mean.'

'Oh – right.'

She sounded less sure than she had when she was asking for money. But I figured she was on the hook now. She would be thinking there was more where that came from.

'We could go to my place, but my sister's there,' I lied. 'We'll have to find someplace else.'

'Uh-huh.'

Promise had been replaced by reluctance in her tone now. She was trying to hide it, though without success. I decided that maybe I'd been wrong to think she was on the hook; now that she had fifty bucks, all she wanted was a way out of the transaction before she had to deliver her end.

We were already approaching the outskirts of Albany, although I was still unfamiliar with the detailed geography. It was pitch dark outside, and I could see nothing in my headlights except an empty road with what looked like an abandoned industrial landscape on both sides.

'This looks OK,' I said, pulling the car off the road onto some wasteland. My headlights swept across a curious-looking house. Tom Freeman would later describe it to me as looking like an exposed tooth in a well-worn gum. It was abandoned, though not quite a ruin, but with its windows broken or boarded up and tiles missing from the roof. There was a strange tower at one corner, like an imitation Gothic castle.

'OK for what?'

I gave her a look that said I knew she was kidding and I didn't mind. But it was a look between equals. There was no room to change her mind now.

'Get out of the car,' I said, doing so myself.

She didn't move. 'It's creepy. I don't want to stay here.'

'It's not creepy. Get out of the car.'

I walked a few yards, enjoying the chance to stretch my legs and take in the cool night air. Part of me, I knew perfectly well, was secretly hoping she would take the money I had given her and just disappear. It would be better for both of us if she did. If I'd stopped in town, or even at a gas station somewhere, I was fairly sure she would have done just that. But out there? That was another question. I realized I was playing some kind of game, one that I had not chosen to play, but to which I was now committed.

I stopped as a distant, twanging discord reached my

ear. I listened a moment, turning, trying to figure out where the sound was coming from. Then, further up a gentle rise, and only now visible as my eyes got used to the dark, I saw faint, strobing patterns of light reflected in the night sky. By chance, I realized, we had stumbled across the rock festival she had been looking for. It was only a few hundred yards away, just over the horizon. She had said it was supposed to go on around the clock for three days.

'Come out here,' I called back to the car. 'There's something you should see.'

This time she didn't even answer. I bent down and peered into the vehicle. There was no sign of her.

How little we know ourselves, even those of us trained to peer below the surface of human behaviour. A moment earlier, I had thought this was what I'd wanted. And so it had been. But not, I realized now, for the reasons I had thought. I had wanted her to run not to end this thing, but to make it happen. I *wanted* this betrayal, this insult. Only this would release the things I had kept locked within me for so many years. The genie was out of the bottle now. I did not know if I would ever get it back.

I saw a flash of movement not far away. It could only have been her. I started after her. My eyes were well accustomed to the dark by now, better than hers would be after sitting in the car with the dash light in her face. A couple of times she made a wrong turn and had to double back. She didn't know where she was going. Neither did I, but all I had to do was follow her, getting closer to her with every mistake she made. It was not long before she tripped and fell, and I was on her. She started to scream, but my hands were already at her neck, and she fell silent.

It would surprise many people to learn that I believe in God. It strikes me that a rigorous application of Occam's Razor to the mystery of our being leaves us with no credible alternative. Any other explanation is both over-complex and incomplete.

That I do not automatically assume He is benign might come as less of a surprise. I believe that He is beyond good and evil, which are merely categories we have invented to rationalize the capacity for pain and pleasure with which He has endowed us. The Devil is our invention, not His.

We exist for His amusement. He plays with us.

When it was over, and my head began to clear, I realized I faced serious problems. I had taken a risk, a reckless one. Someone could have seen the car, noted the licence plate. No reason why they should and no reason to think they had. But I had been foolish to gamble on it not happening.

I looked around. There was no sign of any kind of life. But I could see from the sky that dawn was not far away. I had to dispose of the body.

My gaze fell on the old house, with its absurd tower and its weed-clogged garden. I picked her up and ran towards a half-rotten door leading into what must be the basement.

Inside, I dumped her on a rough earth floor. It was too dark to see properly what I was doing, though a faint dawn light was starting to filter through a small skylight. I realized I had cut my hand. My blood was mixed with hers. And other things. DNA profiling was by then a perfected forensic tool. I could not afford to have the body found.

I went out to my car, and was alarmed by how visible it had become in the dawn light. In the distance I could still hear the sound of electric guitars and strident caterwauling, but there was nobody in sight. All the same, I moved my car to a concealed spot amidst some run-wild overhanging trees, then opened the trunk in search of something I could use to dig a grave. All I had was a small snow shovel and a jack that I could use as a pickaxe to break the hardened surface of the earth down in that cellar.

As I hurried back, checking all around for any signs of movement, I saw something that almost stopped my heart. A man, dirty and unshaven, ran out of the door I was heading for and through which only moments earlier I had carried the body. I was fairly sure he hadn't seen me, but he was moving as though he'd seen something – something that had half-scared the life out of him. Perhaps he *had* seen me. Perhaps he'd been in there, in that cellar, all the time, though that would not explain why he should be running away only now.

And was he alone? He seemed to be, but I could not be sure. I could not be sure of anything, yet I had to act. If he got help now, I was finished. I had to stop him somehow. It was a moment of the worst panic of my life.

I watched him as he scrambled through long grass and undergrowth and up a slope towards a road. I had to stop him before he got there. I sprinted across at an angle, but didn't make it in time. He was already out in the open, running as fast as he could, intent, I could only imagine, on raising the alarm.

As I ran after him along the road, I heard a truck approaching. It wasn't a big truck: a pickup, with a single driver, who must have been very drunk from the way he took the corner as he came into view. He was having trouble holding his vehicle in any kind of straight line. The man I was chasing leapt out in front of him, waving his arms. I doubt if the driver even saw him – he might have seen some blurred image, and certainly should have felt or heard the impact. But he didn't stop, just floored the accelerator and sped off as fast as he could to get out of there.

The moment the truck appeared, I dived into the bushes. The driver couldn't possibly have seen me, even if he had been capable of seeing anything clearly. I waited for a moment to be sure he wasn't going to stop, turn around and come back, but the sound of his engine faded into the distance.

I crawled out of my hiding place and headed towards

where the man I was chasing had landed – on the edge of a ditch, with his limbs spreadeagled and his head at an angle that made me think his neck must be broken, though I couldn't be sure. I checked him over. He had a pulse and he was still breathing – just. His forehead was gashed and bleeding heavily. I suspected he might have brain damage, because he barely stirred when I covered his mouth and nose – and kept them covered till he stopped breathing altogether.

There was no one in sight as I looked around. I stayed low as I moved away and started back towards the over-grown hollow and the basement of that strange old house. I was satisfied that, so far, my luck had held.

The man I would later come to know as Tom Freeman was dead.

51

A shallow grave was the best I could manage for the girl. Any stray dog would have had little trouble uncovering the remains. There was also the risk of children playing. Anyone could get in there, just as I had – and, apparently, the man whose life I had ended. Aside from which, there was always the risk of someone buying the building and knocking it down to put something in its place. One way or another, she was sure to be found, and I could not rule out the risk of a DNA trace leading back to me. In the end, I had only one choice: buy the place myself.

One advantage of being the child of a lawyer is that you tend to find out for free tricky things that other people have to pay dearly for – such as how to buy a piece of property without revealing your identity. Using the name of Adam St Leonard, a name I got off a tomb-stone in Albany, and for which I eventually obtained a driver's permit and a passport, I tracked down the title to the building. The owners were so astounded that anyone should want to buy it that they practically gave it away.

After that, I flew to a couple of sun-drenched islands to sign the necessary papers, and the house was bought by a company whose origins were shrouded in mystery.

My original plan had simply been to keep the place for long enough to remove all traces of the body. But then I had an idea. Why not keep the house permanently? Not to live in myself, of course. I would continue to occupy the bright and elegantly furnished apartment I had bought on Sycamore Avenue thirty miles away. But I had already noticed a creeping yuppiedom on the fringes of Grover's Town, or 'Death Valley' as it was known locally. So I decided to convert the place into apartments. The investment paid off handsomely. Everything was rented within a month of my appointing a realtor to deal with that side of things – everything, that is, except the ground floor and basement apartment, which I retained in the name of the fictitious owner of the building, Adam St Leonard. I didn't want strangers nosing around down there – ever.

Four years passed, during which everything in my life ran smoothly. Then, one day, my colleague Bella Warne told me about a family called Freeman who were having problems with their three-year-old daughter. At her request, I agreed to see them right away.

I know of no way to describe the totally unprepared-for shock of seeing the man I had left dead in a ditch four years earlier walk into my office. Only by a superhuman effort of self-control did I avoid giving myself away.

Oddly enough I never felt even for a moment that I

could be mistaken, that this was not the same man. His face had etched itself into my memory though not because I was haunted by remorse over what I had done. True, I had not wanted to kill him, but at the time I had been left no choice in the matter. Perhaps that was why his face had remained so clearly with me, like an enemy vanquished but in some way honoured.

Could I have been mistaken in thinking him dead? Had I been too rattled by events to finish the job properly? It had to be a possibility, but I did not believe it was the answer. What I believed was that I was facing a man who had come back from the dead.

When I discovered what the problem with his daughter was, I knew why.

In my first sessions with Julia, I quickly established that her 'Melanie' memories were fragmentary and posed no direct threat to me − at least at that stage. What might happen as she got older was another matter.

Amazingly, Tom Freeman had no memory at all of that night when our paths had first crossed. Years later, of course, I discovered that he had an unconscious memory of it in the form of his recurrent dream, which merely reinforced my earlier analysis of what had happened. Drunk and drugged, as he habitually was back then, he had stumbled into the basement of the house in search of somewhere to pass out and spend the night, or what remained of it. He had been there, presumably unconscious, when I arrived with the girl. For whatever reason, he had happened to come out of his drunken slumber during the short time that I was away in search of something to help me bury the body. On waking, he had wrongly assumed that he himself was responsible for the girl's death. Whether, when I first saw him, he had been running away to save his skin or to raise the alarm was anybody's guess. Unless, of course, he got his memory back, which was always a possibility, and one I had to reckon with.

The coming together of our three lives on that night was remarkable in several ways that showed the hand of God, the God I have already described: God the games player, God the maker of puzzles, God Whose thoughts we are as He whiles away eternity by inventing and then dismantling us.

Take, as an example of His games, the situation that confronted me. Tom Freeman had inexplicably survived my attempt to kill him. He had gone on to father a child who claimed she had once been Melanie Hagan. Then, as part of the same extraordinary symmetry, the Freemans had been referred to me and not to somebody else for treatment of their daughter's condition. True, Bella Warne, their doctor, knew I was the best available, but there was no guarantee that I would take the case. I could have been away, unwell, or simply too busy. There were a thousand reasons why Julia Freeman might have wound up in different hands. The fact that she had come to me was more than mere chance.

My first objective, to put it simply, was to drive a wedge

between the two identities vying for control of the child's conscious mind. I could not delete Melanie as easily as a file on a computer, but I could try to ensure that Julia kept the upper hand. In fact this proved relatively easy, using standard game therapy and light hypnosis. I don't want to give the impression that I was lulled into a sense of false security by this, because I remained certain we were far from the end of the story. Melanie had not gone away by the time we stopped our first series of regular sessions: she was merely in abeyance. The only way I could be sure she would never return was by eliminating Julia, which was effectively impossible. My best course was to anticipate and prepare for Melanie's return. I had no doubt that if this happened I would have far more trouble controlling her than previously. Melanie in an older Julia would be harder to deal with than in a small child.

So I began to imagine possible scenarios, and my responses to them. As part of this strategy, I made a point of staying in touch with her parents to monitor her progress. We would meet for a drink or simply chat on the phone from time to time, as well as run into one another at restaurants or various social functions: Saracen Springs was not a large pond, and we were sizeable fish in it. Our conversations were always principally about Julia, but in the course of them I learnt what her parents were up to, where they were going, and every detail was filed away in case of future need.

Whether or not that need arose was up to Melanie Hagan.

52

Five more years passed before I got the call from Tom
Freeman at Niagara Falls to say that Melanie was back.
Two days later, they brought their daughter to my office.
Tom had already told me on the phone that the
'episode', as he called it, had seemingly come to an end
shortly after their visit to Melanie's home. Julia had
taken a few things she claimed as hers – as Melanie's –
but was showing little interest in them and had ceased
talking at all about her 'previous' life.

Although I had seen the child from time to time
throughout the previous five years, it had always been
casually and with her parents. This was the first time I
had been alone with her since our earlier sessions ended.
I sensed at once that Julia was nervous behind the shy
smile and demure manner, as though she feared she was
about to be accused of something she hadn't done.

'Just relax, Julia,' I said, 'like we used to. You
remember?'

She nodded. I talked for a while, in effect putting her

into a light trance, using a variation of the techniques I'd used when she was younger. 'All right,' I said eventually, 'why don't you tell me what happened at Niagara Falls?'

'We went on this boat, and it was great! We had to put on these oilskins so we didn't get wet . . .'

I let her chatter on about her holiday for several minutes, during which time she made no mention of Melanie. Then I prompted her with a question.

'Didn't you go somewhere else after that?'

She shook her head, but with that too firm and slightly tight-lipped way that children have when they are denying something and not simply answering a question. I prompted her further.

'Didn't you take a bus ride and go looking for something . . . ?'

This time she didn't answer, just dropped her gaze and stared at the fingers she was twisting in her lap.

'Julia? Didn't you go to look for a house?'

She answered without looking up, and almost inaudibly.

'Yes.'

'What house were you looking for?'

'My house.'

Still she didn't look up.

'But your house is here, Julia, in Saracen Springs.'

Her voice hardened, but she kept her eyes on the twisting fingers in her lap.

'No, *my* house. *I* wanted to see *my* house.'

'You mean Melanie's house?'

She looked at me now, and her gaze was as defiant as the tone of her voice. The eyes that bore into mine were no longer Julia's, and there was a coarseness in the face that was not Julia's. I recognized that look.

'No, I mean *mine*, motherfucker! Who d'you think you're talking to here? Snow fucking White?'

If she was looking for shock in my reaction, she was disappointed. I just smiled calmly and said, 'Hello, Melanie.'

My lack of concern unbalanced her slightly, but she covered it with aggression. 'Don't think you're going to stuff me back in the box this time,' she said. 'This time I'm going to finish you, fuckhead!'

That has been the pattern of our sessions since. To her parents and the outside world she has remained Julia. With me, in private, she is Melanie. She has abused me and called me every foul name she can think of, most of which I am sure would be unknown to Julia.

When I got the call from Tom a few days later to say that he had found the house from his nightmare, I realized that his memory was beginning to return, as I had anticipated it would, albeit only partially and obliquely for the moment. But things were moving fast now towards their close.

Only my foresight and my well-laid plans can save me now. And I believe they will.

53

They arrive a little before eleven thirty, but I am ready for them. More ready than they know.

'I hope you parked in my garage, Tom, like I told you,' I say.

'Sure. That's a big help.'

It is interesting that neither Tom nor Clare has ever asked why I have extended the privilege of parking in my private garage to them alone and to no other patients. Proof perhaps of the old adage that you do not look a gift horse in the mouth.

'Julia,' I say, 'why don't you go talk to Sally for a moment while I have a word with your father.'

She likes my receptionist, and heads off happily to her office. I steer Tom into the waiting room.

'So how are you feeling this morning?' I ask. 'You certainly look better.'

'I went to an AA meeting last night. I managed to get home without stopping for a drink.' He gives a quick self-deprecating laugh. 'I'd forgotten how bad it could be.'

'You made it, that's all that matters,' I say, taking care to sound encouraging, not patronizing.

'I wouldn't quite say *all*,' Tom says. 'I mean, where exactly are we now? What is it you said you have to tell me?'

'Just give me ten minutes with Julia, that's all I need. Then I'll have Sally get her back to school. After that, I'll be right with you.'

Tom sits down with a newspaper as I leave him, closing the door behind me. As I walk down the soft-carpeted corridor, I can hear Julia chattering happily with Sally Young.

'Hello, Julia. How are you today?' I say.

She gives me her usual big smile. 'I'm fine, Dr Hunt, thank you.'

I tell Sally to go over to the hospital and check out some records, then go straight to lunch. The records are, of course, a blind. They are real enough, but I do not really need them. And Sally is delighted to have an extra hour for lunch.

'Come on in, Julia,' I say, holding open the door to my private office.

I was not sure at first, whether Julia herself remembered anything of what happens in these sessions; gradually I became certain she remembered nothing. This morning, as always, she walks ahead of me and settles in her usual place, then turns to look up at me brightly, ready to begin. Only when the door closes, with the muted click of its latch, does the transformation take place.

David Ambrose

'OK, big boy, what's it gonna be? Blow-job? Ass-fuck? Whatever does it for you?'

The voice is different. The face. The whole posture of the body. A total transformation – from an innocent nine-year-old to a precocious, foul-mouthed and foul-minded strumpet of fourteen.

'Stop it, Melanie,' I say with exaggerated weariness, because I want her to think that she has worn me down and my defences are flagging. 'You know nothing like that is going to happen here. How could it?'

She gives a self-satisfied, knowing smile, enjoying the power she thinks she has over me.

'You're gonna have to kill her in the end,' she says. 'That's the only way you're ever going to silence me, you know. You're going to have to kill the brat. That fucking Julia.'

'How long are you proposing to go on with this?' I ask, slumping into my chair, exhibiting all the body language of defeat.

'That's for me to know and you to find out.'

'So you still think there's some purpose to all this?'

'Oh, I *know* there is.'

She continues to smirk at me in that 'I've got a secret' way. There is not even a residual trace of Julia in her. Melanie, as always, has taken over completely.

'You're going to have to kill her,' she repeats. 'I'm not kidding, you know.'

I look at her, not troubling to disguise my disdain for her strategy. In the past I have let her think I was afraid, that she was in the driving seat. But that has been *my* strategy. And now, though she does not know it yet, she has been outmanoeuvred.

'Why would I kill Julia Freeman?'

'I told you – because it's the only way you're going to silence me.'

'But why should I bother to silence you, so long as you keep these crazy accusations between us in this room?'

'What makes you think I'll do that?' she says, giving me that sly, sidelong I'm-cleverer-than-you look she probably practises in her mirror.

'I've already told you what will happen if you start telling people I killed you ten years ago. They'll put you away in a place for very sick children. That's all you are – a sick and harmless child.'

She gives a throaty laugh. 'I bet you wish you could be sure of that. Safer to kill her, big boy. Kill the brat – and then what? Make it look like an accident?' She laughs again, a harsher sound this time. 'Suicide? That would be a good one if you can pull it off.'

She is watching me carefully, avid for a twitch of unease, any hint of fear.

'You're leaving me no choice, are you?' I say quietly, as though accepting my fate, acknowledging that she is in control.

'You'll never get away with it, you know. She's not like me. She's got her folks, and they're going to get *real* pissed if anything happens to her. But you can't shut

me up without shutting her up. So admit it, big boy.
I've got you cornered. You're fucked – right?'

'You're very clever, Melanie,' I say. 'Too clever for
me, I'm afraid.'

She likes flattery. It is a weakness I make use of. All
the same, her logic is impeccable. I've known that for a
long time.

I get to my feet, cross the room, and pull open a
drawer. Her eyes follow me every step of the way.

'What the fuck is that thing?'

She points at the object I have just taken from my
desk. I am mildly surprised she doesn't know what it is.
In her world, the world she inhabited before her death,
she might, I thought, have come across such things.
Apparently not. No matter.

'Have you never seen one of these?' I say casually,
holding it out for her inspection. 'It's a stun gun. There's
a battery in the grip that creates an electric charge at
this point – here – powerful enough to render a full-
grown man physically helpless for several minutes. So
imagine what it will do to you.'

Her eyes light up. She thinks she understands what
is happening. She thinks it is what she wants, that she
has won.

'Hey, big boy, you're really going to do it, aren't you?
Cool.'

'Yes, Melanie, I'm really going to do it. But not the
way you think.'

I take a step towards her. Her eyes are fixed in

fascination on the object in my hand. She doesn't even try to pull away.

Tom sits hunched forward, elbows on his knees, hands clasped together as though in prayer. He looks up as I enter the room. He barely registers the object in my hand until I touch him on the shoulder with it. He convulses like a man suffering an epileptic fit, then slumps back, dazed and physically helpless.

He does not feel the hypodermic as it punctures the soft flesh at the base of his neck.

I drag him down the rear stairs which lead directly to my private garage, then manhandle him into the trunk of his own car – having pulled on the gloves which I shall wear until the whole of this operation is complete. Next, I go back for Julia, and load her too into the trunk of her father's car. Anyone observing the car emerge from the automatic door would see only a driver in a hat and coat with an upturned collar, who could as well be Tom Freeman as anybody else. But nobody, as far as I am aware, actually sees me.

It takes twenty minutes to reach the garage rented in the name of Adam St Leonard in Broadlands, a bleak stretch of low-rent housing where few people watch, and even fewer give a damn about, anybody's comings and goings. This garage also has space for two cars, although until now there has only been one, an ageing black Mercedes, kept there. It, too, is owned in the name of Adam St Leonard. The only prints on it, when it is eventually found, will be those of Tom Freeman and his daughter, just as the only car found in this garage will be Tom Freeman's. The conclusion will be obvious: that Tom Freeman has been for many years leading a sinister and shocking double life.

Once inside, with the door safely closed, I transfer the two unconscious bodies from the trunk of Tom's car to the Mercedes'. Then I put on the moustache, heavy-frame glasses and distinctive hat of Adam St Leonard, and set out for the house in Grover's Town where this whole extraordinary affair began.

PART THREE

'Judgement'

54

Tom's first thought was that it must be his dream again, the nightmare that he knew so well. But in the dream there was light – enough at least to see where he was and the horror that lay at his feet.

He raised a hand to his eyes, and felt a slight restriction on the movement. He realized he was fully clothed, even down to his shoes. He felt his body, his arms and legs, his head, and concluded he was uninjured, in one piece.

Was he blind? Why was there no light? Literally none.

Where *was* he? Not in bed, not his own bed: not any kind of bed. He was not *in* anything but *on* something. He felt around and traced the shape of some kind of couch, covered in what felt like polished leather. His groping hand found a floor just a few inches lower. It was uncarpeted and felt like it was made of concrete.

The silence was total, like a hermetic seal wrapped around him – so tight and so total that for a moment he feared that he might have gone deaf as well as blind.

But he heard himself calling out anxiously, 'Is anybody there?'

There was no response. Only the sound of his own breathing. When he held his breath, all he could hear was his own heartbeat.

He struggled to recall the last thing that had happened. He had taken Julia to her appointment with Brendan Hunt – it was going to be her last, or near to last. He remembered arriving and talking briefly with Hunt, and Hunt saying that if he would wait a few minutes, there was something he wanted to tell him.

Had Hunt come back? Tom struggled to remember, rewinding the scene in his mind and replaying it from the beginning. Yes, Hunt had come back. He remembered the door opening. He had looked up – and seen something odd.

What was it?

He played the scene again. It became more clear with repetition. Hunt had been holding some kind of gadget; he remembered a length of chrome, or something like it, and a stubby grey handle. He didn't know what it was, though for some reason he'd vaguely recognized it. He'd started to get to his feet . . . and then he'd passed out.

But no, he hadn't passed out, it was something else. He remembered that he'd thought he must have had a stroke or a heart attack. Everything had gone into slow motion. His legs had given way. He had struggled to sit up, to pull himself together and get to his feet, but his limbs would not respond. He felt like a man underwater – drowning.

The hypodermic. The rest of it came back now – Brendan Hunt had jabbed a needle into him. That was all he remembered. It made no sense. Why would Hunt do that? Why had he, Tom, let him?

Suddenly he remembered what the gadget was that he had seen in Hunt's hand. It was a stun gun. A friend of his had bought one after being mugged. Hunt had touched him on the shoulder with it, and that was when he'd become disoriented, unable to coordinate his movements. After that had come the needle, then blackness – the blackness he was still in.

He swung his legs off the couch and felt for the floor with his feet. Nothing stopped him: he was not tied down. Still seated, he stretched his arms, partly because he suddenly felt the stiffness that came from lying too long in an uncomfortable position, and partly to feel for obstacles around him. He found nothing, so he tried to stand up. He felt strangely unsteady, the aftereffects of the drug pumped into him, perhaps – along with the surprising difficulty of keeping his balance with no visual reference to guide him – but after a moment he was all right. He had his bearings: at least he knew which way was up and which was down.

Holding his hands out in front of him, he began exploring the darkness, moving cautiously, knowing he was in an alien place where every step could bring him up against something hard or send him over a precipice.

But as he edged his way forward the floor remained firm beneath his feet.

His left hand, waving around, connected with something. He stopped, turned towards it, and brought his right hand over – something hard, part metallic but part cushioned in a way that made him think, after several moments of exploring it, of a dentist's chair. Could it be? Surely not.

But why not? Anything was possible in that sightless vacuum.

He moved on. After a few steps his shins encountered a low wall. It was made of brick or concrete blocks on the side towards him, but smooth metal on the other. He moved along cautiously until he reached a corner, then turned and followed the wall until it turned again. It was some kind of shallow basin, square and large enough to be a child's play pool. So far as he could determine, it was empty, but the metallic lining sloped down from all sides to what felt like a drainage point in the centre.

A few steps back, and he found himself against another wall – brick by the feel of it, but older, rougher brickwork. Inevitably, he thought again of his nightmare; but this wall, though made of brick, was not crumbling. He felt his way along and came to a kind of door, made of steel he thought, and solid: there was no hollow echo or suggestion of a shift when he pushed at it, then hammered on it with all his strength. Nor was there a handle. He could not find a lock or even a keyhole. Perhaps it was just a panel, not a door. Or perhaps it could be opened only from the other side, like a prison cell.

He was being held prisoner. There was no question in his mind of that. Just as he knew he was being held by Brendan Hunt.

But why? Could Hunt believe that he, Tom, was the killer, as he'd accused himself of being? Had he decided to lock him up out of harm's way until . . .

Until what? Why would a sane man do this? The question echoed in Tom's head. He felt a strange fluttering sensation in his chest, as though his heart had missed a beat; then the cold prickling of gooseflesh on his skin. Was he saying that Brendan Hunt was insane?

He couldn't believe it. He couldn't even be sure that what he was remembering had actually happened. Perhaps it was just a fantasy produced by his dysfunctional brain, and there was some other explanation for his being here.

He was moving faster now, less carefully, blundering over and around things that he no longer even tried to identify. His hands swept the walls in search of any crack or crevice that might offer a way out. He did not even realize he had hit a switch until an electronic clunk above his head brought two strips of harsh white light flickering into life. He breathed in the light through every pore of his body. The relief was indescribable. But moments later he would have welcomed back the darkness.

It was more than a cellar – it was a dungeon, though there were no chains or shackles, no racks or wheels or instruments of torture – except, now that he looked at it more closely, what he had taken in the darkness for a dentist's chair. It was indeed something very similar, though with straps to hold its occupant in place by force. And behind it was a rocking horse with an obscene penile attachment to the saddle. He must have knocked against it in his blundering around, because it was still moving gently back and forth, as though below some unseen rider.

He turned and saw what he'd taken for a child's play pool. It took on an infinitely more sinister and suggestive aspect in the cold glare of the overhead light. Its lining was zinc or stainless steel, inclining, as he had thought, to a central drainage point. A hosepipe attached to a tap on the wall was coiled at one corner. Something about it made him think of mortuaries and pathology labs.

Built into the wall on his left was what looked like a small furnace. A steel pipe that could be a smokeduct had been plumbed to the wall, with a couple of narrower pipes alongside it, and several electrical cables had been stapled to the wall above it. The work was neat, but looked somehow amateurish. Perhaps, he thought, because it was the kind of work you *had* to do yourself, because you could never tell anyone else why you wanted it doing. He closed his eyes in denial of his thoughts, and in defiance of the revulsion that threatened to overwhelm him.

He started to call Julia's name. As he did so, he turned – and for the first time saw a staircase in one corner: a set of open wooden steps, leading to a trapdoor in the ceiling.

He was immediately across the room and struggling with the catch on the trapdoor, but it was locked on the other side. Absurd of him to expect anything different. He beat at it till his fists hurt, then crossed back to the steel panel he'd hammered at in the dark. Now more than ever it looked like a door, but with no lock or handle on his side. He kicked and hammered on it some more, until he was forced to give up or risk hurting himself badly.

Despite his efforts to suppress them, pictures began forming in his head. About why this room existed. About what had happened here. He closed his eyes, but the pictures only became sharper. He would go mad if he did not get out of this place. If he did not get an answer to the question into which his nightmare imaginings had poured their poison.

What had happened to his daughter? What did Hunt want with her? What had he done to her?

He heard a lock being slipped across the room, where the wooden steps were. The trapdoor was opening and the lower half of a man came into view.

Then a hand with a gun in it: at least, a sort of gun. 'It's a little like the thing I used on you before,' Brendan Hunt said, following Tom's gaze, 'except this works at a distance. And I need to keep a distance between us now.'

A red spot suddenly appeared on Tom's chest. 'It's laser guided,' Hunt said. 'Can't miss.'

Tom raised his eyes to meet the other man's. 'Where's Julia?'

'She is unharmed, not far from here.'

'I want to see her.'

'Soon enough.'

Tom started forwards, but stopped when Hunt lifted the gun and the red spot hit his chest again.

'Stay where you are.'

Reluctantly, telling himself he had no choice but to play for time, Tom obeyed.

'Melanie Hagan,' he said. 'That was you?'

Hunt nodded his head, almost imperceptibly.

'But . . . Why?'

A ghost of the Brendan Hunt he had known crossed the features of the man Tom was looking at. It was almost a smile – but not of amusement so much as of despair at the shallowness of human understanding.

'You're too smart to expect a simple answer, Tom, and we don't have time for a complex one.'

'I want to see my daughter.'

'You will. Now go stand in the centre of the floor and stay there.'

He gestured with the stun gun. Its little red spot now appeared in the centre of the floor. Only when Tom had gone to stand there did Hunt come down the last step into the basement, using his free hand to swing the trapdoor shut above his head.

'You see that desk over there?' Hunt said, using the red spot to identify a metal desk against the wall with drawers down both sides. 'I want you to take something out. I don't know which drawer it's in. You'd better try them all.'

'What am I looking for?'

'A tele-command – it's in one of those drawers.'

One by one Tom pulled them open and pushed them shut. 'There's nothing here,' he said.

Hunt did not seem surprised, just reached into his jacket with his free hand and produced a small object from an inside pocket. 'Foolish of me,' he said, not disguising the fact that he was play-acting. 'Here it was all the time – catch!'

Tom's hands sprang automatically to catch the object that Hunt tossed to him.

'Press A2 13Z,' Hunt said.

Tom did nothing. 'You're trying to get my fingerprints on everything,' he said. 'That's what you're doing, isn't it?'

Hunt gave another faint smile that made him resemble the man Tom had once known. 'Very astute of you, Tom. That is exactly what I'm doing.'

'You mean,' Tom started to say, though the thought was in place before, in his shocked state, he could find the words to express it, 'you mean . . . you want to make out that this place is mine?'

'This place *is* yours. The whole house. The house of your dreams, Tom. You will be found with an ID in your pocket for Adam St Leonard, its owner. It will be obvious that you've had this alter ego for some years. Those who know you best will find it impossible to believe, but the evidence will be overwhelming.'

'This is madness. You can't get away with something like this.'

'Oh, I think I can.'

'What are *you* doing here, anyway? You're not even wearing gloves. You're getting your own prints everywhere. How will you explain that?'

The same ambiguous smile hovered around Hunt's mouth as he delivered the reply he had so carefully prepared. 'You kidnapped me and brought me here – by threatening harm to your own daughter if I didn't obey. That is what I will tell the world when I get out of here.'

'You're insane. You're totally insane.'

'What an inspired diagnosis, Tom. Tell me, where did you complete your psychiatric internship?' Hunt's smile vanished as quickly as it had appeared. 'We're wasting time,' he said, glancing at his watch like a school teacher telling his class to pick up the pace. 'We haven't all night. Enter that code I gave you.'

'Do it yourself,' Tom snapped, and tossed the telecommand contemptuously on the desk.

Hunt looked at him like an adult whose patience is being tested by a fractious child, and who knows that any moment he is going to have to be stern.

'Tom, even if I do it, your fingerprints will still end

up on those buttons. That's easy to arrange. And you will have died without the comfort of knowing that your daughter has gone painlessly before you.'

Once again Tom felt that strange implosion in his chest, as though he had been hollowed out and left breathless by what confronted him.

'What have you done with her, you madman?'

'Nothing yet. What I finally do is up to you, Tom. Her death is in your hands.'

'You aren't making any sense, you crazy fucking—'

'I'm trying to tell you that you're dead, Tom. Already dead. You're a ghost. Can't you understand that?'

He spoke with a force, with a light of mad conviction in his eyes, that silenced Tom.

'I killed you, Tom. That night you dream about. You were in the house that night, *this* house – and you found the body. I saw you running away, and I went after you. But before I could do anything you were hit by some drunk in a truck who didn't stop. I went over to see if you were dead, but you weren't. So I killed you. I stopped you breathing. You had no pulse.'

He paused, his eyes boring into Tom's as though trying to physically burn his message directly into the tissue of his brain.

'I couldn't take the risk of your leading people back here.'

Again he paused to let his words sink in. And maybe to savour the satisfaction it gave him to speak them.

'You have to understand, Tom, that you have no right

to be alive. Which means that your daughter had no right to be born.'

There was a twitching at the corners of his mouth, a tightening and relaxing of the lips, repeated several times. It took a moment for Tom to realize that it was a kind of smile.

'It is the work of a God sorely in need of entertainment, don't you think? How dull His world would be without us.'

Tom had no thoughts to offer in response to the madness of the man who stood before him. 'You poor sick fuck!' was all he said. The words came from him like a sigh. Like a dying breath. Like a dead man's final curse. They made no impact on Brendan Hunt.

'There's no more to discuss, Tom, we're wasting time. Are you going to enter that code or not?'

Tom's eyes went to the tele-command lying where he had thrown it on the desk. He reached for it.

'What was it again?'

Hunt repeated the code. Tom pushed the buttons with numbed, unfeeling fingertips. The steel door in the wall swung open, away from them. Beyond it Tom saw a black Mercedes in a garage. The car was not a recent model, twenty years old at least.

'It belongs to you,' he heard Hunt saying, 'under your alias of Adam St Leonard. Your fingerprints are already all over it. It's the car you always use when you come here, as you have, from time to time, for many years. You keep it in a garage, also rented under the name of

Adam St Leonard, in which your own car will be found. Your double life will become a legend, Tom. I myself am already planning an article and possibly a book about you. Now go open the trunk.'

Moving like a zombie, conscious of the fact that playing for time was still the only chance he had, Tom stepped through the door into the darkened garage. He saw, beyond the car, another and larger steel door, as solid-looking as a bank vault. He recalled that he had seen this door from the outside, touched it even, only yesterday, when he had found this place. It was the door that had replaced the old wooden one in his nightmare.

'Open the trunk – and bring what's in it back with you.'

As he moved towards the car, Tom glanced right and left in search of something, anything, that might serve as a weapon. There was nothing. He reached the Mercedes and flipped open the trunk.

It was what he had feared, but had refused to imagine. His limbs turned to lead, he could not breathe. Julia lay unconscious, or dead, it was impossible to tell which. He reached out; she was warm to the touch. He bent down and put his face to hers; she was breathing. With a smothered sob of relief he gathered her into his arms.

'She's asleep, Tom. And if we do this right, she won't ever regain consciousness. It's up to you.'

Tom turned to face Hunt where he stood framed in the doorway, and started towards him. There was nothing else for him to do, no escape, no hiding place. Yet do something he must. He swore it before God – in Whom he did not believe, therefore who was his absolute last chance.

'What are you planning to do?' he asked.

Hunt contemplated him a moment, then spoke more like a prosecuting counsel than a man imparting information.

'You suffered a psychotic breakdown in my office this morning. Your daughter had said something, in my hearing, something that made you face up to your double life. The increasingly flimsy barrier you had kept in place until now finally gave way. You came back here because the part of you that is Tom Freeman, and only Tom Freeman, had to see this for himself. And because the other part of you, Adam St Leonard, has always known it must end like this. You will murder the child who has been your accuser – your own daughter – then take your own life.'

Hunt paused as though to let the surreal nature of this statement sink in. His gaze held Tom's unwaveringly as he went on.

'You will also take my life – or think you have. You will have shot me at close quarters before putting the gun to your own head. It will be a serious wound, one that could very easily have killed me had it gone a fraction more this way or that. Fortunately I am a doctor, so it will not. Of course, you will already be dead when I am shot, but then I will put the gun back in your hand. The picture will be quite convincing, and entirely consistent with the story I shall tell the police.'

Tom's gaze went to the stun gun in his hand. 'That gun?'

Hunt slipped his free hand into his jacket and pulled out a small pistol. Tom was no expert on guns, but any fool could see that it was lethal.

'Look at me,' Hunt said, glancing down at his two hands filled with weapons. 'I look like Jesse James.'

'If only you were human, you might.'

Hunt smirked faintly at the remark, then indicated with a nod of his head the grotesque object that still reminded Tom of a dentist's chair – perhaps because he refused to let his mind dwell on what other uses it might have.

'Put her in that,' Hunt ordered.

'What d'you mean?' Tom said, without knowing quite what he intended by the question. It was a perfectly clear instruction, without ambiguity; yet the implications of putting his daughter in that thing were so unthinkable that he refused to understand the words.

'You know what I mean,' Hunt said. 'Settle her comfortably in the chair, then start fastening her in place.'

No choice. If there was a hell, then this was it. No nightmare Tom could wake from could be worse than this reality. He did as he was ordered.

'You'll find it large for her, but it was designed for occupants of Melanie's age. Please fasten the straps. They're quite simple.'

It was true: they clipped neatly into place, one by one. He fastened four of them. As he reached for the fifth, he turned slightly so that he had Hunt in his sight-line but without looking at him. The pistol was back in Hunt's pocket, only the stun gun was in his hand.

Click. Another one, the fifth. Tom reached for the sixth, lower down, bending his knees and spine into the crouch from which he was going to spring with all the speed and power he possessed. From the corner of his eye he saw Hunt watching him, but did not think he knew how closely Tom was aware of him. His muscles were taut, his balance right, he must spring before Hunt realized he was about to move.

Tom was halfway across the distance between them, moving faster and with more force than he thought possible. But even in the blur of his own speed, he saw the red spot on his chest, and two small objects coming towards him, with two hair-like wires snaking out behind them and connected to the stun gun in Hunt's hand. He felt his body explode in a blinding flash of pain. He did not feel the impact of hitting the floor. He thought he was dead.

But no, he was still there. In that living hell. Like before, only worse if that was possible. His body did not respond to his orders. He even had trouble formulating orders. His thoughts were scrambled and fragmented. He had lost all contact with himself. He thought he was going through physical convulsions, though he could not be sure.

He saw Hunt looking down at him with more indifference than triumph, as though this had been inevitable. Tom realized that Hunt had been ready for his move long before he made it.

That had been Tom's last chance.

And Julia's.

Both to Hunt and to himself, Tom was now just a bystander, no longer part of the equation. For him, even a simple movement was impossible. The world around him was as fragmented and disjointed as his thoughts. But he had the impression, quite suddenly, that some time had passed. He thought he might have blacked out, moments only, but something had changed.

She was awake – Julia. Still strapped down, a prisoner, but awake and shouting something at Brendan Hunt. He could not hear what she was saying, only distorted echoes as though from a great distance. Her face was contorted with a fury that shocked him. He had never seen such rage in her before, nor such a strength behind it. This was not his child he was looking at, or any normal child.

Something else was happening now. It took Tom's addled brain some time to realize that Hunt had taken the pistol from his pocket and was putting it to his daughter's head. She was laughing at him, a laughter that spat contempt and loathing. The sound of it down the long tunnel that connected Tom to the world was terrible. Strapped down and helpless, the child was defying the man who was about to kill her, challenging him to do his worst.

It was Melanie Hagan Tom was looking at, not his

daughter. Yet it was his daughter's head Hunt was going to blow off.

Tom tried to move, but he was still weak and helpless as a new-born foal. His head swam, he thought he was going to vomit. He fought for breath.

The gun was pressed against Julia's forehead. Tom could see a white ring in her flesh around its barrel. Still she laughed.

Hunt pulled the trigger . . .

Dear God . . .

Nothing happened. A dry click.

Hunt did something with the gun and pulled the trigger again.

A dry click. The gun was jammed.

Julia was laughing louder, a harsh, violent sound, with her head thrown back only to snap forward and spew forth a new torrent of abuse.

Hunt was pulling the trigger time after time, growing paler and more frantic with each dull click.

It could not go on.

Yet it did.

Tom realized he was being given one more last chance. He did not understand why he was being given it or how, only that he must not let it pass.

Hunt was not ready for the weight that slammed into him. In his frustration with the misfiring gun, he had forgotten about Tom, and the attack sent him sprawling on the floor. Tom did not know where he himself had found the strength to move, let alone to pummel and kick, tear and slash at his opponent with his bare hands. His fingers curled like steel around Hunt's wrist, forcing him to open his hand . . .

There was an explosion, then another. The gun had fired twice. Tom was not hit, nor was Julia. The bullets had gone wide, but the noise seemed to have galvanized Hunt, given him back the advantage that had briefly been Tom's.

Another shot. Tom became aware of searing pain – aware, though he did not truly feel it. It was as though the pain was happening to someone else, to an unknown body that he was inhabiting and coldly registering its condition.

The gun went off again, but its bullet merely spat up chips of concrete from the floor. Tom had his hand on it now. With his other, he delivered a massive punch to Hunt's face. Cartilege crunched and blood flew. Hunt staggered back, stumbled against the low wall around the shallow zinc basin, and fell into it.

Tom had the gun now. Hunt pushed himself up on one elbow and put a hand to the shattered centre of his face, then looked in disbelief at the crimson mess that covered his fingers. He looked at Tom, and Tom saw in his eyes that he knew Tom was going to kill him. He knew that Tom would not permit him the mercy of the law. He would end his life now, without a second's hesitation.

'No!'

It was a command, and it had come from Julia. Tom

turned and saw her standing. The straps that had been holding her helpless were now unbuckled, hanging loose. She could not have unfastened them herself, yet there she was – this slim, small figure standing with a power and a presence about her that was not his child's, not any child's. This was something from elsewhere, an unknown, perhaps unknowable, force.

'You're too late,' Tom shouted back at her. 'I'm going to finish him off and get my daughter out of here!'

'*I* brought him here. He is in *my* power. *I* will deal with him.'

The voice was no more Julia's than the twisted lips and blazing eyes that burned into him as though he was as much the enemy as Hunt.

'You are both in my power. You have been all along.'

Tom saw Hunt move again. He raised the gun to fire – and gave a cry of pain. The gun fell to the floor with a clatter. Tom opened and closed his hand. It was red and stinging. The gun had burned like a hot coal when he had tried to pull the trigger.

Melanie's furious gaze, superimposed like some collage in living flesh and blood on Julia's face, remained on him. 'I brought him here for *us*,' she screamed. 'For *all* of us. We *need* him here – to burn in hell!'

Hunt was on his feet now, blood streaming down his neck and turning his shirt into a sodden mess. He was staring at the child as though confronting a horror that not even he had ever imagined. He took a step towards her, unsteadily, drawn it seemed against his will.

Instinctively Tom moved to block him, to get between them and protect his daughter at whatever cost. But he was thrust aside. Not by Hunt: by some force he did not see. Or perhaps simply by the agonizing cramp in his side where he had been hit by the bullet moments earlier. He had felt nothing until now, but suddenly his body convulsed and wrapped itself around the pain as though to smother it. Irrationally, his head was filled with a strange odour. He wondered whether it was some by-product of his injury, an olfactory hallucination in a nervous system that senses the approach of death?

He fought to stay upright, to beat back the pain, but its tentacles reached into every part of him. He fell on his knees, holding his side, then rolled over, helpless, foetal. And he saw something across the room.

One of the pipes on the far wall had been torn open by a stray bullet. That smell was no hallucination: it was escaping gas. The room was going to fill with it, and they would all die if they did not get out. Tom tried to cry out a warning, but a searing stab of renewed pain snatched his breath from him. He looked towards Hunt to see if he had seen what Tom had seen, but Hunt's gaze was elsewhere – and everywhere.

His eyes were flickering left and right, wide with a terror he seemed not to comprehend. He was seeing things, Tom realized, that he himself could not: things which, from the way Hunt was cowering back from them, were closing in on him from all sides. He was trying to get away from them, but there was no escape.

Hunt's victims had come back for him. He was staring into a hell that he had made himself.

Tom looked at Julia. She had not moved. Her gaze was fixed on Hunt, unflinching, murderous.

As Tom watched, something else started to happen. With an incongruity that now barely startled him, he found a corner of his mind light up with a memory from childhood – that old trick of playing with a magnifying glass, focusing the sun's rays onto a sheet of paper until it burst into flame. He remembered some of the boys he had known doing it with insects, and worse. Or just the backs of one another's hands. The power of that focused light had been frightening.

Now he found himself observing not the effect of focused light, but something else. He didn't know what name to give to it, but Hunt was being burned by it. Burned like a victim at the stake. He could not move except to beat uselessly at the flames that were starting to engulf him. At first it was just his clothes, then his hands and face began to char and blister as though from some raging fire on the inside of his own body.

Fire . . . gas . . . and fire . . . Tom remained rational enough to understand the danger of this combination. He had to get his daughter out of there before the place went up like a bomb. He had no reserves of strength, yet he drew on something, hauling himself to his feet through layers of pain, each one of which tried to beat him back. The ghastly spectacle of the burning man was forgotten. Tom was deaf to his screams. Julia was all he could – must – think of. He forced his body to turn and move towards where she stood.

She was gone.

He panicked for an instant, then he saw her. She was lying on the floor, crumpled, with her arms flung out. She was dead, or she had fainted; he had no time to find out which. Defying the screams of pain from his own body that drowned out even the howling of the burning man, he stooped and gathered her up in his arms. She did not move.

Blind to everything but his determination, he carried her towards the stairs, praying only that the trapdoor would open and that there was not a hidden catch he wouldn't find in time.

Mercifully, it moved at the touch of his shoulder. Tom thanked Providence for the hydraulic hinge that let him slam it back without having to let go of Julia. With a last superhuman heave, he lifted her dead weight up and through the gap, then hauled himself out after her.

Behind him, Hunt's screams were no longer human. Without wanting to, knowing there were only seconds – if that – to spare, Tom took one last look back.

Hunt's clothes were burned off and his flesh was on fire, but he was still alive. And screaming. And beating at the flames that were devouring him.

Tom reached for the trapdoor as the gas finally ignited. A pillar of flame shot up and hit the ceiling of the room he had climbed into, then curled back down again in search of whatever else was there to consume.

Using his whole body as a lever, Tom slammed shut the trapdoor and imprisoned the inferno below.

He stumbled to where Julia lay, still motionless. Mercifully, the escaping flames had not touched her. Neither of them was burned, though the kitchen he found himself in was filling with smoke as the smaller fires now started to spread. He gathered her once more into his arms and carried her out into what looked like a hall.

She stirred. She was breathing. She was, thank God, alive.

He could see windows, thick blinds over them so he could not tell if it was light or dark outside. And doors. All he had to do was find a way out, before the whole place went up.

55

It was the hospital Tom had woken up in ten years earlier, imprisoned in neck brace and plaster, to be delivered a death sentence unless he mended his ways. This time it was not a young doctor who sat on the end of his bed but Murray Schenk. And although Hunt's bullet had shattered two of Tom's ribs and punctured a lung, he was able to speak. Movement, however, was out of the question, too painful to attempt.

'The good thing is,' Tom was saying, 'the best thing of all, is that Julia remembers nothing. It's as if that whole part of her life has been wiped from her memory. Of course it wasn't in fact *her* life at all, so maybe it isn't so surprising.'

Schenk nodded thoughtfully, taking the information in but obviously preoccupied. He had barely spoken a word since arriving ten minutes ago.

'What's on your mind?' Tom asked.

'They've found seven bodies,' Schenk said dully. '"Remains" would be more exact. Buried under the floor.'

337

'Oh, my God. I was afraid of something like that.'

Schenk's gaze flickered up to fix on Tom's. 'Why d'you say that?'

'It's consistent with what she said. "I've brought him here for *us*," she said. "For *all* of us. To burn in hell." I told you that, didn't I?'

'Yeah, I believe you did.' Schenk fell silent.

'Will they be able to identify them?'

'Oh, they've done that already.'

'*How*?' Tom's voice reflected his surprise at the speed of this.

'He'd kept certain things. Personal things – kind of trophies. A piece of jewellery, a pocket book, even a mobile phone. It's a thing that killers often do. Sex killers. Serial sex killers.'

'Dear God.' Tom's soft whisper carried all the force of his bewildered revulsion. 'I was going to say it's almost beyond belief. But it *is* beyond belief. No one could believe a thing like this. It has to be real.'

Schenk nodded solemnly once again. 'Tom, there's more to it,' he said, clearing his throat and shifting his position slightly. 'Hunt had written up a note the night before all this happened – the fire and everything. They found it in his office. It seems he wrote it after you'd called him to come and pick you up out here – after you'd found the house.'

The tone of Schenk's voice warned Tom he was about to hear something that he wasn't ready for. 'A note?' he said warily. 'What kind of a note?'

'About you. He said he thought you might be on the verge of a . . . a psychotic break, I think he called it.'

'Have you seen this note?'

'As a matter of fact, I have. It's in his own handwriting. The gist of it is, he suspected you might have been living a double life.'

The case against Tom took shape with mesmerizing speed. It was only a matter of hours before certain routine enquiries were set in motion as a result of Brendan Hunt's carefully recorded misgivings. First, all Tom's credit card and cellphone records were subpoenaed for as far back as possible. This allowed his movements to be checked against the last reported sightings of the seven girls whose remains had been found buried beneath the cellar of the house. In each case, Tom had been close enough when they disappeared to have been the one responsible. He lay immobilized in his hospital bed and listened in disbelief as the evidence piled up.

'For Christ's sake, Brendan Hunt knew me all those years. We stayed in touch. We talked about Julia. We talked about a lot of things – what I was doing, where I was going, the projects I was planning. He knew my movements. He must have followed me around, snatching these girls so that he could ultimately frame me. Can't you see that?'

Murray Schenk, and the two detectives who had accompanied him on his second visit to Tom's bedside, listened stony-faced.

'What about the garage in Broadlands?' one of them asked. 'The place has been rented in your name for the past eight years.'

'But didn't anyone ever meet me? I mean, this man who was supposed to be me?'

'Everything was done through banks and realty agents. They've traced the payments to a Bahamian account – also in your name.'

'But somebody must have seen this man coming and going. Surely at least one person, one time.'

'All anybody ever saw was a man in dark glasses with a moustache and a hat.'

'That could be anybody!'

The silence that followed made it clear that, as far as they were concerned, that 'anybody' could perfectly well be Tom.

'We found a false moustache, dark glasses and a hat in the trunk of your car,' Schenk said.

'That wasn't my car!'

'The Mercedes? It's in your name.'

'Look,' Tom said in desperation, 'are you sure you've gone through Hunt's home as well as his office?'

'With a fine-tooth comb. There's nothing out of order, no loose ends.'

'There *has* to be something, somewhere. It's not possible that anybody could have got a thing like this so perfectly right. There has to be a transfer deed, a receipt, records in a bank vault somewhere – *something* to prove that Hunt set this whole thing up.'

'We're working on it, Tom,' Murray Schenk said uncomfortably. He wanted to believe this man whom he'd come to like, but it was hard when every day brought some new and damning revelation. 'Meanwhile, if you want my advice, you should get yourself a good lawyer – now.'

The first thing the lawyer checked out was the possibility of DNA evidence. But there was nothing on the human remains found in the house to identify the killer. There was only the circumstantial evidence, all of which pointed faultlessly to Tom. After that, the lawyer's only suggestion was that Julia be hypnotized, in the hope that she might remember something of that day in the cellar – enough, perhaps, to corroborate her father's story. It was by no means certain, he warned, that such testimony would be regarded by a court as unbiased or even admissable, but it was their best shot. It was obvious to Tom that the lawyer thought he had an unwinnable case and was merely going through the motions.

Tom and Clare discussed the idea of involving Julia. She sat by Tom's bed and held his hand. Not for a moment had she wavered in her belief in his innocence, but the strain showed in the dark shadows beneath her eyes and the lines etched at the sides of her mouth that had not been there two weeks ago.

'If it's our only shot, we have to take it,' she said.

But Tom had thought this through and made his

mind up. 'I'm not going to let it happen,' he said firmly. 'She's come through this unscathed, and that's the way she's going to stay. If we make her relive the whole thing, who knows what the consequences might be?'

'What about the consequences if we don't?'

'I'll take my chances. I'm sorry, Clare. I'm sorry about everything. But we don't have a choice.'

PART FOUR

'AFTERLIFE'

56

'So, even now, you still believe that your father is innocent?'

'Yes, I do.'

The old woman turns her gaze from the window, with its sweeping view of downtown Chicago Lakefront in the shimmering summer heat. Her eyes have something impenetrable in them. I am not sure whether it is sadness, or civilly concealed dislike, or perhaps mere vacancy.

'Well, I suppose I have to say that such loyalty does you credit. I would have hoped for the same, had I ever needed it, and had they lived, from my own two children.'

Suddenly there is less ambivalence in her gaze. Her eyes burn into me with open dislike. She does not want me here and regrets having agreed to see me.

'Miss Freeman,' she begins, and I realize she is about to tell me that the interview is over, 'I don't know what you expected from me, but I cannot help you. I am sorry for your sake, and for your sake alone, that your father has been in prison for thirteen years. Personally, I am content for him to stay there for the rest of his life, as I believe he is likely to. He killed my son; he killed at least seven young girls; and he almost killed you.'

She must be close to eighty, but she has a steely self-possession and her mind is sharp. And she is very angry. I understand that, but it will make it hard for her to help me.

'But Mrs Hunt,' I say, preparing to repeat the argument I have put so many times and to so many people over the past few years, 'if my father intended killing me, why did he save me from that fire the way he did?'

She looks away dismissively, as though my question is unworthy of her time. 'I do not understand the workings of the criminal mind,' she says brusquely, 'even less of the criminally insane mind. Nor was that an area of special interest to my son, so I am not surprised he failed to detect the madness in your father – until too late.'

I persist. 'That doesn't answer the question, Mrs Hunt. If my father had been considered criminally insane, he could never have stood trial.'

Her eyes flash once again in my direction. 'But he did stand trial, and he was found guilty.'

'I am questioning that verdict.'

She gives an impatient sigh, a short, sharp exhalation of breath that warns me I am running out of time.

'This is pointless,' she says, making a flicking motion

with one hand, as though removing some fleck of dust from her lap. She sits rigid, in a straight-backed chair, wearing a long black dress with a ruffled high collar that looks too hot for this weather, except that the room is air-conditioned to the point almost of chilliness. I wonder if she always wears black, in memory of her dead children. I wonder if she ever goes out. Something about her makes me doubt it. Something about her makes me think of Miss Havisham in *Great Expectations*, although the apartment is spacious and filled with light. She also reminds me, with her silvery hair cut severely short, of one of those despotic ballet teachers you see in films, tapping her cane on the floor of the rehearsal room to terrorize her pupils.

'Before the trial,' I begin again, trying to sound as though I have more to say that is deserving of her attention, 'my father's lawyers wanted me to be hypnotized to recall that day. He refused to allow it. His reason was to protect me, even though he knew I would corroborate his version of what happened.'

This time she blows a puff of air out through her nose. It is a meticulously calibrated snort of contempt.

'Are you seriously suggesting that any court would accept the evidence of a child, based upon hypnotic trance?'

'No. I realize now it wouldn't have helped my father's defence. The judge would have thrown it out of court.'

'Besides, you may well have recalled a version of events inimical to your father's plea of innocence –

which would certainly explain his consideration for your welfare.'

This last is said with an acid sarcasm that leaves me in no doubt that I have failed with this woman. When we began our conversation she was merely an opponent; now she is an enemy.

I cannot give up. I must try to go on.

'Except that when I volunteered later to be hypnotized, when I was old enough to make the decision for myself, I remembered everything that went on that day. Your son was killed by some kind of paranormal manifestation of Melanie Hagan and all those other girls he had murdered—'

'I will not listen to this!' She hits the arm of her chair with the flat of her hand.

'It's the truth. And I'm going to prove it.'

I am losing my temper, just as she is. It will not help. I must control myself. I think for a moment that she is going to get to her feet, but she just swivels in her chair to face me squarely.

'Let me give you some advice, Miss Freeman.' She makes it sound more like an ultimatum. 'Drop this obsession and get on with your life. You are an attractive young woman. How old are you?'

'Twenty-three.'

'You have your life ahead of you. Your *own* life. Live it.'

She glares at me, wanting some sign, some acknowledgement, that her message has struck home. I drop my eyes and look at my hands, loosely clasped in front of me.

'Mrs Hunt,' I say, keeping my voice level, my manner respectful and polite, but also trying to make her understand that I am not going to go away and let this matter drop, 'a year after your daughter died, her best friend Naomi Chase also died. I've read the public records: it was a particularly vicious sexual crime.'

Now she is on her feet, even before I have reached the end of my sentence. For some reason, with this mention of Naomi I have finally crossed the line.

'Are you suggesting, Miss Freeman, that there was some connection between those events?'

I stay seated and look up at her. Her whole face is drawn back into a mask of withering disdain.

'Don't tell me it has never crossed your mind, Mrs Hunt.'

Her eyes narrow, becoming black pinpoints of fury. I think she is about to strike me, but she holds back.

'Get out, Miss Freeman. Get out of my house. Now!'

There is no more I can say. I get up and start for the door, leaving behind me a silence so charged that I am waiting for an explosion. Or a blow. Or something sharp plunged deep between my shoulder blades.

Of course nothing happens. Nor did I expect it would. All the same, it is a long walk to the elevator, and I am as much relieved as I am disappointed to find myself on the street minutes later.

57

I walk by the water's edge. There is a strange stillness in the air, as though nature is holding its breath, waiting mischievously to release the storm that must come soon.

The more I think about it, the more sure I am that Brendan Hunt's mother is hiding something, or at least suspects something that she prefers to leave hidden. What convinces me is the way she reacted to my linking the death of her daughter with that of Naomi Chase. She had not been surprised by the connection, simply angry and alarmed that I had spotted it. In all the months and years I have spent finding out everything I could about Brendan Hunt, nothing stood out as suspiciously as the coincidence of the deaths of those two girls when he was a boy.

I am on my way to see Warren and Samantha Chase, Naomi's parents. They answered my original letter sympathetically, agreeing to meet with me, and they were helpful on the phone when I called to make arrangements. I check again their address against the street map I have bought. I calculate that I have time to walk, which means I can save money on a cab. But I must walk slowly; I do not want to arrive on their doorstep flushed and perspiring from the heat.

This is my first visit to Chicago. It is a beautiful city, the tall buildings at its centre glittering like a massive jewel box thrown open to the sun. I wish I had the time to look around and get to know it properly. Perhaps some day I will. Perhaps some day I will have time for many things – such as living my own life, as Mrs Hunt so self-interestedly advised me to do.

Yet my father has given me the same advice more than once. I have had to promise him that I will not spend my life trying to clear his name. But of course I will, if I have to. Each time I see him, caged behind that glass partition, I know I have no choice. He has become not so much old in prison as a man without age. His skin is drawn tight over his bones, and his hair is grey and cropped short. He exercises a great deal, because there is so little else to do. He is fifty-seven years old, and has that lean, hardened look that I have come to know is the mark of a 'lifer'.

The Chases live in a large prairie-style house on a wide tree-lined avenue. I can see, from what little I have read about the city's architecture, the influence of Frank Lloyd Wright. There is great wealth in this city, and I know that the Chase family, like the Hunts, have enjoyed their share of it.

A maid opens the door, Puerto Rican I would guess. She smiles pleasantly and asks me to follow her. I am taken into an open living space, one side of which seems to be all glass and looks onto an enclosed garden with rocky waterfalls and rich green ferns, broken here and there by slashes of bright colour. Warren Chase stands waiting for me. He is tall, casually dressed with a natural elegance. I take his outstretched hand.

'Thank you again for agreeing to see me.'

'Not at all. You're very welcome.' He must be in his seventies, and has the air of a retired academic more than the aerospace executive I know he was. 'My wife will join us in a moment,' he says. 'Please sit down.'

But he has seen my gaze wander over to the display of family photographs nearby. I know they have two children apart from Naomi, an older son and younger daughter, both now with children of their own. He picks up their pictures one by one to show me, telling me their names. In addition there are at least half a dozen pictures of Naomi, from her first steps to one that must have been taken not long before she died. This one is of the whole family on their boat out on the lake. Her best friend Cassie Hunt is in it too. Warren Chase does not comment on these pictures; he knows I recognize the girls.

When we turn back to the room I see that Mrs Chase has joined us silently. She is a delicate, pretty woman, slightly birdlike in her movements and with a quick smile that lights up her face. Both she and her husband, I can already see, have that quality of reaching out, of giving their whole attention to whoever they are talking to. At least that is how they make me feel. It is a special sort of kindness, maybe one that comes from having suffered a tragedy in your life that has made you more sensitive to the pain and needs of others.

The maid is setting a tray of tea and small things to eat on a low table. Mrs Chase sits next to me and serves.

'Your letter touched us both deeply, Miss Freeman,' she says. 'We don't know much about your father's case, only what you've told us, but he's a fortunate man to have a daughter like you working for him.'

'Thank you,' I murmur. It always embarrasses me to be paid compliments for doing something I have no choice about. How could any child not do the same? I am not special.

'How did your meeting with Judith Hunt go?' Warren Chase asks.

I describe it briefly. He nods thoughtfully, as though it is pretty much what he expected.

'Judith has increasingly withdrawn from the world over the years. We used to be good friends, but now we hardly see each other. After Cassie's death her marriage broke up, and she went through a long, bad time. She pulled out of it eventually, but she was a changed woman. One understands, of course. Then Brendan's death . . . that was the final straw.'

I do not mention the possibility of a link between the two girls' deaths, not yet. Instead, we speak of how

I went about discovering everything there was to know about Brendan Hunt, and tracking down everyone I could find who ever knew him. 'I've only read the official reports of Cassie Hunt's death,' I say, 'plus what I found in the newspaper libraries. I wondered if there was anything you might know of that hadn't been published.'

They exchange a look. I think perhaps I have touched on something that has remained unspoken between them. Warren Chase answers my question guardedly, choosing his words with care.

'Brendan was the last person to see his sister alive. According to him he tried to save her but it seems he didn't have the strength.'

According? It seems?

'Did you ever suspect there might have been more to it?' I ask.

Again their eyes connect before Warren Chase continues.

'We used to hear hair-raising tales from Naomi about the things they got up to and the fights between them. We just dismissed it at the time as the usual brother-sister rivalry. But then, after what happened . . .'

He parts his hands slightly to suggest an open question, and possibly an open mind. I notice the way his wife is still looking at him, confirming the suspicions my questions are beginning to arouse.

I ask, 'Was Brendan Hunt ever questioned about his sister's death?'

'Only briefly,' Warren Chase says, 'just to establish the facts as he recalled them. The coroner's verdict was accidental death.'

I let a silence hang between us for a moment before I ask my next question. 'About your daughter's murder,' I say, 'I understand there was never any suspect in the case.'

'The police never came up with a serious lead,' he says. 'Their best guess was some kind of itinerant killer, who was probably miles away by the next morning.'

'There were no fingerprints in the house other than family and friends?'

'Correct.'

'But those fingerprints included some of Brendan Hunt's.'

'It was my sister's house,' Samantha Chase says. 'Brendan was in and out of there as frequently as anyone.'

'What about DNA?'

Warren Chase makes another of those vague gestures with his hands and shoulders that speaks volumes of regret about what might have been, if only. 'It happened a good fifteen years before DNA typing became possible,' he says.

'But there must have been . . . traces.' It is as delicate and neutral a word as I can find for what I mean. I have read reports of the case, and what was done to their child does not bear thinking about. 'If anything has been preserved,' I say, 'they could still run tests now.'

Samantha Chase looks down as though to get away from this thought. Her husband frowns and seems momentarily at a loss, perhaps embarrassed and even angered by what he has to tell me. 'It's beyond my comprehension, but apparently nothing whatever was kept. I asked about it in the eighties, when I first read about DNA profiling. I couldn't believe it when they told me. I mean, all right, nobody can anticipate what technological breakthroughs might occur in ten or fifteen years, you can't be prepared for everything. But you'd think in the case of an unsolved crime . . .'

He shakes his head and leaves the sentence, though not the sense of it, unfinished.

'So nobody,' I say after a moment, 'absolutely nobody ever connected Brendan Hunt with your daughter's murder.'

'The question didn't arise. It crossed nobody's mind. He was a child, for heaven's sakes.'

There is disbelief in his voice, though whether in response to the idea of a child committing murder, or to the fact that nobody contemplated such a possibility at the time, I do not know.

'I have a feeling it might have crossed his mother's mind,' I say, 'though she would never admit it, even to herself.'

No one speaks. Then Samantha Chase says, very quietly, 'If that's the case, it might explain quite a few things. About Judith, I mean.'

Another look passes between herself and her husband,

some kind of understanding. He nods his agreement with what she has just said.

'Mind you, Miss Freeman,' he says, then adds as an afterthought, 'Julia, if you don't mind my calling you that . . .'

'Please do,' I say, relieved to drop the formal mode.

'You know, Julia, I would never, not even in my wildest dreams, have entertained such an idea as you're suggesting. Neither of us would. But in the light of what you've told us . . .'

Again he leaves the sentence unfinished, though the thought is complete.

'I have no proof,' I say. 'And apparently there's not much chance of finding any. But I'm grateful to you for listening to me.'

Suddenly I cannot say any more. A wave of terrible depression overwhelms me. I realize I have been holding it at bay for months now, even years, forcing myself to believe that eventually I would find something, some long-forgotten detail, that would lead me to the discovery that would change everything. But now it seems that I have failed, as I was always bound to. It is a hopeless task that I have set myself.

I must leave now, quickly, before I lose control. These people do not need my tears. I hope I do not seem rude. 'I've taken up enough of your time,' I start to say, but have to clear my throat and swallow hard to get the words out.

Samantha Chase's hand is on mine, firm and

reassuring, holding me. 'Stay where you are,' she says. 'You're having supper with us.'

I start to protest. 'No, you're very kind, thank you, but I . . .'

'Really. We want you to. Please stay.'

Suddenly I realize how much I also want to. 'Thank you,' I say, in a whisper. My eyes are pricking. Damn!

But I hold on. I am going to be all right.

58

Over supper Warren Chase asks me what I do when I am not busy trying to be a part-time sleuth, though he does not put it quite in those terms.

'I'm a nurse,' I say.

They nod their approval, the way people often do when they hear this. But a look of concern passes over Samantha Chase's face.

'This must be costing you a lot of money, the travel, everything you've been doing. Is anyone helping you?'

'No – I've managed to fit in some additional private nursing recently. It pays well.'

'And what about your mother?' Warren Chase asks. 'You live with her, you said. How is she coping with it all?'

They listen sympathetically to my rather flat recital of the obvious – that life is not easy for the wife of a murderer, a man dubbed by the press as 'The Monster of Hell House'. Her business fell apart after my father was arrested. All her clients evaporated in less than a week, every one of them with hand-wringing excuses and expressions of sympathy, none of which changed the simple fact that they no longer wished to be associated, however indirectly, with the name of Freeman. She was forced to sell the house in Saracen Springs and we moved to the outskirts of Philadelphia, which was close enough to where my father was in prison to make visiting him possible and not ruinously expensive. She found work as a book-keeper for several companies on a freelance basis, but whenever our history was uncovered, as it invariably was, she was quietly let go. For a while she worked on checkout in a supermarket, but for the past three years has worked for a contract cleaning firm. She is one of a regular team who goes into the offices of a large insurance company between ten at night and six in the morning. We spend as much time together as we can at weekends, sometimes visiting her family. She has no friends, apart from some of the women she works with, most of them Mexican, one or two from eastern Europe.

'And what about you?' Samantha Chase asks. 'Did you have problems at school?'

'I had to move once,' I tell her, 'when the bullying got too bad. But that was not long after the trial. After that, I was luckier. Freeman isn't too uncommon a name. People didn't always make the connection automatically.'

It is almost ten when I leave. Warren Chase has insisted on calling me a cab which, despite my protests, is pre-paid on an account he has with the firm. They

A Memory of Demons

both hug me at the door. 'Now remember,' he says, holding me at arm's length with his hands on my shoulders, 'any kind of help we can give you, anything at all, you only have to ask.'

'Please believe that, because we really mean it,' his wife says.

'Thank you,' I say, feeling tears well up again, knowing I must get away before they do. 'I'll remember.'

'Be sure to stay in touch,' he says.

'I will,' I promise.

I am grateful for the taxi, realizing that I am more tired than I thought. Also, my hotel is in a part of the city where I do not particularly like the atmosphere at night. From the way he accelerates away after dropping me, I suspect the cab driver feels likewise. I start up the three or four steps to the hotel door, and am reaching out for the bell that will bring the night porter to open it, when I sense more than see somebody watching me. I turn my head to look, telling myself as I do that this is probably a mistake; I should ignore whoever is there, press the bell, and get inside to safety.

The street is patchily lit, and I can just make out the silhouette of a man. He is slim, not very tall, and seems to be wearing a long overcoat. As I look, he takes a step forward.

'Miss Freeman?' he says.

'Y-yes,' I say warily, surprised to hear my name.

'Julia Freeman?'

'Yes.'

David Ambrose

My hand is still outstretched, ready to press the bell, but I hold back for some reason. The man takes another step towards me. I can see his face now. It is thin, clean-shaven, sallow-looking. His hair, which is jet black, is brushed straight back and glistens with some kind of gel. It is difficult to guess his age; he could be forty or as much as a decade or more older. We regard each other, I on the steps looking down at him, he looking up at me. He seems about to say something, then changes his mind. For a moment I have the strange impression that he himself knows no more than I do what he is doing here.

'Yes?' I say, prompting him. 'Can I help you?'

'I . . . I think we should talk,' he says, as though it requires something of an effort to make up his mind about this.

'What about?' I ask, still not moving away from the door of my hotel, though I have lowered my hand from the bell.

He frowns, as though struggling to recall why it is he wants to talk to me. There is something strange about him, something wrong. I am starting to feel alarmed.

But then he says, 'It's about Brendan Hunt. I think I can help you.'

59

The street is oddly quiet, more so than I have known it over the few days I have been here. A single car crosses an intersection in the distance, but apart from that there is no traffic, nor can I see anyone walking.

I have stepped down to the sidewalk and now stand facing the man. He is short, barely my height. His hands remain thrust deep in the pockets of his belted overcoat. He could whip out a knife or gun, I tell myself; but somehow I do not think he is about to.

'Who are you?' I say.

He frowns, looking down. I cannot make out whether he is wondering if he should tell me his name, or trying to remember it.

'Lenny Rearden,' he says eventually, and looks at me, as though he has clarified something in his mind and now recalls what it is that he has to do. 'My name is Lenny Rearden,' he repeats. 'I was at school with Brendan Hunt. I . . . well, I should have given you this some time ago. You, or somebody. It could have made a difference.'

Without my quite noticing the movement, he has taken one hand from his pocket and reached into his coat for something. Now he is holding out a folded square of paper, inviting me to take it.

'What is it?'

'You'll see. Take it, please.'

I do as he asks, opening up the paper in the light of the yellowish street lamp. It is a faded piece of newsprint, cut from a larger page. And it is in German, a language I studied for a time at school, but which I do not speak at all.

As though in answer to the question I am about to ask him, he points at the smudged picture of a teenage girl at the head of the story. According to the caption, her first name is Hannah; the second I can barely read, let alone pronounce.

'We went on a school trip once, to Germany,' Lenny Rearden is saying. 'One night in Hamburg we were let off the leash for a couple of hours. We did the strip clubs, porno shops, the obvious stuff for a bunch of horny fifteen-year-olds from the Midwest. At one point I saw Brendan Hunt talking with this girl in an amusement arcade. I only got a glimpse, but I'm sure it was her. Then they disappeared. When I saw him later I asked him what had happened with the girl. He said there wasn't any girl, I was mistaken. Then, the next day, I saw this in one of the local papers.'

He pauses, his eyes still fixed on that piece of faded newsprint as though it is a cue-card he is reading from, and on which he has lost his place for a moment.

'What am I supposed to do with this?' I say. 'How is it going to help me?'

He blinks as though trying to clear his thoughts, then shifts his gaze from the paper and refocuses on some point in space in front of him.

'I never told Brendan I'd seen this. I never told anyone. I didn't want to believe it, I guess. Or couldn't. But I've kept it ever since.'

'Please,' I say, 'just tell me what I'm supposed to do. I don't understand any of this.'

Now he looks at me, and again I get the strange impression that it takes him a moment to focus, to remind himself who I am and why he is talking to me.

'Check this out,' he says after a few moments, as though this advice is one of several alternatives he has had to choose from. 'I should have done something about this years ago. In a way it's too late now. But maybe not.'

I look at him, praying that he's not some lunatic, the kind of weirdo who goes to the police and confesses to every major crime he hears of.

'Keep that,' he says, 'it's yours now. Just check it out, that's all. I have to go.'

He takes a couple of steps back, looking at me earnestly as though to be sure I have understood him, then turns abruptly and starts to walk away.

'Wait,' I say quickly. 'Where will I find you?'

He pauses, swivelling briefly to look back at me.

'You won't need me. That's all you need. Just do as I say – check it out.'

Again he starts to walk away. I feel frustrated and helpless.

'How did you know about me?' I call after him.

'It doesn't matter,' he calls back. 'Just do it.'

I look down again at the piece of paper in my hand, with its impenetrable language and its smudged picture of a girl who could be anybody. I must at least get a phone number for him. I look up.

But he has gone. I can still hear in the distance the sharp click of his retreating footsteps, but he must have turned into an opening on his left that I cannot see from where I stand, and I do not feel inclined to chase after him in the dark. I will find him again if I have to. Lenny Rearden.

For the moment all I need is someone who understands German.

60

It has only been two months, but they have felt like years.

Murray Schenk agreed to help me out. He must be in his middle or even late seventies now, but he has changed little. He still fishes. And he still thinks about Melanie Hagan, and my father. He has never been sure that justice was done, and it troubles him deeply.

As soon as I had the newspaper story translated into English I took it to Murray. It contained all the details he needed, including the name of the investigating officer – who, he was able to find out with a few phone calls, was still alive. The crime itself was remarkably similar in its violence and sexual savagery to the murder of Naomi Chase.

I decided I would tell my mother nothing of what was going on. To get her hopes up only to be disappointed yet again was too cruel. There is a dullness and a sense of defeat in her eyes these days that I find unbearable. Her face is lined and thin, her hair almost entirely white. I shall need to be sure before I say anything to her.

It took every last cent I have, what with plane fares to Europe and lawyers' fees, together with a host of connected expenses. But today the call came. Now I am sure.

She sobs helplessly, like a child. I hold her in my arms.

The Germans had kept DNA samples from the murder scene. They match exactly Brendan Hunt's. Both Murray Schenk and the lawyer who defended my father at his trial say that there is no doubt that the case will be reopened. Equally, there is no doubt that my father's conviction will be quashed and he will be freed. There will be compensation, our lawyer says, probably substantial, though that matters little to my mother and myself. Nonetheless, it will be useful. My parents will have to rebuild their lives from nothing. They will need money.

I have put my mother to bed. She is exhausted. I even suggested she take a sleeping pill. That is something I rarely advise, but she is too excited to sleep otherwise, and she needs a good night. Tomorrow she will wake up to the dawning realization that her nightmare is over, that the good news she thinks she has only dreamed about is actually true, that her life is about to begin again.

The doorbell rings. I look at my watch. It is after eleven. I do not know who can be calling at this hour. I look through the spy-lens, and see Murray Schenk. I open the door.

Something in his face makes my heart tighten, creating a hollowness in my chest, filling me with sudden dread. He has come with bad news, I am sure. Something has gone wrong.

'Easy,' he says, 'take it easy,' steadying me with a gentle hand. 'I just want to talk, that's all. Nothing's happened. Well,' he corrects himself, 'I can't say nothing. But nothing necessarily bad.'

We sit down in our small living room. Murray Schenk unbuttons his coat but keeps it on because I have turned the heating off and the air is already chill. He is frowning, unsure where to begin, or how.

'This man Rearden,' he says eventually, 'you couldn't find him in the phone book, you said. You never saw him again after that night in Chicago?'

'Never. You know that. Why?'

Schenk chews on his lower lip a moment.

'Come on, Murray,' I say, 'what's this about?'

He looks at me. 'Well, it doesn't make a whole lot of difference now, because we checked out that piece of paper like he said . . . and, well, it all fell into place.' He pauses. 'But you didn't get that newspaper clipping from Lenny Rearden. So I was just wondering if you'd tell me where you did get it.'

I stare at him, dumbfounded. 'Murray,' I say, 'it happened exactly the way I told you it happened. Why would I lie?'

He shrugs. 'I don't know. Maybe you're protecting somebody. Or maybe the guy, whoever he was, lied to you and said he was Lenny Rearden.'

'I don't get this. Why shouldn't he have been Lenny Rearden?'

Murray Schenk's gaze is absolutely steady, and there is some emotion in his eyes I cannot read. It is a cop's trick, perhaps, or just the habit of a lifetime, an instinctive ability to mask, when necessary, his true feelings from the person he is talking to.

'Lenny Rearden was killed in an automobile accident in Texas,' he says flatly, 'ten years ago.'

For a moment I think that I am going to faint. I remember thankfully that I am sitting down, then wonder – absurdly – what happens if you faint while you are sitting down. Do you roll forward to the floor, or fall back safely?

Murray Schenk is watching me, observing my reaction.

I begin to stutter. 'But . . . but you just said . . . it checked out . . . that report . . . the DNA . . . everything.'

'Sure, it checked out. But the guy who gave it to you doesn't.'

I shake my head slowly. I have no words. I do not know what to think.

'What did he look like, this Rearden guy?'

'He was shorter than you,' I say. 'Trim build. Long overcoat. He had dark hair, brushed back.'

'Is this anything like him?'

Schenk leans over and hands me a small black-and-white photograph.

'That's him,' I say. 'That's the man I met. Lenny Rearden. I don't understand.'

Schenk looks back at me. 'Nor do I.'

We sit in silence for some moments.

'For God's sake, Murray, what are you telling me? That I saw a ghost?'

He shrugs. 'I would say, on that count, that your guess is as good as mine. If not better.'

'But . . . is this going to make any difference? To my father?'

Murray turns his mouth down at the corners, tips his head slightly to one side and then the other. 'No reason why it should. Though I don't see a whole lot of need to tell everybody about it. The information you got from this guy, whoever or whatever he was, was good. That's all that matters. There's no reason to believe you acquired any of it, including this piece of paper, by illegal means.'

Again he pauses, his eyes on mine.

'You didn't, did you?'

'No,' I say, 'absolutely not!'

'In that case, I think we're fine.' He gets to his feet. 'Forget this conversation ever took place. Nobody else is going to ask you about it.'

I walk with him to the door, where I give him a hug and kiss him on the cheek. He says he'll come by tomorrow to see my mother. She needn't know about this either. He leaves, and I lock the door behind him.

There is no sound except the distant traffic. I look in on my mother. Her breathing is deep and steady. The sleep of the just – with a little help from pharmacology.

In spite of what I have just been through, or perhaps because of it, I feel exhausted myself. I head for the bathroom, push open the door, and pull the cord that switches on the bright and unflattering overhead light.

I scream.

In the mirror, I see someone standing in the corner behind me, by the shower stall.

I want to run, but I cannot. I cannot move. I am paralysed by fear. I can feel the hairs on the back of my neck, stiff like bristles.

Melanie Hagan leans casually against the wall, smiling curiously, her eyes on mine. I am not sure how I recognize her. Although for a time in my childhood I was possessed by her, we have never met.

Until now.

She is unchanged from the day she died.

I see her lips move in the mirror. When I hear her voice, it seems closer than her physical presence, like a whisper in my ear. 'Remember me,' she says.

Somehow I break the spell and turn.

Nobody is there. I am alone.

I look back in the mirror.

Her reflection has gone.

I try to tell myself I imagined it. But I know I did not. She was here.

The light goes out, plunging me abruptly into utter blackness. Suddenly I am chilled to my bones, and have the feeling that I am falling helplessly through space.

I cry out. I scream, and go on screaming . . .

61

A light goes on. I am not sure where. I can see the angle of a door, my door. It swings back. My mother hurries in. I know it is my mother, though I see her only in silhouette.

And I know this is my room. I am back, for some reason, in Saracen Springs.

My mother kneels by my bed and puts her arms around me, the way she did when I was a little girl.

'It's all right, darling. You had a bad dream.'

I start to say, 'No, it wasn't . . .'

But my mother has switched on a light. I see myself in the mirror on the wall opposite. And I see my mother.

'Mommy, I was . . . I was trying to find a way to help Daddy . . .'

'You had a dream, my darling . . .'

'No, I . . .'

Again I look into the mirror. I am ten years old. And my mother is exactly the way she always has been: young looking, beautiful, no longer the worn-out old woman I just left.

But that was no dream. It was something more. I know it. I have never been as sure of anything in my life. I have to persuade her. I have to make her understand what just happened.

'Mommy, we have to call Mr Schenk!'

'Sssh, now, try to go back to sleep.'

'He has to go to Germany. There's a policeman there . . .'

'Darling, stop it, please . . .'

'You have to believe me! You *have* to, Mommy!'

'All right, all right, we'll talk about it in the morning.'

'No, now! There's man in Chicago who can save Daddy, but he's going to die. He's called Lenny Rearden. We have to find him . . .'

62

Tom had not been expecting a visit from Clare that morning. From the time of his transfer from the prison hospital to the county jail, after the court had refused him bail, he felt he had been treated more like a man already proved guilty rather than one awaiting trial. Visits were restricted, and he had to allocate the hours available to time spent with his lawyer as well as his wife. Julia, who had visited him in the hospital, had not been allowed, at his insistence, to see him in prison. They had already arranged that when the trial began she would be taken on a long vacation by Clare's parents as a way of shielding her from the ghoulish publicity that the case was certain to attract.

He followed the guard to the room where he spoke with his visitors through bullet-proof glass, their voices distorted by the less-than-perfect speaker system. The first thing he noticed was that his lawyer was present on the far side of the screen as well as Clare. And for the first time ever there was the hint of a smile on his face.

But it was Clare's eyes that told Tom at once that something had happened. Something they had been praying for. A miracle.

'Darling,' she said, one hand pressed flat against the glass as though to defy the separation it imposed between them, 'it may be a while yet, but we're going to get you out of here. We found a man in Chicago, Murray Schenk has been over to Hamburg, there's a DNA match between an old crime and Brendan Hunt . . .'

'Hold it, hold it,' Tom said, trying to slow her down. 'What's this about Chicago? And Hamburg?'

'It's too complicated to explain now—'

The lawyer cut in. 'Tom, they're dropping the charges against you. There's paperwork to be done, but as soon as it's finished you'll be released.'

'It's true, darling,' Clare said, tears of happiness running down her face now. 'You're coming home.'

Tom stared at her, with the numbed, unthinking conviction that this had to be some kind of mistake.

Or a trick.

But this was Clare. How could it be a trick?

'You're coming home,' she said again.

Acknowledgements

Anyone interested in the notions underlying this story should read Tom Shroder's excellent book, *Old Souls: the Scientific Evidence for Past Lives*, published by Simon & Schuster in 1999. In it he examines in depth the work of the remarkable Dr Ian Stevenson, whose website (www.childpastlives.org/stevenson.htm) is well worth a visit.

Aside from the particular thanks I owe to my editor Suzanne Baboneau and my agent Irv Schwartz, I want to thank my old friend Barry Hanson for his helpful comments on certain key aspects of the story. I also thank Ian, Gabriel and Sabrina Chapman for their illuminating comments on a first draft which I thought was finished, but wasn't.